Helen Garner

and the

Meaning of Everything

Helen Garner
and the
Meaning of Everything

Alex Jones

PUNCHER & WATTMANN

First published in 2006.
Second, corrected edition published 2007.

Published by Puncher and Wattmann
PO Box 441
Glebe NSW 2037

http://www.puncherandwattmann.com

fiction@puncherandwattmann.com

National Library of Australia
Cataloguing-in-Publication entry:

Jones, Alex
1938 -
Helen Garner and the Meaning of Everything

ISBN   9781921450051

I. Title.

A821.3

Cover design by Penelope Robards

Printed by McPherson's Printing Group

to my muses

PUNCHER & WATTMANN

Alex Jones: Helen Garner and the Meaning of Everything

Alex Jones, after a brief career in the law, spent his working life teaching at the University of Sydney. His interests there have included Old English, linguistic theory, the literature of fantasy, and Australian English, both written and spoken, but he counts as his greatest intellectual influence time spent working on the Gurindji language at Wattie Creek (NT).

Acknowledgements

Thanks are due to Pan Macmillan Australia for permission to make the quotations from *The First Stone* and *Joe Cinque's Consolation* and to Penguin Books Australia Ltd for the quotations from *Monkey Grip* and *The Children's Bach*. I am also particularly grateful to Helen Garner herself for her generosity in authorizing the quotations from *Cosmo Cosmolino*, including the extended passage on pp. 41-42. The references in the text to *Monkey Grip* and *Cosmo Cosmolino* are to the McPhee Gribble editions (Melbourne 1977 and 1992 respectively); for *The Children's Bach* the text cited is the edition published by Penguin Australia (Melbourne 1996), while *The First Stone* and *Joe Cinque's Consolation* are cited from the Picador editions (Pan Macmillan Australia, Sydney 1995 and 2004).

Thanks also to Anna Rose, who gave me permission to quote from a piece she had written for *Honi Soit* on the understanding that this wasn't to be 'some dreadful right-wing book'. I hope she isn't too disappointed.

My daughter Sophie provided much of the inspiration for the character of the narrator's daughter in this story: I can only thank her for giving me such a model of what a daughter should be, and hope she doesn't feel traduced in the process; thanks to my son Anthony as well, for asking questions that clarified my thinking at various crucial points in the composition of this work.

1

*α – the initial situation**

'Make it about the rabbit.'

I was in the courtyard at the time, just close to finishing a reflective pastie. 'Refective' I wrote at first, fingers preferring a neologism to a cheap rhetorical device. I find that a little bit of this sort of self-examination: standing outside oneself, maybe just a pace to the rear like a ghostly Duke of Edinburgh, head cocked attentively, hands tucked out of sight behind the back – that gets me through the day with some satisfaction. Whatever process it is that mediates between subconscious impulses and socialized behaviour will now and again throw to the surface a whorl, a flower-like pattern or arabesque, almost, it seems, for the special delight of that second invisible self. Years ago, and not far from here, I once ran into a young woman who had been a student of mine, now with a couple of toddlers in tow. 'Are these dear children yours?' I had asked her then – no, they were her sister's, she was looking after them for the day – and so we parted. But the pleasure of that briefly renewed acquaintance was more than doubled by realizing in recollection the undoubted subconscious question: 'Are these the children of dear you?', and how it had been rearranged and socialized so that it could be asked without a stammer and answered without a blush. (The subconscious doesn't speak English – it has its own language).

Getting through the day: that was the thing. I could have done some cleaning, I suppose; I could have worked at some home improvements; but if Johnson had no passion for clean linen,* I have none for a cleaned or improved home. The cleaner pushes the vacuum around now and again and mops the tiles and what not, and that has to do. Cooking, yes: I think I've perfected the classic pork pie over the last couple of months – get the fennel seeds just right and hold the salt till you've reduced the stock – don't put it in with the meat. Etc. You will have your own favourites, and easily spend a few hours on each of many days getting them just so. I like to read the newspaper, sitting in the sun at the spindly-legged Italian table on the terrace. Do that to start the day, because it will often take quite a while – and a trip to the shops will fit in well later in the morning to choose an appealing piece of fruit for lunch: a ripe fig earlier in the season or a pomegranate, or a Seville orange to eat slowly, segment by segment, in the winter sunshine: fanciful melodic bursts of mandarin or orange or grapefruit played against the harsh continuo of that bitter, bitter, bass.

I have not long retired, you see. 'Unemployed at last,' I said to L, my partner, quoting the only sentence of *Such is Life* that I ever expect to read. It's a cheap edition that we have, printed by some local house in a close-set, unattractive font, but it shows a certain seriousness to keep it on the shelves. She is actually my wife: I said 'partner' to sound more modern – I try to live in the world. 'Begin as you mean to continue': perhaps that worked for marriage in the 18th century; there was no divorce in those days. I would rather say 'Begin *as if* you mean to continue'. How we tiptoed around each other at first, cautiously waiting for the social senses to catch up with the flesh. So then we both laughed, out of self-satisfaction and loyalty respectively – and that sort of loyalty is not so easily found. Which is why I think it's just as well to leave the house every couple of days, particularly when L 'works from home' as they say, to pick up my emails, say hello to former colleagues, and so on.

And that explains why I was now in the courtyard, an eating place at the university where I used to teach. What did I teach? Rhetoric, I suppose, if the medium really is the message. The courtyard is popular at lunchtime, today no less than usual. Rustic tables, or tables become rustic from long exposure to the weather, are crowded together with little lanes between, and faced by benches each holding three or four people. I was on one end of a bench; next to me a quiet girl, her eyes under a dark fringe fixed on a biology textbook, sipped at a bottle of water from time to time. Sitting down, I had pondered for a moment on the role of the fringe as an index of social class, but saw little evidence to take me one way or another. The rest of the table was occupied by four raucous young men making hearty lunches of institutional food of some kind I hesitated to identify. I couldn't follow what they were saying – it seemed to revolve around a commerce assignment that had just been handed back, and was punctuated with cries of 'Mate!' and high fives whenever another friend came past or joined their shifting group at the table.

I'm too deaf these days to make any sense of a situation where a lot of people are talking at once. It's just a wall of sound to me, so I bit away at the pastie, now and then dropping a flake of pastry, or flicking one away just to see the pigeons wheeling and crowding from one place to another. But then came one of those random pauses, the sort that happens when waves pursuing their own peculiar rhythms each come to a trough in the same instant. And in that instant I heard the words:

'Make it about the rabbit.'

I looked around. A pair of young women sat facing one another at the next table. *Sisters,* I thought, *the older one's tough, the young one's miserable.* * The older of the two, Elizabeth, as I called her to myself, seemed to have been the speaker. She was a slender young woman of say 23 with a light, even, tan. I silently amended the name to Elisabeth, to take account of this suggestion of Germanic background. She was wearing a high-necked t-shirt of some light colour, and the styling of her ash blonde hair reminded me of a canary palm over-enthusiastically trimmed by a local council. All it needed was a humorous mouth to make a poor man's Meg Ryan; being a poor man could have its upside, it seemed. Vicki, the younger of the two, was turned a quarter away from me. I wasn't aware of much more than the bulging left rear quarter of an 18-year-old midriff over the waistband of her jeans, and a general air she had of being a cheaper edition of her older sister. A book was open on the table between them, and the body language with which Vicki was addressing herself to her sister suggested desperation – an appeal for Elisabeth's help before some great approaching challenge.

Then there was a clatter of plates, and the young men stood up together, sweeping the thick white crockery into a redoubtable pile, with empty bottles of sports drink and styrofoam cups making outworks and flanking turrets to the central castle. The fringe girl worked on her hydration. Elisabeth took a calamari ring from a cardboard packet and bit it in half with a decisive movement. The sun had gone round, and the shadow of my hand began to creep up the side of her shirt. It would have seemed indelicate to guide it in any way; I was just happy enough to let nature take its course. But there was only so long that I could pretend to be interested in the stub end of the pastie. I dusted myself down, this provoking a fresh feeding frenzy among the pigeons, got to my feet, and edged out of the seat, where I promptly fell over a maroon sports bag with the badge of some suburban high school that one of the young men must have left behind. For a moment I canvassed the possibility that the offender had been of Middle Eastern appearance, and dispatched, perhaps by Osama himself in envy of our Western way of life, to wreak havoc on the campus – but came out of that instant of reverie to find myself doubled over the edge of the adjacent table. One hand was flailing in the direction of the body its doppelganger had so recently caressed, the other planted squarely on Vicki's open book. Between my splayed fingers I read the title: *The Children's Bach.*

*

Either the trip downtown was quicker than usual, or I was in a dream. Sometimes, caught up in a train of thought, I've shuttled backwards and forwards on the more physical train – rattling off to Strathfield or sliding back to Central when what I wanted was Redfern all the time. But the motion of the train is more seductive: the bus is another matter. The sudden jolts of braking and acceleration that give a mini-rollercoaster to the standing passengers don't soothe you in the same way. Nevertheless, I was way past Town Hall before I recollected myself, and so, to give myself time to wring the last drops of satisfaction from trying to make sense out of Elisabeth's delphic words, I decided to go home by ferry.

The afternoon was windy by now, and most of the buskers, never so enthusiastic on a weekday in any case, had disappeared. I edged behind the small unimpressed crowd standing loosely around a young man who voiced his didgeridoo in recurrent belches. The ferry was waiting; I took a seat on the western side. Reflected from the rising chop, the sunlight that glared through the glass diffused a pleasing warmth around my left hand ribs.* I closed my eyes and thought about rabbits. Flopsy bunnies; Miffy; the velveteen rabbit yearning Pinocchio-like for authenticity; the rabbits swelling across the paddocks like surges on the grey North Sea that drove my grandfather, perhaps always a man poised on the verge of hysteria, to despair. The sea slapped at the hull, the ferry edged out from the pier with a deep-throated swoosh; the deckhand coiled the white cable that had held it to its mooring – a thick rope of cotton, or sisal perhaps. It put me in mind of a young model you see now and then in the background of a TV commercial who has coarse white hair like sisal or horsehair. I thought of the coarse guard hairs of a rabbit's pelt above the soft, woolly layer below. I thought of Elisabeth's hair – did I recall steel-grey roots, like the underfur of a rabbit, or was that just an effect of the light?

The mood lasted me across the water; then, a clatter of rails, the deckhand straining the white cable against a purchase on the shoreside bollard, and it was time to get off. Would I ride on to Lavender Bay and walk back? With a little skip I crossed the short gap above the water, khaki-grey in the shadow like the fur of a you-know-what.

The approach of home turned my mind to more serious matters. Long days at work make L hungry by the time she gets home. She works in public relations and marketing a couple of days a week – her firm, though she just consults for it now. You have probably seen some of her work – remember those discreet ads for Santa Sophia School that just show a high blank wall with a pair of closed gates and the words 'You wish'? By the second week they had doubled their waiting list. They are one of the clients she still keeps; the name might sound like a convent, but it isn't – it's one of those schools founded by radical feminist bluestockings just after the First World War. This particular one, Dr Edith V, was much devoted to the sanctity of wisdom, but gave the spelling its Spanish flavour as a nod to a 15th century Andalusian nun whose mystical writings she found disturbingly exciting. Since that time, and partly because of the founder's shrewd choice of site, the school has flourished: good results, social cachet, old girls in positions of influence all round the state, and indeed the country – twenty grand won't buy you better. But all this has its price, of course, and by the time L comes home she badly needs to eat and unwind. My role is to listen to the gossip, to reassure her if necessary that all the day's decisions have been correct, and to lay a suitably filled plate in front of her at precisely 8 o'clock.

So it was that I was beginning to saute some lentils when the phone rang. This is a job that takes time, because, absorbed in some reverie or other I have burnt the saucepan before now, which makes it liable to stick. I stirred attentively, with an intermittent jab at any lentil that seemed to want to remain unstirred. The message could go through to the keeper, I thought, and kept stirring.

'Hello, it's Gracie here. I know you're there, Dad. Pick up the phone.'

I dropped the spoon. Gracie is our daughter – a corporate lawyer at one of those firms whose name would be a household word if they didn't keep changing it every time they merged with one of their competitors.

'Hello, Gracie,' I said.

'Why didn't you answer straight away?'

'I'm cooking – oh, just excuse me for a moment,' and I ran back and lifted the saucepan off the stove. One or two lentils showed early symptoms of scorching, but their condition was certainly retrievable.

'What are you having?'

'I was thinking of dhal, maybe poured over some broccolini and baby carrots, with basmati.'

'Sounds lovely – listen, can you and Mum look after Billy tomorrow?'

Billy is her child.

'What's happened to child care?'

'It's enrichment day: once a term they have a day when every child is taken out by a relative. Mum knows about it.'

'You mean they enrich themselves by taking your fees and farming out your children.'

'Something like that. Well I knew I could count on you.'

'I suppose it's all right; I'll get Mum to ring you. Hey, on another topic, I know you keep up with things – have you read *The Children's Bach*?'

'The one about the rabbit?'

'*What?*'

'There's a rabbit – but, actually, come to think of it there are lots of rabbits in Helen Garner. A *leitmotif.*'

'Sounds like a heavy motif to me.'

'You know we bill in six minute increments. Save the facetiousness for your wife. She's made a career out of appreciating it.'

'OK, Mum will ring you tonight. Bye.'

I brought the saucepan up to heat again and opened the fridge for the jug of vegetable stock made the day before. You read people saying that it bruises the lentils if the stock isn't at room temperature, but that sounds like nonsense to me. *Shish* modulated to *shoosh* as the cold stock hit the hot metal, steamed and then broke into bubbles of steadily swelling circumference. I stirred in respectful homage to the spirits of yesterday's garlic and celery that drifted around the kitchen. Would L like it better with or without cardamom? One thumbnail slit open a pod, and let two or three of the scarlet varnished seeds fall into the pot. The other spices were waiting in the mortar already pounded, and in another twenty minutes I had gone as far as I cared to: lentils still lumpy enough for authenticity, but not irritatingly *al dente*. Then it was just a matter of trimming the vegetables and readying the rice so that everything might converge on a point of satisfaction at about one minute to eight. By the time I heard L's key in the lock I was slumped in front of *Big Brother*.

'Hello darling,' she said. 'Why is that girl crying?'

'She was fined for mentioning Marty and Jess.'

'I'd fine her for the way she's hanging out of that swimming costume. I don't know how you can watch such rubbish.'

We often have this conversation: it's part of the bonding that married people do, so I gave the expected response:

'Because it's such pure television. It dissolves the illusion that there is a *signifié*.'

If our roles had been reversed, L's reply would have been 'Whatever you reckon', but she is much too dignified for that, so we came to a momentary check. I helped by giving her another opening:

'Gracie would like you to ring her.'

'Have I got time before dinner?'

'No, I don't think so; dinner's just about ready.'

As the program dissolved into a commercial I ran out to get the dinner served. I heaped a satisfactory tablespoon of rice onto each plate, and with careful tongs* made a nicely oblique disposition of the vegetables before pouring the dhal over about half of each. The orangeness of the carrot, the greenness of the slender broccolini reposing on the rice, the nether extremities of each just hinted at below the steaming beige of the dhal, made me think of naive and alien bedfellows half glimpsed beneath a doona in some vegetable *Big Brother*.

L took a forkful.

'I hope it's to your liking.'

'It's very nice; but you know me – I'd be happy with just a boiled egg. Do you mind if I finish mine in front of the television?'

'I thought you didn't like *Big Brother*?'

'I can't stand it, but if I don't start unwinding now I'll be up half the night.'

'Do you have a lot to unwind from?'

'Remind me to tell you the latest about the headmistress.'

'I'll talk to you later.'

By now, as the dhal seeped away, the modesty of my vegetables was only tenuously intact, so I forked up a little rice to cover them before taking another mouthful. Sophia's new headmistress had been a topic of hilarity between us for some time. Recently recruited from overseas, she was a woman bent on remaking the school in the fancied image of some young ladies' seminary of ancient foundation. This was beginning to express itself in more and more baroque ways. I pondered the balance of flavours: did carrot and onion alone give enough sweetness to let the cardamom come through? Perhaps half, no, quarter of a teaspoon of palm sugar another time. Then in the background I heard the blare of the next commercial break and the sound of L getting up to dial Gracie's number. Her end of the conversation came dimly through the closed door.

'Is everything all right?…oh, just some sort of curried chickpea stuff your father made…yes, of course darling, we'd love to…'

I disposed of the vegetable lovers. Nothing but a small heap of rice like a crumpled sheet bore witness to their passing, less than a forkful, now thoroughly infused with dhal. L came back into the room.

'Do you mind if I have some more? I just don't know how you think of such interesting meals. That would be nice enough to serve when people come.'

'Is someone coming?'

'There was a woman I met at the school today; she would like Santa Sophia to take her daughter. I thought it would be nice to extend the hand, so I've asked her to morning tea on Saturday.'

'The trouble is, you ask these people, and the next thing you know they retaliate, and so it goes on. The cycle of abuse.'

*

The alarm went at six. L had stretched herself into an elongated lump under the covers, for all the world like a slender broccolini – broccolina? – waiting the attentions of some eager young carrot. I punched her awake.

'Oh,' she groaned, 'is it time to get up already?'

'Gracie will be dropping Billy off first thing. At our age it looks more seemly if we're dressed.'

L disappeared into the shower. She has always had a strong belief in the redemptive possibilities of each new day, so she seeks a baptism, as it were, as soon as possible. A more sluggish convert, I turned over for a few more minutes. Adult baptism would do me. Nevertheless, by the time Gracie breezed in immaculately suited and holding little Billy by the hand, I was not only dressed but already cutting a carefully-judged slice from the squat, crusty, sourdough loaf I had baked earlier in the week.

'Ra-ra,' said Billy.

'He wants to have a go on that plastic tractor. Look, darling, it's just outside the back door.'

Gracie turned to me, waving something photocopied on red paper with a border of gumnuts.

'There's a form here the childcare people would like filled in about what Billy does today. It says they want it detailed enough that they can evaluate his kin interactions on a number of developmental scales.'

'Don't say "enough that".'

'*Enough for them to be able to.* Does that make you happy?'

'Next thing to ecstatic,' I said. 'Say goodbye to Mummy, Billy.'

'Bye-bye mum-ma,' Billy piped in his winsome fashion.

'Just before you go, you say there are rabbits everywhere in Helen Garner?'

'Well you know what rabbits are like, Dad,' Gracie replied, and with a huge smirk of self-satisfaction she swung out the door, just calling a happy farewell to L as she disappeared.

'Toat, gam-pa,' said Billy, just as I had spread a little honey on the sourdough.

'He'd like a piece of your bread,' said L, coming into the room. 'Grandpa will cut a piece off for you, Billy.'

I held it out, and Billy put one corner in his mouth; then, with both hands by his sides, he opened his mouth again and let the offering fall, leaving a trail of honey down the front of his jumper.

'I expect he doesn't like sourdough,' said L. 'Would you like a lovely piece of banana, Billy?'

I left her casting round for a sufficiently appealing foodstuff and carried my coffee and the newspaper onto the terrace.

'Don't imagine that you can just opt out,' called L from inside as she sponged up the remains of a rejected rice cracker from the kitchen floor.

'I wouldn't dream of it, but I would like to go in today. Gracie gave me an idea that I want to follow up. You know Helen Garner?'

'Not personally, though I've got a vague feeling I might have met her when she spoke at a WEL do that I went to with Edna Q. But I know who she is, of course.'

'Edna Q? Wouldn't that have been WILPF?'*

'Hardly; Helen Garner is younger than we are. Those WILPF people dated from the Spanish Civil War.'

'Well apparently Helen Garner has some sort of a thing about rabbits, and I want to do some research.'

'If it will keep you happy.'

'By the way, what were you going to tell me about the headmistress?'

'I might tell you tonight, if I've forgiven you by then for jumping ship.'

'Love you,' I said.

'I love you too, but it's not unconditional love.'

*

The library received me with a rush of warm air.* Mindful of the ways of coincidence, I half expected to see the pythoness of the day before, but apparently she had retreated to her grotto. I crossed the floor, indelibly marked by the imprint of stilettos once dear to me. At least it would have been except for two things: they made you take off your shoes in those days, and in any case the floor had been resurfaced. But the impressions remained *in posse*, as it were.

At this time there were few students at work on the computer catalogues — just a couple of forlorn Asian girls defying the printed notices by sending emails to loved ones at home. Most of the people at our universities who can read books aren't even out of bed before twelve. I soon had the call numbers for Helen Garner. There was a pale, limp young man at the circulation desk – a former protege of mine. Timely forewarning of a plagiarism charge a few years ago had earned me some residual gratitude.

'Where will I find these?'

'Helen Garner's a bit out of your way, isn't she?'

'Knowledge is indivisible, Garry.'

'Well I'd look on the eighth floor. The undergraduate copies most likely aren't on the shelves.'

'Thanks.' I pushed through an indolent crowd of undergraduates waiting for the lift, and bounced up the stairs. By now the warm air had a clammy undertone, like a wine cellar or an abandoned railway tunnel, and I began to sweat. By the time I reached the eighth floor at last, I half expected to see dripping water, and glow-worms between the bays. But there they were, the modern Australian novels, and piling the works of Ms Garner into the crook of one arm, I made for a desk. There was a lot to read – not least the sad graffiti all over the desk and the adjacent wall – but I had more serious interests. I began on *The Children's Bach*, just riffling through the pages at first to get the feel of the narrative, and then more and more intently. Yes, there the rabbit undoubtedly was. A sort of parallel to Athena, I thought – first caged, then set free. But as I reread the book, the wisdom of Elisabeth's words struck me: the story of the Fox family, of Dexter and the wifely Athena, was in a sense a framing narrative – the true drama was enacted by the rabbit: the Athena that might have been. Caged and cringing in its hutch at first – then running free, the hutch at last consumed with the pizza boxes and newspapers in that final incineration. Vicki, no doubt, had been due to give an oral presentation on the book or something of the sort, and Elisabeth's sage advice had given her a line that any tutor would have had to approve.

But what about other rabbits, if others there were? I opened *Monkey Grip*, then suddenly realised after half a dozen pages that the day had worn along, and I would need to be getting home and buy something quick for dinner. I bundled up the rest of the books and headed for home.

Sometimes the butcher's window is a source of inspiration; so it was today.

'What can I get you, sir?'

I would have resented the honorific, but I knew how random it was.

'Two veal cutlets, thanks.'

'That'll be nine bucks, mate; have a good evening.'

Veal cutlets on a celeriac mash I thought. I could almost hear L's voice saying: 'Chops and some mushed up vegetable stuff your father made,' as she replied to Gracie's duty call of thanks.

I opened the door.

L was sitting with a cup of coffee; in her hands she had an email that was folded over; she looked up as I came in.

'Did you have a good day?'

'Yes, thanks. How about you?'

'I had a lovely time with Billy. Do you know, he can write all his letters backwards.'

'Is that good?'

'Well it shows how intelligent he is; he's not even three yet.'

I looked at some pieces of paper on the floor with squiggles of crayon on them.

'What's that?'

'I think it's I; or maybe it's S like a snake – he really is an amazingly bright child.'

This time the ball was in my court, so I said 'Whatever you reckon.'

'Don't say that, it sounds so dismissive.'

'What's that you've got in your hand?'

'I was going to show you last night: it's an email from the headmistress.'

She handed it to me. The babyish Geneva font, like kindergarten printing, seemed to rob the missive in advance of any gravitas it might ever have had. It was headed 'Naming the library'. The Santa Sophia Foundation had recently presented the school with a new library, which from lack of space stood partly over the playground. Its supports appeared flimsy, but the Old Girl architect had assured the school council that they were an outstanding piece of contemporary design, the carbon fibre technology adapted from mast designs used in the Sydney to Hobart fleet. I hoped there wouldn't be a southerly. In its entirety the message read:

I think *In Grallis* has a certain ring to it

'Has she finally snapped?'

You may not have picked up the allusion, but the school crest has three Ss intertwined, with the motto *Non cerebra in grallis* (we are not brains on stilts)* – it's taken, I believe, from one of the lesser Roman tragedies: the *Amazonia* of Persius, I fancy.

Before this topic could develop further, L had set out in another direction:

'Gracie wanted to know what happened to the survey.'

The survey? Then I remembered the morning's piece of red paper.

'It's in my pocket I think. I must have been using it to take notes on.'

A quick check of my inside breast pocket revealed nothing. I had a mental vision of myself sitting at the library desk with the numbers in front of me, jotted down for convenience on that piece of red paper. I recollected the folded edge of the same piece of paper idly stroking the hairs on the back of my neck against the grain as Athena, herself at the hairdresser's, listened to a conversation about colonic irrigation. Was it already time for me to revisit Jim's Continental Hairdresser and renew acquaintance with hits from the 70s and old copies of *Who Weekly*? Then I saw myself closing the pages of *Monkey Grip* and inserting that same folded red paper to keep the place. I retrieved the survey and handed it to L.

She unfolded it and began to read, squinting a little at the difficulty of making out the text of the document against the crimson background.

'They could have made it a bit more user friendly.'

'Isn't red the Chinese colour for happiness? Quite a lot of the parents might think that was important. Specially when the child's privacy is involved.'

'Yes, and I suppose they had the layout feng shui'd to stop the privacy leaking out through the bottom right hand corner.'

L manages to support both the Luddites and the Enlightenment simultaneously, so this sort of conversation has the potential to go on for ever. Now she started again:

'What's this scrawl?'

I played for time.

'What scrawl is that?'

'Just up in the corner here under the Bib and Bub logo?'

I knew L was upset, or she never would have soiled her lips with a word as newfangled as 'logo'. There was no denying it was my own handwriting, nor that the content was some of the more picturesque graffiti from the desk where I had been sitting. For a number of years I had sporadically been putting material together for a pilot study called something like 'The Permanent in the Ephemeral − Changing Fashions and Sexual Invitation'. Perhaps an Australian Research Grant would come of it one day.

'I know your work is very clever and important, but we can't possibly send this in with that sort of filth written all over it. Next thing we knew, Billy would be taken into care.'

'I don't think Community Services have a big enough budget to follow up every case.'

L thought for a moment. Then the Luddite came to the surface.

'Sophia's junior school go in for this sort of nonsense − they got back a bundle with the analysis just the other day. I saw it in the Office. I'll take one of those and send it off for Billy.'

Her contempt for educational research was equal to her contempt for privacy and feng shui combined.

'But won't Gracie find out?'

'She'll never know. The relative gives the survey back in a sealed envelope with the child's name written on the outside. Gracie won't see it.'

If you are going to seek redemption every morning, it probably helps if your sense of sin has some foundation. I went off to peel the celeriac.

*

L was away to an early meeting the next morning, and neglecting the paper I made for the terrace with a pot of tea and the copy of *Monkey Grip* that the previous day's domestic urgencies had forced me to lay aside. Apparently the novel had in its time been prescribed for more than one popular course, for the text bore underlinings and highlightings in several styles and colours. Paragraphs with the strongest appeal had been underscored so emphatically with a ballpoint pen that the corrugated imprints on the reverse of the page made reading near impossible. The carolling of magpies in the nearby trees along with the cheepings and chirrupings of other birds I was unable to identify, the at first tentative and then grateful warmth of the autumn sunshine, the aromatic vapour of the second-finest Assam tea (I don't buy the finest − it's too absurdly expensive), combined with the shimmering of the type on the insanely corrugated pages to produce an effect not far from stupor. And then I saw it: *cradling the rabbit with my cardigan.**

I tried to push the paper flat with a fingertip, and felt it, furred as it was by generations of abuse and now warm from the sunshine, almost like the ruckled skin of the little creature. I backtracked several pages to fix in my mind just how this rabbit fitted into the story, while hypotheses multiplied in my brain. *Nora is the younger counterpart of Athena.* I flipped back to the title page to confirm that this was the earlier publication. *Nora seems to be a self-possessed young woman, but her inner self just wants to be cuddled. The rabbit has been saved from the dogs. Nora is creating for the inner self that confining hutch of domesticity from which Athena will need help to release her. Nora and Athena are successive surrogates for Helen Garner.* Had there been a shocking pink fluorescent highlighter near to hand I might well have picked out the phrase that wrapped the rabbit in the cardigan for the benefit of future readers – though it could hardly have been noticed amid the profusion of other visual aids with which the text was embellished.

Yes, I thought, as I read on with refocused attention, in some ways *The Children's Bach* is *Monkey Grip 2.* Should we call it *Monkey Grip 2: the Children's Bach* in the film version, or would we just bring out the similarity by casting the same actors? I played in my mind with various casting possibilities. Or would it be one of those parallel things like *Sliding Doors?* For both books have the same disillusioning visit to Sydney, the same family trip to the country, the same late scene at the swimming baths. That could be a reason to cast Gwyneth Paltrow, always a good thing, though the scene might have to be moved to California. I tried to picture Gwyneth Paltrow on Nora's eternal bicycle. How L would have hated those inner-city alternative-liver faux-green people with their bicycles and their macrame shoulder bags! At least Athena had a car. Trapped or not, she had certainly made a step up. But still, Gwyneth Paltrow would look good on a bicycle. I saw her in a sort of flat cap, rather like in *Shakespeare in Love.*

'I'm taking it as a sort of fantasy autobiography,' I said to L when she got home that evening. 'Reality v. wish-fulfilment, look on this picture and on that. There's a Hegelian dialectic, with false consciousness as a necessary step towards liberation. I don't actually know anything about Helen Garner's life, but they say *Monkey Grip* can be read as a *roman à clef* if you were there at the time. And the rabbits link it together.'

'Sounds fascinating, I'm sure,' said L. 'I'm glad you've finally found a real interest. I hope you've remembered that the van Tromps are coming tomorrow.'

'I was planning to spend tomorrow reading *Cosmo Cosmolino.* And anyway, who are the van Tromps?'

'You remember, I told you I'd met a woman who was sending her daughter to Santa Sophia, and I wanted to be friendly.'

'I don't think you mentioned the name. Are they Dutch? I've often found them a very aggressive race of people. You know, in Amsterdam they think nothing of pushing people off the footpath. I suppose it comes of having so many of them in such a small country.'

'What an absurd racist generalisation — anyway, you can't call the Dutch a race.'

'In that case, it isn't racist.'

'*Touchée*,' said L, 'but Rita van Tromp is just as Australian as you or I.'

'Me,' I said, to make it clear who was to have the tactical high ground. I wasn't letting her say *touchée*, with or without a final e, and get away with it.

'As you or I *are*,' said L.

'Is there a Mr van Tromp in the picture?'

'I don't think so, just the mother and daughter, I believe.'

'I dare say she pushed him off the footpath.'

'Very likely; what I gather is, the daughter has been living with her father in Melbourne and she's now coming up here to stay with her mother.'

'I expect she'll prefer it here; it can't have been comfortable living on the footpath.'

L let me have the last word, and we turned to other occupations. She had a presentation for a new client to work on, and was soon staring as fixedly into her laptop as any gipsy into a crystal ball; for my part I went off cackling to bend my mind to the morning tea.

*

Morning tea can be a problematical time for entertaining if you don't know the people. My natural instinct is peasant-style, or English country kitchen if you like: scones and jam and hearty cups of tea. Mrs van Tromp, however, as a person thinking of enrolling her daughter at Santa Sophia, presumably had plenty to throw around, and might be accustomed to something a little more upmarket. But is there such a thing as an upmarket morning tea? Morning tea as I understand it is essentially an English concept, and from what little I know of upmarket English folk I would expect them still to be sauntering down to breakfast at ten o'clock, lifting the cover from a dish of devilled kidneys or ringing for a fresh pot of coffee. The fresh pot of coffee I could do, but devilled kidneys, no. Who ever heard of having kidneys for morning tea? Had it been afternoon tea now, cucumber sandwiches and cake would have afforded no difficulty.

After some thought, I settled for traveller's gingerbread,* and I will just drop in one word of advice: leave out the rosewater, you'll find the mixture is wet enough already. Something the squire's rosy-cheeked kitchen girl might hand around steaming hot from the oven before the hunt, I fancied, and gingerbread itself could be taken as a courteous acknowledgement of the van Tromps' putative Dutch antecedents. Tea and coffee we could provide as they might prefer.

Having made this resolution, I was happy enough to sleep on it, but such was not to be. L lay quietly for a long time — too quietly, I couldn't help thinking — and then began rolling and flapping about like a beached tuna. I tried to ignore her. Then she began to groan.

'Whatever are you up to?' I said. 'You're carrying on like a fish in labour.'

'I can't help worrying about what Gracie is going to do when she finds out about the survey.'

'You said she wouldn't find out.'

'I shouldn't have taken your advice: I've been worried sick about it ever since. Why didn't you talk me out of it?'

'We could have sent in the original, but you wouldn't have it.'

'How could we, after you'd besmirched it like that?'

There was no reasoning with L in this mood. I got up and went downstairs. With any luck *Big Brother — Up Late and Uncut* would still be on.

*

The van Tromps arrived on time. No sooner had I lifted the gingerbreads from the oven, each appealingly dimpled as a kitchen girl's cheek, than the doorbell rang and L hastened to answer it. I have heard of women keeping a freshly ironed apron next to the front door to cast aside as they welcomed visitors, but L's social self-confidence had no need of props. Besides, she knew that whatever domestic achievements were on show, she would automatically be thanked for them: not even her most feminist friends could seriously entertain the thought that these were areas where a man might contribute.

Our visitors were a typical family, or part of one, at least. Have you noticed that when advertisers show a generic family on the television you will have a ruggedly cheerful father, a beautifully turned out mother, a wholesome-looking teenage boy with an open expression and his hair nicely cut – not too long, but not aggressively short either – and a younger child, boy or girl, who looks a bit of a tearaway but would clearly be a lot of fun to have around the house. Specially if you were that sort of a father. And then there is the goth teenage daughter. Mother and daughter, such were the van Tromps.

I took in the daughter with a cursory glance: the straight black hair parted in the middle to reveal a scalp the colour of candle wax, its dull sheen echoed by the stud in her lower lip; the arms and shoulders strikingly thin, though well this side of anorexia, but so swaddled in a black crocheted shawl that every other detail would have to be supplied by the imagination. Her impossibly long black-stockinged legs – an effect created no doubt by an impossibly short skirt – were as spindly as those of any Italian table and finished in a pair of shoes of at least twice the bulk that could be necessary to accommodate feet of any proportionate size. Do people still wear Doc Martens, I wondered, or is there some new brand that is even bulkier? Walking around in those all day must do wonders for your lower body strength. *They reminded her of the ankleboots worn by Ant and Bee in a book her mother had read to her,* I thought.

Such was Poppy van Tromp, though as I say I gave her little more than a fleeting glance. My eyes were drawn rather to her mother, and with a dawning dismay I hoped I could manage to conceal. For Rita van Tromp turned out to be none other than Rita Rizzo, a young woman who had cut a destructive swath through my colleagues during my junior years as an academic. I well remembered one of those colleagues, a very young man whose byronic appearance belied a rather prudish and retiring nature, who had been on the receiving end of one of her infatuations. She burst into his room one afternoon wearing nothing but a plastic raincoat, and he had been hard put to bundle her into a wardrobe in time when the professor knocked at his door. As soon as the professor's business was concluded, he had run and slammed the door behind him, so he confided over a beer at The Courser's Arms. His hands still shook from his experience, and the beer slopped wildly over the laminex table and dribbled to the floor. He was too frightened to go back — would I talk to her and get her to go away?

Our parley had been brief, and mostly conducted through a closed door; I hoped the merciful effects of age would prevent recognition. Did L and I need such a disruptive influence in our lives? I kissed her by way of greeting, contriving to turn my face away as far as it was possible to do so. There is a lot of kissing at Santa Sophia. Myself, I am not a huge fan of the passionless kiss — perhaps I was spoilt by a former girlfriend — but I had learnt that it was expected in these circles. If there were some of L's school acquaintances that I was a good deal readier to kiss than others, that was in the nature of things, and I did my best to conceal it. But Rita's kiss was formality itself — so far, so good — and we proceeded to the morning tea.

L had optimistically set places on the terrace; as we walked out, Poppy's legs formed a decorative counterpoint to the Italian table. The conversation flowed. Rita's former husband Philip, it seemed, had snorted himself into a stroke. There appeared to be plenty of money in the background, so lengthy life-support would not be a difficulty, but in the meanwhile there was Poppy to look after. Naturally, Rita wanted the best for her child (though her secret history made it easy for me to guess how Philip had been awarded custody); naturally, again, she had thought of Santa Sophia. L was bright and gracious through all of this as she always is, while Poppy sulked in silence with her legs drawn up and the shawl gathered even more encompassingly around her slender form. Compact and black, she might have been one of those dormant funnelwebs people find in the bottom of their swimming pools. Her hibernation, however, was not so profound as to stop her making steady inroads into the gingerbread.

We traversed the major attractions of Santa Sophia: the excellence of its facilities, the accessibility of the staff, the friendliness of the parents, the superiority of its exam results, all this interspersed with tantalizing snippets of autobiography from Rita, and smiling assent from me whenever it was called for, or L said 'Don't we, darling?' or something of the sort. In the circumstances my participation had been a little more guarded than might otherwise have been the case, and I was now beginning to feel it was time for the occasion to draw to a close. Natural misanthropy could have brought me to this point, joined with a disinclination either to forgo my lunch or share it with the intruders; today these natural impulses were compounded by my fear that at any moment Rita might discover our previous acquaintance and launch into an unwished-for intimacy. Had I not known what reprisals such an act would provoke from L, I might have been tempted to a definitive movement, such as gathering up my cup and plate and carrying them to the kitchen.

At this point, however, the doorbell rang. I got up. Standing on the porch was a well-built man of perhaps 35. He was wearing a black leather jacket, black jeans tucked into heavily buckled boots that reached to mid-calf, and black gauntlets profusely studded with silver spikes. Only put back the motorcycle helmet which he had removed, and which now hung from one of those disproportionate paws, and he could have passed for Darth Vader. We looked at one another for a moment. We might have continued to do so, except that Poppy now squeezed past me, jumped up, and hung soundless with both arms wrapped around the newcomer's neck. He, for his part, dropped the helmet, shook off the glove and held out a large powerful hand in my direction.

'Dave,' he said.

I waved them in with my other hand, in what I conceived to be a graciously seigneurial gesture. At which point Dave produced an enormous bunch of flowers which I hadn't previously noticed – he must have been holding them behind his back.

'Could you look after these, mate?' he asked.

I made for the laundry; Dave and his mute burden sought the terrace.

What was the significance of the flowers, I wondered, as I plunged the stems into a bucket of water. What was Dave's role in the van Tromp establishment? Could I evade detection until Rita had left the premises? And what fresh insights awaited me in *Cosmo Cosmolino*, if I should ever be permitted to begin reading that work?

These, as Les Paul would say, were questions.

2

*A – villainy**

The last of my questions at least, it seemed, was not destined to receive a speedy answer. As soon as our guests had left, Rita to travel by some means undisclosed, Poppy on the back of Dave's bike, L was keen to dissect the experience of the morning.

'I think she's quite charming.'

'Rita? Do you know who she is?' I told the story.

'Well, I've often heard that story from you, but I had no reason to connect it with Rita van Tromp. Aren't you overreacting? We've all done things when we were young that we may not be 100 per cent proud of.'

'I bet you never walked into a tutor's room in nothing but a plastic raincoat.'

'I'm not saying whether I did or not: you'd only cast it up against me.'

'Look, if I'm repetitive, perhaps it's because she is seared so deeply into my memory. Believe me, that woman is poison. Promise me you'll never oblige me to be in the same space with her again.'

'That could be a little difficult. When you were doing whatever you were doing for so long, I told her you'd be happy to give Poppy a few pointers.'

'You did what?'

'Well you see the syllabus is so different at Santa Sophia, and the school she's been going to in Victoria didn't believe in exams or some such foolery, so naturally the poor child has no conception of how to study.'

'But what do I know about the high school syllabus? Do we even know what subjects she's going to do?'

'You academics can turn your hands to anything – don't tell me you couldn't master the high school syllabus in every subject in a couple of days.'

Even if L's flattery went some way to mitigate the outrage of her promise, those last words sounded ominous.

'A couple of days?'

'Yes, we fixed up that you'd see her on Monday afternoon – you won't be doing anything then.'

'I had planned to get on with my research.'

'That'll keep. So what did you make of Poppy?'

'I don't know how she'll fit in at Santa Sophia. Do they take girls with black hair?'

Almost to a girl, it seemed, Santa Sophians had smooth shining hair of an immaculate blondeness.

'I expect they'd have to. There are anti-discrimination laws about that sort of thing. Anyway, Poppy's hair is dyed.'

'Do they take girls with dyed hair?'

'She'll just have to undye it, I'm afraid. I thought she was probably rather sweet under all that nonsense.'

'I'd have to plead insufficient information. But I liked the boyfriend.'

'That can't be Poppy's boyfriend. She's barely fifteen.'

'So how do you account for Dave, then?'

'Apparently he taught at Poppy's school – I wish I could remember the name: Something Girls' High. Started with a c, I think.'

I tried vainly to picture a school that could have Poppy for a typical product. Charles Addams meets the Castle of Otranto?

'C that says *kuh*?'

L ignored this interruption.

'Computer Studies and Industrial Design were his subjects, I think Rita said. But he's spending some time with them now till he finds his feet again. He and the school parted ways; a clash of philosophies, according to Rita.'

'I can see that: the school's philosophy would be that it didn't want its teachers sleeping with fifteen-year-old girls.'

'It's dreadful the way you jump to conclusions. If a quarter of what you think is true, the man ought to be in jail.'

Johnson's words about jail floated into my mind. Secure in Pentridge, Dave might not have been better housed and better fed, but knowing what I knew there was no doubt that compared with Rita's establishment it might provide better company.

*

Coming away from this exchange, and reflecting on the events of the morning and the nameless horrors that might await on Monday, I had a feeling that comfort food was required. Comfort with a capital *kuh*. Lamb and roast vegetables would do for a start, with some green I had yet to decide on, and I'd make a pumpkin soup in sufficient quantity to leave some over for a quick meal on Monday evening – that is, if the worst should occur and I was detained at Rita's. There was a leg of lamb in the freezer; I would work on the soup while the meat defrosted. Filled with foreboding, I peeled a pumpkin.

This soup, I like to think, is my own invention, though doubtless untold generations of Italian peasants would rise up and claim priority. Untold if you can't count beyond twenty or so, that is, for I doubt there were many pumpkins grown in Italy before about the middle of the 16th century. The ingredients are simple: pumpkin, water, and salt or sugar as required. Your more insipid pumpkin might need quite a lot of these last. Then basil – lots and lots of basil. You finish it off with some yoghurt or sour cream or whatever you happen to have, a bit of crusty Italian bread on the side, and Bob's your uncle. It's the basil, you see, that makes that intriguing difference. They will all be pushing out their plates for another helping while you happily reflect that you have not only fed but satisfied an army, and all for next to nothing. A person that lived on pumpkin wouldn't need to spend much.

With such and similar thoughts and deeds the afternoon wore away. Meanwhile the leg of lamb, with a little help from the microwave, had defrosted. I inserted the point of the knife and began to ease the meat free from the bone. There is nothing to this job that can't be done in quarter of an hour, or that the butcher couldn't do for you in two minutes. Perhaps some of those spiky little leaves of rosemary in the cavity, as Elizabeth David might have it, and then tie it up. I opened the drawer where we keep such things, and looked for the string.

'Do you know where the string is, darling?'

'Wherever you normally keep it, I suppose,' replied L distantly from another room. She was in out of body mode, roaming virtual space on some business-related quest. While she was thus occupied, my more carnal concerns could carry little weight. But then I myself, lesser and more earth-bound shaman though I was, received enlightenment.

Our laundry, adjoining the terrace on one side, contains the few gardening implements that L and I possess. Neither of us has much of a way with plants, so there is not much growing except for a frangipani of majestic proportions, and a vine which is trained to shade the terrace in the warmer months. There flashed before my eyes a picture of a day last summer: L tiptoed on a stool, doing her best to secure a trailing vine shoot to a wire above her head.

'Whatever is that in your hand?' I had asked.

'A bread tag: it was the only thing I could find.'

'Be careful: I was reading that a lot of older people die from swallowing bread tags.'

'I'm not trying to swallow it; I'm trying to tie up the grapevine.'

'I'll get you some string.'

'People die of swallowing string too, you know,' she had said. 'Remember

> *at last he swallowed some which tied*
> *itself in dreadful knots inside?'**

'Henry King was a child. A person of your age would be in much more jeopardy from a bread tag.'

And so I had brought the string, which then in all likelihood had been heedlessly left in the laundry. I went in search of it.

The most obvious feature of the laundry today, however, was not string. It was an outsize bunch of flowers – Dave's unaccountable baggage – standing where I had left it in its plastic bucket on top of the washing machine.

It certainly represented much money. There were lilies of more than one kind, which I vaguely supposed might still be in season. There were strelitzias, or something like them. There were what I took to be members of the orchid tribe. There were unnameable blooms and blossoms. There was foliage. Then there were things that I had to assume were organic in origin, but looked more like something out of Hieronymus Bosch. As I remembered the sequence of events that morning, the flowers could not have been for Poppy. For who then? Rita? Or some third unknown? Certainly they were not for us. Dave had clearly forgotten them – perhaps he would return. Time would tell.

The string revealed itself; I secured the meat with three or four ties, then making small incisions between the strings I pushed in slivers of garlic. The general effect, with ridges of meat bulging up between the bands of string, each ridge ornamented with the protruding ends of half a dozen pieces of garlic, was powerfully suggestive of one of Dave's studded gauntlets. It seemed that I would not cease to be reminded of the events of the morning.

Then there were the vegetables. Now you may think Jamie Oliver is a bit of a lightweight, but for very eatable food that's totally of today, I say he's spot on. Just slice up the vegetables – potato, probably, with some onions and kumera – and toss them a bit in the baking tin with oiled hands. Sprinkle in some salt, freshly ground pepper – I keep a little mortar that I use mostly for pepper – and maybe some dried oregano, and bake it under the meat. The beans (I had decided on beans) could cook while the lamb was resting.

'Aren't you leaving the dinner a little late?' called L at half past six. Travels in cyberspace must have made her hungry.

'The leg of lamb that can't be cooked in an hour and a quarter hasn't trod grass,' I replied confidently, turning the oven to its highest setting. Now for some comfort.

*

There are domestic tasks to be done in even the most carefree household, and ours at the moment, or at least my part of it, was not that. L passed the laundry door the next day just as I was bundling a navy-blue towel into the washing machine. The flowers had been moved to a corner.

'You're not putting that in with the whites, are you?' she asked.

'There you betray your superficial acquaintance with housewifely skills,' I replied. 'The towel is clearly a white, whereas this,' and I held up a white t-shirt, 'is just as clearly a dark colour, and will be washed with the socks. I'm afraid you wouldn't stand up very well against Athena. Helen Garner specifically mentions the careful darns in her jumper.'*

'I despise women like that,' said L. 'They're like little girls playing in the dollies' corner. I should hope I've got better things to do with my life than darn jumpers.'

'A common theme of religious thought has been that it isn't the act itself that's important, so much as the spirit in which it's done:

> *Who sweeps a room, as for Thy laws,*
> *Makes that, and the action, fine.'**

'I don't suppose George Herbert could have been a man, by any chance?' retorted L; 'Do the words "false consciousness" mean anything to you?'

'Are you suggesting that Helen Garner is actually a man?'

'I wouldn't go as far as that, but if she really imagines housework can be enough for a woman of spirit, I'd say she needs to take a long hard look at herself.'

L's words provoked a fresh train of thought: could it be that a religious subtext underlay *The Children's Bach*? I had done my reading of that book in the library and so had no copy near to hand, but the story was clear enough in my mind to suggest a tropological interpretation would not be far to seek. A *Pilgrim's Progress*. Finding only betrayal in the land of Egypt — this played by Sydney, in a typical Melbourne perspective — where she had been lured by seductive but ultimately empty promises, Athena has toiled back through the wilderness to Melbourne – you notice that she returns by train though she had come by air. Anyone who has sat up in the train from Sydney to Melbourne will appreciate that it's an appropriate symbol for forty years in the wilderness. There are always bits in the middle of the night when you're not quite sure which way the train is going, and I'm certain that the last time I did it we must have passed through Uranquinty at least three times, the station sign banging in the wind and dimly lit by one of those overhead lamps that were the last word in illumination in 1915. And now, returned to Melbourne, in her spiritual re-invigoration she perceives it to be the Promised Land. But if Athena was the human soul, where would that leave the rabbit? And what became of the doubling of the story with *Monkey Grip*? There was something there, but puzzling as to what it might be, I continued to brood right through the pumpkin soup.

I was having a second bowl of this in front of the television when the phone rang.

'Will you answer that?' I shouted to L. 'I'm watching *Big Brother Live Evictions*.'

Apparently it was Gracie, just ringing to keep us up to date with some of the clever things that Billy had been saying. During a lull in the televised hysteria, L's voice came through the door:

'…oh, pumpkin soup, with some herb thing your father knows about…yes.'

The screen reclaimed my attention. Then I let out an involuntary howl of dismay.

'I have to go, Gracie,' and L banged down the phone. 'Whatever's the matter?'

'I just realised that I forgot to record my vote. All that Rita business completely drove it out of my mind.'

'I thought you were having a heart attack at the very least. You shouldn't frighten people like that.'

'My vote could have made all the difference. You know what they say about evil triumphing.'

'I doubt it. After all, what are you against all those teenage girls that watch *Big Brother*?'

What indeed, I reflected, and what's more I was slated to take on just such a teenage girl the next day. Some of the sweetness seemed to go out of the television.

*

At least I deserved a toothsome lunch before setting out. I bought a new loaf of sourdough from the excellent local delicatessen-cum-supermarket which is one of the joys of inner-city densities. You don't have to be shooting up all the time and riding round on bicycles like those people in *Monkey Grip*. The rest of this loaf would go well with the reprise of the soup, but meanwhile I would make a hearty lamb sandwich. I carved off a slice or two from the lamb, ruby-red jelly glistening in the bottom of the plate. That could contribute to some future meal. In the meantime, the rosemary-scented lamb, set off just with some tomato and a leaf of lettuce, made as fine a meal as I could imagine – worthy of a more auspicious occasion. Then it was time to go.

Rita's home was a longish but quite possible walk – no more than three quarters of an hour. Nora perhaps could have managed it more quickly on her bicycle, but I was not Nora. I had printed out a few of the more likely-looking syllabuses from the Board of Studies website, and these I carried in a plastic shopping bag. I thought this would strike the right note of academic unworldliness without descending to the level of macrame. Whether Poppy would be alive to such subtleties remained to be seen.

My chosen route lay past Luna Park, which appeared to be open. At least the rides were operating, though whether there was anyone on them was unclear. I peered through the fence. There were none of the crowds of sailors and prostitutes there would have been in my young day. Had the park been commandeered by some small group perhaps, like Wally World by the Griswold family in the climax of *National*

Lampoon's Vacation? What an artist Chevy Chase was, I reflected, and chuckled to myself as I replayed various scenes in my mind. What about the aunt on top of the car? Someone had told me that story a few years ago as a personal experience of a friend of theirs in South Australia. What liars people were!

The dismissive *Pfff* of contempt which escaped me at this moment, following as it did on the chuckle of a moment before, drew some odd looks from a group of Japanese tourists busy photographing one another on the boardwalk. On a Saturday or Sunday afternoon this area would have been full of wedding parties posing against the undoubtedly spectacular vistas of the harbour for innumerable photos while their impatient guests hung around elsewhere, desperate for a drink. Today it was almost deserted. I pushed on past what looks like a Victorian shooting box, but always turns out disappointingly to be a heritage item connected with Sydney Water. I dare say they pump sewage from one side of the harbour to the other, or something. No doubt it will come in useful if ever there is a sewage shortage down south.

Like an alpha male of any of the species to which I have sometimes been likened, I have my regular tracks. Now as I came up the steep flight of steps from the harbour, I felt that I was beginning to pass beyond the boundaries of my own territory and entering realms of which I knew little. There were many ways leading from this point, all of them more or less unfamiliar. Nevertheless, as I drew nearer the area in which Rita's establishment was to be found, I began to be seized with a growing sensation of *déjà vu*. I checked the address, which L had written on a piece of paper.

'Do you know where you are going?' she had asked me that morning. 'I wrote down the address for you.'

I gave it a cursory glance and noted the suburb.

'There are so many Chinese people around these days that I'm sure I'll find someone to translate,' I said. L's writing is notoriously incomprehensible.

'I don't know what you're carrying on about. If anything, my writing is too unformed and girlish. I don't think it's changed since primary school, and I won a certificate in fifth class then for having the neatest books. I would show you, except that my mother threw it away years ago when she was tidying up. Some people have been kind enough to say that my writing is just like my lovely open personality; what they would make of those cramped little glyphs of yours I don't know – they look as though they could have been scratched out by a garden gnome.'

The full significance of this simile escaped me, but 'glyphs' was pretty good; people don't pay her all that money for nothing.

'Well I suppose I'll just play it by ear.' I had said. Now I looked carefully at the address for the first time, and a terrible certainty took hold of me. Rita's was the very street, probably the very house, perhaps even the very apartment to which I had made my way years ago as an uninvited, unwelcome, even, though I hate to say it, maudlin caller on a once-loved someone – she of the kisses, to be precise, so let's call her K (if only because she came before L). The whole scene was etched indelibly on my brain, and unreeled itself like one of those movie clips people send you that clog up the email for about half an hour. I could see the stairwell with tiles shoulder high and inset panels of salmon-colour and off-turquoise. Not marbled, pearlised I think the word is, and those little white six-sided ones on the floor and black edges and a wrought iron balustrade. A bit like an aquarium or down in a rockpool looking up. Just outside the door there was something in a brass pot – perhaps an aspidistra, but when I tried to focus I wasn't sure any more. Then K was opening the door, the dark heavy door they have in blocks like those, and I saw her and past her to the water, and the sun was just high enough not to dazzle but low enough for the light still to move across the pictures as a ferry went past; watercolours mostly, or perhaps lithographs – under glass at any rate. And the glass shone and the walls were glazed too, the way people had them then, but not perfectly flat, so the light varied and the reflections varied too and moved and the plants, there was one on a bookcase I think, with leaves that stuck up – mother-in-law's tongues, they're called – moved like seaweed as stripes of light slid up and down. What were they saying, those tongues? Nothing to my advantage.

Now it was I, the caller, who was unwilling, fearful that the door would open on the Gorgon head of Rita. As with *Monkey Grip* and *The Children's Bach*, I seemed to be playing a scene with all the same elements, but with the implications of the roles unaccountably rearranged.

'*Childe Roland to the Dark Tower came*,' I muttered to myself as I applied my finger to the bell. There was a buzz from within, and Poppy opened the door. Of Rita there appeared no sign. Things were looking up. The apartment, since my last visit, had acquired a few obvious signs of wealth, but was otherwise little changed. There were black Italian leather sofas flanking a glass coffee table. There was a small sculpture of some sort where the pot-plant had stood in years gone by. The profusion of pictures that I remembered, or thought I remembered, was gone, and the walls, no longer glazed, were painted in some matte finish just a fraction removed from white. The longest of the walls in this sitting room held a largish painting which appeared to be of some distinction. Poppy motioned me to a seat on one of the sofas, and took her place on the other. Against the black leather one was conscious of her rather as a difference of texture than as a presence. Her pale hands and face appeared to float free. I put the plastic shopping bag down on the coffee table: it struck a welcomely familiar down-to-earth note.

Gradually, during the course of the afternoon, I elicited from Poppy the names of the subjects she would be studying, though her participation in the dialogue was more by inclinations of the head and movements of the arms and shoulders than by articulate speech. That seemed to be a medium foreign to her.

I explained how she should attack the various subjects; I gave her tips about organising her work. I suggested all the hundred things that roll off the tongue of anyone who has been teaching young people almost as long as they can remember. At last we came to English. Poppy's class were reading a number of novels: Rita had bought copies of them, and Poppy produced them now – a low, uneven stack of multicoloured covers reflected in the glass of the coffee table. Uppermost in the pile was *The Great Fire*.* I put my finger on it.

'I'd start with this one,' I said, 'it should appeal to you. It's like *Lolita* retold as a Mills & Boon.'

Poppy shot me a look of sheer hatred, but like thunder after this lightning came a deep burst of laughter, and Dave emerged from some inner room.

'That's a good one, mate,' he said. 'It was sounding like a bit of a dry argument there for a while — could you handle a beer?'

'I have been known to drink one from time to time.'

'Just hang on, and I'll get us some out of the fridge.'

Poppy had disappeared. While waiting for Dave to return, I went over for a closer look at the picture. It was a harbour scene in early morning light with the suggestion of the remains of winter fog, as if a grey scrim had been dropped between the viewer and the scene. About two thirds of the way to the left and above the centre of the picture was something which, though distant, was unmistakeable as one of those huge angophoras still common in the bush around Middle Harbour. I studied the picture. It could almost have been a Streeton, though if it had been it would probably have been called something like *Winter's Trophies*. This one had a small brass plate fixed to the frame which said simply: 'Long Bay — 1895'.

Dave pushed a stubby into my hand.

'Cheers, mate,' he said.

'Cheers, Dave,' I replied, and felt cheered indeed as I took a gulp of the ice-cold liquid. The Gorgon's lair had something to be said for it.

'You see that tree?' said Dave, indicating the object of my own recent scrutiny.

'Yes; is there something special about it?'

'That's the very tree where Barcroft Boake* committed suicide. Hanged himself with his stockwhip.'

This was an unsuspected side of Dave; it was up to me to respond in kind:

'Sounds like a made-up name, doesn't it, Barcroft Boake? I wonder if he was really called that. And I've never understood how you would go about hanging yourself with a stockwhip.'

I tried to picture some cunning flick of the wrist which would send the thong over the branch of a tree and back round the stockman's neck, then jerk him from the ground to hang twitching at last from the angophora.

'He was gay, you know,' went on Dave, undeterred.

'Would that make it easier?'

I thought of a well-loved teacher from my youth, a gentle pedophile who had shot himself rather than face exposure.

'I've done a lot of reading of those blokes,' said Dave. 'When I was younger I did a few things I'm not so proud of.'

These words recalled my recent conversation with L, and I had a flash, if 'flash' is not too graphic a word in the circumstances, of Dave wearing nothing but a plastic raincoat. I dismissed it as quickly as it came. Then I looked again at Dave, now less formally clad than at our last meeting. In the light of this new information, the whole picture of the man, from his ponytail to the powerful forearms with their amateurish tattoos, said 'prison' just as clearly as if Dave had spelt it out, beginning with p that says *puh*. Dave had improved his time by reading in the prison library, I guessed, and this was the foundation of his unlooked-for familiarity with the unfortunate bush balladist. I had misjudged him. Dave really was in a position to weigh the company of Rita against that available in Pentridge. I wondered which he preferred.

*

L was already home when I got back.

'Good news for Rita,' she said; 'Mrs Smith in enrolments says that hopefully they'll be able to take Poppy in a couple of weeks.'

It is far too late in the day to defeat this Germanism, but a rearguard action could still win some credit, if only from L.

'I expect she means she hopes,' I said. 'It might be worth checking whether your enrolments woman changed her name from Schmidt to avoid internment during the war. The only time I recall meeting her, she certainly looked old enough.'

'That was rather uncalled for,' said L. 'I don't see what her age has to do with it.'

'If they can take her in a few weeks, why not take her now?'

Then I remembered: at Santa Sophia the whole term is planned as a military operation, and when I say 'military', I'm not just using the word idly. Dr V the founder of the school, though she despised male violence in all its forms, had embraced the metaphor of warfare to inspire the girls as foot-soldiers in the struggle for women's rights. The headmistress was commander-in-chief, the teachers her lieutenants, and with the help of their leading girls they planned each term for the capture of certain strategic objectives on the road to knowledge. Sometimes repeated assaults would be required, but the goal once attained – the mastery of simultaneous equations or whatever it might be – the results were signalled back to the headmistress, who rewarded outstanding individual efforts by adding a stripe to the girl's blazer, or something of the sort. The induction of a new recruit in mid-campaign would take careful thought. Here a Teutonic background might well be a plus, and I silently congratulated whichever previous headmistress had first given Ms Schmidt her stripes.

By now *Big Brother* was beginning to beckon. I could easily reheat the soup in one of the commercial breaks.

'I hope you don't mind having soup again this evening, darling,' I asked preemptively.

'I'll be happy with whatever you care to make. You know me, darling – just a dry crust would suit me down to the ground.'

Nominations were going well. One of the contestants was talking to Big Brother: 'I don't think she's being herself,' he was saying, 'and that affects my time in the house because it makes me uncomfortable if someone's not completely honest with me.'

'What a lot of gibberish,' said L, coming in. 'I hope he's the next to go.'

'It will all depend on the nominations,' I replied. 'I didn't think you followed *Big Brother*.'

'I should just about hope I've got better things to do,' said L, ' but you can't help picking up on a few of the threads. The way that man went on in the spa last Thursday was just disgraceful.'

A domestic idyll, in other words. I was just beginning to feel completely relaxed for the first time that day when there came a knock like thunder at the outer door, followed by the sound of the same door being thrown open. Gracie stormed into the room. She is the most courteous of daughters, and though of course she has her own key, I had never before known her to enter the house without invitation. Something must have moved her powerfully.

'Whatever do you and Mum think you're playing at?' she demanded. I am accustomed to standing in the front line in this sort of encounter; people think L is far too sweet-natured to instigate any wrongdoing.

'Look what they gave me at the childcare this evening.'

She was holding out a fax. Reading upside down, I saw the letterhead of a well-known organisation for educational research. She handed it to me.

Dear carers, I read, *Billie is a very disturbed little girl.*

'You'd think they could spell the child's name correctly,' I said. 'It doesn't give you much faith in the quality of their research.'

'Don't try to change the subject,' snapped Gracie. It was obvious what had happened: L, in selecting an already completed survey from the Santa Sophia junior school, had made an unlucky choice, and no doubt there was some question, unnoticed by either of us, that had revealed the child's gender. I played for time.

'It's just a silly misunderstanding,' I said, 'and Mum has been feeling really upset about it.' Then I had an inspiration. 'Actually,' I continued, 'she got you something to say how sorry she was about the whole affair.'

I went out to the laundry. The flowers were still there. A few were no longer in their first youth, heads drooping rather too listlessly or petals browning around the edges, but the general effect was little diminished. I nipped off a few offending details with a finger and thumb, and returned to where Gracie was standing, mystified at our apparent foreknowledge of her anger. Her mood brightened a little.

'These must have cost a fortune,' she said.

'As to that, I won't comment,' I replied, 'but if they go any way towards showing how inexpressibly contrite your mother and I are about the whole unfortunate business, we would think any expense was justified.'

'Very nicely put,' said Gracie. 'Thankyou for the flowers: now I have to get back to Billy. Don't think that you may not still be punished in some way.'

'Give my love to dear little Billy,' interjected L, and shut the door after our temporarily bamboozled daughter.

'That was a close call.'

'Rather too close,' said L, 'but at least I'll be able to get a decent night's sleep for once; I've been worried sick these last few days. It was a bit unfair the way you took all the blame and I got all the credit.'

'Notice anything about these shoulders?' I asked, flexing the items in question in what was intended as a display of unquestionable virility.

'They're very broad and I love you very much.'

'I love you too,' I replied, 'and if we're quick we won't miss much of *Desperate Housewives*.'

'At times like that, I know exactly how they feel,' was L's rejoinder.

*

The next day dawned fine and mild. Carefree as I now was, it seemed a perfect opportunity to make my long-deferred start on *Cosmo Cosmolino*. Much as Sherlock Holmes prepared for a problem by packing a favourite pipe, or Pope's Baron inhaled the vapours of coffee while seeking inspiration for his assault on Belinda, I brewed a pot of Darjeeling. Its smokier essence, I felt, would help me distil the significance of *Cosmo Cosmolino*, and in so doing resolve some of the questions that had so multiplied since my reading of the two previous books.

I put on a jacket against the chill which settled on the terrace these early mornings.

> *Now something something something the returning year,*
> *And winter, ruffling the dark waves, was here.*

Returning or *revolving*, I wondered to myself, perhaps a little bit rusty now on Virgil's words. And *ruffling* sounded wrong on second thoughts — perhaps it should be *roughening*. What translation was I quoting from, and could I be said to be quoting from any if I couldn't remember the words? One of my retirement projects had been to read the *Aeneid* right through — in Latin, that is — but for the moment Helen Garner must take precedence. I looked down in the direction of the harbour. The waves did seem a trifle darker, and the masts of some boats at anchor swayed like wild metronomes in the wash of a passing vessel. I poured a cup of tea, settled myself on a spindly Italian chair, and opened the covers.

On a first breeze through I picked up the outline of the story. *Cosmo Cosmolino* took us, I found, among a group of ageing counter-cultural leftovers. Both the characters and the setting — Sweetpea Mansions, a rambling Victorian house as I imagined it, somewhere in suburban Melbourne — could have been straight from the imagination of Patrick White. But were they just a house and a set of characters? In the text of the novella the bodily imagery was so profuse — even a superficial reading showed there was scarcely a part of the body left unmentioned — and the characters themselves so much more like humours than mere people, that the house and its inhabitants together could be read as a body in mid-life crisis, lurching hopelessly and ineffectually towards desires that could not be fulfilled.

Considered as humours, I thought, Helen Garner's Janet and Ray divided Jung's rational types between them, while the same could be said of Alby and Maxine vis-à-vis the non-rational. I went inside to find my copy of *Psychological Types,* turning *Cosmo Cosmolino* face down on the table to keep the place. I weighed it down with the teapot. Though not quite so energetically pre-loved as *Monkey Grip* had been, this library copy had suffered much, and would surely suffer more. The Pentagon would certainly have approved this relatively mild torture, inflicted as it was in the interests of extracting information.

Jung gave me just what I was looking for:

> *There is little effort to respond to the real emotions of the other person; I read, they are more often damped down and rebuffed, or cooled off by a negative value judgement. Although there is a constant readiness for peaceful and harmonious co-existence, strangers are shown no touch of amiability, no gleam of responsive warmth, but are met with apparent indifference or a repelling coldness. Often they are made to feel entirely superfluous. Faced with anything that might carry her away or arouse enthusiasm, this type observes a benevolent though critical neutrality, coupled with a faint trace of superiority that soon takes the wind out of the sails of a sensitive person.**

Right on, Carl, I thought: if this wasn't Janet to a t, it was pretty close. She would have liked children, but rashly had her tubes tied; she would have liked a husband, but found herself abandoned after a late and short-lived marriage. She longed for intimacy without knowing how to achieve it. Ray by contrast was a thinker: he had a belief system, had plans; he worked, saved money, longed for a materially provided and well-ordered life surrounded by the furniture Alby was going to bring. Maxine would be intuitive: 'unconscious images acquired the dignity of things.' She looked for angels, she sensed auras, told fortunes; she created fantastical works of art out of rubbish and discards, dreamed of the magic cosmic child she was to bring forth. Alby was the introverted sensation type – longing to re-enter the past, imagined, unlimited world that the house represented to him. One striking passage caught my eye:

> *These ten years, no matter where he travelled, he had kept a picture of the household folded in his mind, as an image of the way a life might be lived. He treasured the tomato plants heavy with fruit, the trim rows of lettuces; the washing flying high and fading on the line, straw brooms with their driving rhythm, the casual giving and lending of everything you needed, the unlocked doors and windows through which fine breezes wandered: surely he must have lived through a winter here, but all his memories were of warm air and thin clothing, and every day was Saturday. Any room you peered into had its little drama going on: two women haranguing some poor bastard about housework; a couple of blokes in armchairs with cups*

of tea on the floor beside them, arguing about a strike or a distant war, or working away on acoustic guitars, learning and teaching; a girl in a floppy, flowery dress mending a bike or covering page after page of her diary, never needing to cross out, or reading the long summer afternoon away with the book propped on her chest, while round the next half-open door a lover, pale with jealousy, leaned over a table to snoop on a letter; upstairs in their wide front room the kids — whose were they? which ones actually belonged to the house? — paraded about in dress-ups making imperious gestures, or crawled naked up the bunks, or madly scribbled with the pencils, colouring in; along the hall someone waddled backwards on her haunches, painting the skirting-boards blue, or teetered on a ladder with a roller tray and the radio; if you tapped on the bathroom door you would be screamed at by someone inside who was trying to develop photos; downstairs a visitor picked out a walking bass line on the gutted pianola; on the back verandah somebody's boyfriend since last night sat grinning, head bowed, caped in a towel, submitting to the application of shit-brown gobs of henna; and three times a day the food hit the table, great crocks and tureens of it, coarse with garlic and beans, weird salads hacked to chaff, onions, brown rice, the occasional sausage, vegetable curry that burnt your mouth when you gulped it and later tortured you with farts — but filling! In this house you could fill up, you could eat and hold out your plate for more, and everyone welcomed you, at first; everyone loved you, provided you could crack a joke or stagger round the yard on stilts or grab a guitar and play.*

Well, I had known houses like that, I thought, and not all of us thought they were paradise, not even at the time. If you did, it probably helped to be a wide-eyed twenty-something, and in Melbourne into the bargain.

The passage reminded me of something, and making my way inside again I searched for a while before finding, pushed into a bookshelf, a copy of the student newspaper which I had brought back from one of my trips to the university. This is what I read:

Soon the old factory was filled with people moving in, surrounded by dogs and kids running around, people setting up a kitchen, making clothes from the old textile samples, lugging water from a fire hose up the stairs for the toilets (no running water in the building) and setting up the sleeping areas. Once all this housekeeping stuff had been sorted, the serious stuff began. Over the weekend, panels and workshops were held on a massive range of topics including gender and sexuality, whiteness, graffiti and stencilling, zine-making, indigenous sovereignty, environmental campaigns, kids and activism, anti-capitalism and desire, radical queer activism, reclaiming spaces, borders and refugees, and heaps more... Each night, the forest blockaders from Goonerah Environment Centre (GECO) cooked sensational vegan food, so good that you'd never guess most of it was sourced from the dumpster bins of Melbourne. You'd be amazed at the perfectly good food that bakeries and fruit and veggie stores throw out each day!

All it needed was Alby on stilts to make the picture complete. Yes, I thought, the paradise is still there – Alby's only problem is that he isn't twenty five years younger.

Here there was food in plenty for thought, but considering the hour, something more directed at the outer man might be in order. To have attacked the lamb once more might have seemed not only repetitive but even greedy. L was just as fond of roast lamb as I was, and there was probably enough for a couple more meals, besides the Scotch broth which I had designed to make of the shank. Fruit would be a suitable alternative. I quartered one of those little navel oranges that can be such a delight at the beginning of the season. They hadn't seemed quite as sour this year as I could have hoped; I had quizzed the high priest of our local temple to the fruit and vegetable deities.

'Sorry, mate,' he had replied, running a proud and watchful eye over the apples, bananas, cucumbers, not to mention produce from every other letter of the alphabet. 'People often won't buy the good stuff, they're too ignorant. Do you know, it's hard to shift black muscatels these days; the customers don't like grapes with seeds.'

It's not only Alby has lost that freshness of youth, I thought darkly, dreaming of an innocent, pristine world where every orange was so sour that your teeth would feel like tingling fur when you had eaten it, and every grape as packed with seeds and honeyed sweetness as a pomegranate. Stilt-walkers would be a small price to pay. Then it struck me – Alby himself was like a living embodiment of the Santa Sophia motto: he had no brains, and he was on stilts. Childish though this may have been, it pleased me hugely, in which mood I set out for a walk, needing some time of contemplation to let the studies of the morning sink in.

I took the opposite direction from the previous day. This led me away from the sun and through streets shadowed by houses, and somehow the almost-bare frangipanis and the naked sticks of the prunuses, along with the wind that was today just a little cooler, made the approach of winter seem real for the first time that year. Mine is a winter journey, I thought to myself, and in obvious stages my thoughts flowed back towards the angophora. How carefully it had been placed, I now realised, at the point which divided both the length and breadth of the picture in golden section. The eye was drawn to it ineluctably, just as Boake had been to its physical counterpart. *Du fändest Ruhe dort*, the picture had seemed to whisper even to me, and yes, those sorry events that culminated in the apartment that was now Rita's had brought me as close to suicide as I have ever been. What unbearable sorrow, what anguish, had driven Barcroft Boake to the step that I had not been willing to take?

Then I came out into the sunshine at last at the end of Cremorne Point, and looked back towards the sun, and the city, and the Opera House, and the Bridge, and the shining silver water. There were a thousand thousand attestations of life, and busyness, and I recollected in a corny sort of way that I am far too in love with the pleasure of the eyes and the smell and the touch – and even with the consciousness that delights can still exist though I myself may not ever be lucky enough to have them – to consider leaving the world that contains them by my own consent. In short, I am not the type.

Thus I returned home in buoyant mood, and was beginning to explain to L my preliminary thoughts about *Cosmo Cosmolino* as psychomachia.

'This is leading me to reconsider the earlier books,' I said. 'If this one is about individuation, which is certainly a case that could be argued, perhaps the whole *œuvre* has an overarching Jungian scheme behind it.' I was suddenly conscious of the mixed metaphor, but as L didn't seem to have noticed, I continued:

'I'll have to go in tomorrow, I think, and have a closer look at the characters in *The Children's Bach*.'

'And the rabbit,' said L.

'Don't think I've forgotten the rabbit – it may be the key to the whole thing.'

Had there been a derisive note in that last comment? Any further exchange was precluded by the phone, which now rang insistently. As soon as the words 'Hello, it's Gracie here' sounded from the answering machine, L picked it up.

'No, I haven't the slightest idea,' I could hear her say, and then after an interval: 'Yes, certainly I'll tell him. Goodbye.'

She hung up and turned to me.

'Gracie says there was a card with the flowers.'

'Did she say what was on it?'

'It said "To M in eternal gratitude – Hawkwind." She also said to tell you that you would now certainly be punished.'

'I'll have to handle that when I come to it, I'm afraid.'

'Who or what in the world is Hawkwind? Wasn't that the name of a film with that German man – Dieter Brummer?'*

'The movie you're thinking of,' I replied, 'is probably *Ladyhawke*, with Rutger Hauer. There is a woman, you may recall, who is under an enchantment that turns her into a hawk by day, whereas her protector is a knight by day and a wolf at night time – if I've got it the right way round that is. It's the sort of thing that comes on television at the end of the school holidays when the cricket is washed out. As to Hawkwind, I've got a vague idea it's the name of a band, but whether they still exist, I couldn't say. Whoever he, she or it may be, it is almost certainly not Dieter Brummer, who is someone quite other and different. And Diarmid Heydenreich* is someone else again.'

'I wish you wouldn't say *movie*,' said L. 'You only do it to curry favour when you hang around with young people. I think it comes close to disloyalty.'

'If Madam Chair would grant me a short leave of absence,' I said, 'I could find you an example of the word *movie*, used by no less an authority than *The Sydney Morning Herald,* in the 1920s,* long before you were attending kinematograph performances.'

'Permission denied,' replied L. 'Where I grew up, the children whose parents were vulgar enough to allow them to go to such things called them the flicks.'

3

D^9 – combat with a hostile donor*

L is a dear woman in almost every possible way, but her very presence can sometimes be enough to induce a blight in inanimate objects. At the time of which I am speaking, the mouse of our desktop computer was of the old-fashioned mechanical type, and I was treating it the next morning for a dust-related paralysis – a condition which often seemed to affect it when L had been using the machine for a while. I removed the ball and was scraping away with a pair of tweezers while the cursor juddered around the screen, lurching this way and that when I touched one or other of the rollers. This put me to thinking of those medical shows where the surgeons poke around in a blood-filled hole in somebody's heart or brain, and it seems a miracle that the patient ever survives to walk again, and this in turn led me to the topic of vivisection more generally, and by gradual degrees to the unspeakable experiments Nazi doctors carried out on living victims; finally I came to reflect that a generally Germanic theme had lately entered my life.

It had begun with the complexion of Elisabeth, the full ramifications of whose words I had yet to decipher. It had continued through the laudable thoroughness of Ms Schmidt, the *Winterreise* of the previous day, and the thespian gifts of *Herren* Hauer and Brummer. Not to mention Heydenreich. But in this multicultural land of ours, I reflected, it would not be surprising if now one thread, now another, lies on the surface of the fabric, or hangs loose like a snagged filament in a fairisle pullover. I had once owned such a garment – a favourite of my teenage years – which remained in my wardrobe long after it had sprouted trailing strands of red, yellow or fawn. Fawn, mostly, for that was the dominant theme in the design. It always needed a brisk barbering with a pair of nail scissors before being taken out in public.

And so I continued to reflect on the gifts and the crimes of the

German people, not to mention related topics, until the ball had been restored to its place and the mouse was sliding around freely without even the help of a walking frame. None of these musings, however, prepared me for the example of Hunnish *Schrecklichkeit* that I was soon to encounter.

I had been up the street in search of a green vegetable to go with tonight's projected cold lamb. Had the weather been more summery, salad would have been my automatic choice, but cold meat at this time of the year seemed to demand a vegetable with something unctuous about it, some depth of flavour. I toyed with cabbage as an option, but the altogether richer green of the nearby display of spinach was calling 'buy me' too persuasively. I purchased a bunch.

L was massaging the resuscitated mouse with her fingertips when I burst in.

'Just look at this,' I said, and waved the spinach.

L looked.

'It's a bunch of spinach,' she said. Some of you might have called the vegetable in question silver beet or even Swiss chard, but L and I see eye to eye on this subject. In Australia it's spinach, and if you think the usage of some other country is superior you are always free to go back there. Next thing you'll probably be saying 'aubergine' or 'cilantro'.

'Is there something I'm missing?' asked L.

The extent of my passion can be gauged by the fact that I had shown her the spinach at all: I usually like to keep my culinary intentions private, so as not to diminish the sense of theatre when the meal is produced at 8 o'clock.

'Do you see what they've done?' I asked, turning the stalk end towards her, 'This is no bunch of spinach — it's a whole spinach *plant* that has been sliced off at ground level.'

'Is that bad?' asked L.

'Is that bad? Listen — the whole point about spinach is that the peasant goes out into the vegetable garden and cuts off the leaves and bundles them up as they mature. Then the inner leaves, which haven't had the chance to taste sun and rain and fresh air, will be able to mature in their turn. And so you have a self-sustaining permaculture; the plant is a resource that is continually renewing itself.' I broke open the bunch and held up one of the inner leaves, short and consisting mostly of stalk with only a fringe of pale crinkled green around the edges. 'This baby has been wantonly deprived of life, just to nourish the greed of a multinational. I doubt that it's ever felt the caressing touch of a gnarled peasant's reverent hand. What do you think the Pope would say about it?'

'Something pretty cutting, I'm sure,' said L, smiling at her own wit, such as it was. 'Now, while I love you and all that, I really must get on with the prospectus. We're supposed to be looking at the new draft tomorrow.'

She had three or four prospectuses from other schools lying on the desk beside her. That is how these creative people work — they steal each other's ideas. I picked up one of them and scrutinized the cover.

'What's this on their badge?' I asked. 'It looks like a teapot.'

'I think it's supposed to be Aladdin's lamp,' said L. 'A symbol of learning.'

'But the thing about Aladdin's lamp was that you got what you wanted without working,' I said. 'Sloppy symbolism. I shouldn't think their ideas would be worth much.'

'Not everyone sees as deeply as you do, darling,' said L, and would probably have gone on to draw my attention to some particular feature of this prospectus she thought worth plagiarizing, when our conversation was drowned by a deep, throbbing roar from outside. I went to the window.

'It's Dave,' I said. 'Whatever can have brought him here?'

Dave had resumed his road warrior attire. His Harley-Davidson stood propped on the footpath, unimaginable power instinct in every squat profile.

'No, I won't come in, mate,' he said. 'Just wanted to ask you to do something for me.'

'A pleasure, Dave,' I replied. He produced a form: an application for a reader's ticket to the Mitchell Library.

'I need a reference, mate,' he said, 'and I reckon you owe me after you took those flowers.'

'You left them behind, Dave,' I said. 'We had to throw them out in the end: they were all shrivelled.'

'Well what goes around comes around, I suppose,' said Dave. 'It's all good, mate.'

This singularly modern philosophy reassured me – it didn't seem Dave would have any further intention of calling us to account for misappropriation of the items in question.

'What were the flowers all about then?' I was emboldened to ask. 'What's the story?'

'I've been picking up some casual jobs as a courier,' said Dave. 'Helps with the finances. But after I left your place the other day, it took me a while to work out what had happened to them.'

If I had been Dave, riding off to who knows where with a fifteen-year-old girl wrapped around me, perhaps I too would have forgotten. Perhaps not. It was hard to say. At any rate I took the form, and added my attestation that Dave was of unimpeachable character and in every way suited to be entrusted with the cultural heritage of the State of New South Wales.

'So what are you after, Dave?' I asked.

'Tell you another time mate – it may not come to anything – just something I turned up on the internet.'

With these words he mounted the bike, kicked away the stand, and gunned the machine down the street and out of my life for the time being. For a long while I could hear the fading roar of his passing until at last it died into the background.

When I returned to the house, L was humming the Hallelujah Chorus, a clear sign that the prospectus was going well. Actually it wasn't so much the chorus itself, but the tune, which was the Santa Sophia school song. This was a Latin anthem dating from the school's founder; it had fallen into disuse for many years till revived by the present headmistress, and, perhaps alone among her ideas, was immensely popular with the girls. The main words were 'Feminari!

Militare!' (to play the woman — to be militant); it sounded quite stirring when bawled out from six hundred girlish throats, though I doubted whether the verb *feminor* in the sense of 'play the woman' would have found favour with the better classical writers. I asked L what had pleased her so much.

'This prospectus,' she said, 'the one you were so rude about — it just occurred to me when you went out that the point of getting an education is to make sure that you won't ever have to work, so the Aladdin's lamp image is not so inappropriate after all. And the prospectus itself had lots of good things in it that I could use. The others had far less.'

'Fewer,' I said, not because I really cared, but I was still feeling cut up about the spinach; I had to work off my bad temper on someone.

'You don't seem to have much to do this morning,' was L's rejoinder. 'Why don't you look through these photos and pick out a few that will do for the prospectus? And when you've finished that, we could have a bite of lunch.'

I groaned. L handed me a fat bundle of those folders you get from the chemist, each with about twenty photos. Ninety per cent of them, I knew, would be out of focus or too far away, and most of the rest would have inappropriate backgrounds or feature girls who were scowling at the camera. But whenever a new school publication was being designed, someone had to sort through this heap of mullock in search of the rare item that would say 'this is the school for your daughter'. The final decision would be L's, but she was happy to delegate the preliminary sorting.

'They're a bit light on multicultural content,' I said some time later, having reduced the pile to about a dozen possibles. 'This is where the blondes-only policy really lets you down.'

'I know,' replied L. 'That's why I put in the ones with that GAP student from Kenya.'

'I'd picked up on that already,' I said. 'Don't think I can't read you like a book after all these years. This one with her in could go up there on the cover, and then there were some netball ones that I thought looked quite wholesome.'

'It's a very wholesome game,' said L, 'whereas those basketball uniforms make a girl look like something out of *Sports Illustrated*. And while we're on the topic of unwholesome things, what did Dave want?'

'He was after a reference for the Mitchell Library, believe it or not,' I told her. 'I expect he's planning to corrupt Poppy by showing her some banned etchings by Norman Lindsay.'

'I wouldn't be a bit surprised,' said L. 'He looked like a man that would be capable of anything. And now, would you be an absolute dear and make me a sandwich? There's something I just want to finish.'

I went to the kitchen; salad sandwiches, I thought, would strike a pleasant lunchtime note – but then had a happier inspiration: sandwiches of lettuce with some sliced boiled egg, still warm from the cooking. I put our smallest saucepan on to boil, and cut some crusty slices from a new loaf. L's little finishing touches always take three times as long as she had thought they were going to, so there would be plenty of time to boil the eggs. I find that an egg taken straight from the fridge and put into boiling water for seven minutes is just about perfect: a slight residual runniness in the yolk – not too runny to slice – but with the white firm without being rubbery. L goes for a firmer egg, so I usually allow about eight minutes if I have her in mind. When L boils an egg for herself, she often will let it run for an hour or so, and come back and find the saucepan completely dry.

I had peeled and sliced the eggs and was just anointing them with some coarse salt, rubbing it between finger and thumb as a prospector might assay some rare and precious mineral, when L came in. I handed her her sandwich.

'I don't know how you think of such lovely things,' she said. 'This bread is simply delicious.'

'Do you know that when I was in the supermarket I saw something called 9 Grain Bread?' I asked her. 'I would challenge anyone to think of nine grains.'

'Well there are wheat and barley and oats and rye,' said L, 'and corn, I suppose.'

'In some of the midland counties of England the word *corn* means beans.'

'I wouldn't count beans,' said L, 'but there's rice, which makes six. What about sesame?'

'Sesame isn't a grain,' I replied.

'Well it is in Ali Baba,' said L. 'You remember how Cassim says "Open wheat" and "Open barley" when he can't think of sesame.'

'Well I suppose I'll give you sesame, but it still doesn't make nine. I think they're just playing on people's gullibility.'

'There's millet,' said L.

'You'd have to be joking: have you ever tasted millet? It's more of a broom than a grain. If millet is a grain, so am I.'

'Quite the reverse,' said L, giggling insanely. 'Like most husbands, you're more of a groom than a brain.' Prospectus making seemed to have sharpened her wits. At least I'm not on stilts, I thought.

*

I went off to think about Jung's influence on Helen Garner. Driven off course by the disturbing episode of the spinach, I had shelved my intended journey to the library, and the rest of the morning had been frittered away. On the one hand, Garner's successive central characters, Nora, Athena and now Janet, followed the trajectory of the author's own life and could stand for the ego, which would suggest the role of the self for the rabbit. I relished for a moment the thought that in that case the rabbit contained Athena, which raised the question of which side of the hutch was the outside. But were Javo, Dexter and Alby then successive projections of the animus? I wasn't too clear about the animus, and I wasn't sure that Jung was either. In some trivial sense, all this was obvious – or was it so trivial? If we were to take on Jung's schema as an explanation for human life as a whole, then it becomes a narrative which narrates every author, and must control the authors' artistic creations as well. Was I just finding confirmation that Jung was on the right track? Whether or not that was so, *Cosmo Cosmolino* seemed to involve an active choice of Jungian imagery that went past anything the earlier books would suggest. It was time, I thought, to return to that text and worry it a bit more exhaustively.

My earlier reading had concentrated mostly on the opening and closing phases of the text, and I had to confess that in my haste to get a general picture of the book some of the central sections had been rapidly skimmed or barely glanced at. Now I set myself to read the whole thing through, slowly and carefully. There was a corner of the terrace which still caught some afternoon sun, and I carried one of the outdoor chairs across, placing it to take full advantage of this lingering warmth. Earlier in the season this spot would have been in shade, but the now almost leafless frangipani allowed the sunlight to shine through, barring and crisscrossing chair and page with branching shadows. I tilted the chair slightly, and it teetered in a gratifying balance as I steadied one foot against the wall. All was ready; I began to read.

Now I am quite a fast reader, and though my intention had been to be deliberate, having read the opening sections once already I made rapid progress. I won't say that the pages flicked into a blur like days and nights for H. G. Wells's time traveller, but let's say I was forging ahead. *The telegraph poles looked like a paling fence*, I quoted to myself. And then ironically, just as I was indulging myself with the picture of the police in vain pursuit of my hotrod Lincoln, it happened. You will have seen one of those films that culminate with the criminals' car sailing off into empty space from the lip of an unfinished expressway. Not such a common occurrence in everyday life, I would have to think – in fact I'm not sure that I have ever seen an expressway that was otherwise complete but just ended in mid-air like that. But here was nature imitating art. Less than half way through the story, I came to the episode of Janet and the oval dish. This was the sentence that first caught my eye:

> *They brought her home white-faced and dumb, her plaits standing on end, and from that day on she refused to let rabbit in any form whatsoever pass her lips.**

I read on. Horror upon horror. The vegetable atrocities of the morning had been nothing to this. Images of modern evil! Where were you now, Albert Tucker? The rabbit seller with carcases stretched out skinned and headless on his enamel trays; the old woman with the heap of furry bodies. Had the self been set free in *The Children's Bach* only to come to this? Little more than a page, but how the passage transformed my understanding of the book. I had known about Janet's casserole, but not guessed at its foundation: now it took on the character of a self-immolation. Nor did I fail to notice the bread and the wine — I felt I could ignore the garlic. A Last Supper, and one to which no one turned up! *Go out into the highways and the by-ways and compel them to come in.* My foot lost its position on the wall, the chair overbalanced, and but for a quick grab with one hand I would have fallen into the frangipani. I was shaken.

'I've just had rather a shocking experience,' I said to L, who was still busy with the prospectus. 'I'm sorry to break into your quality time, but it seems to me that *Cosmo Cosmolino*, far from being a Jungian meditation on the mid-life transition, is actually a deconstructive soteriology.'

'It's not quality time, it's quantity time I need at the moment,' said L. 'Didn't I tell you this has to be ready for tomorrow?'

'In fact,' I went on, '*soteriolytic* would not be too strong a word in the circumstances.'

L didn't bite. This was a woman who early on in our relationship — so early, indeed, that we were still communicating mostly in words — had bowled the word *episteme* up to me without batting an eye. She didn't need explanations.

I spent some time pacing up and down in what L tells me is an irritating way; then I remembered the book, and went and retrieved it and put the chair back in its place. Once again, a day had given me a lot to think about. But it was not yet over. Later on, Gracie rang and after a long session with L she asked to speak to me.

'I haven't forgotten your punishment,' she said. This was all right; it surely could not involve anything more onerous than looking after

Billy, and that was not particularly burdensome, though it might have its longueurs.

'But,' she went on, 'after we talked the other day, I decided to read *The First Stone* again, and I have to report there are no rabbits in it.'

'Somehow, I didn't think there would be,' I replied.

*

The next morning the alarm shrilled at six o'clock. It wasn't even light. L was up, and almost, it seemed, before I had time to turn over and settle myself, she was showered and back in the bedroom, bumping around in her underclothes while she made her choice of the day's outfit.

'Is this some challenge you've set yourself?' I asked as the wardrobe door rebounded shuddering from the foot of the bed. 'People are sponsoring you to get dressed inside ten minutes with your eyes closed?'

'I just thought it would be more considerate to you not to turn the light on,' said L. 'I'll have to make an early start because of Billy.'

'But isn't it your big prospectus meeting this morning?'

'Yes that's still on, but Gracie needs me to take Billy to childcare. She has to start early herself – something about a new secretary, she told me – and she can't just dump Billy on the step of the childcare place at seven o'clock.'

'I'll make us some coffee,' I replied. I sat up, pulled my feet into their ugs, and belted my dressing gown around me. The ug boot and the thong, I thought – Lawson could keep the sliprails and the spur: foot comfort is an area where Australia leads the world. The woollen lining, not as yet compacted, gave its almost wiry caress to the upper surfaces of my toes.

By the time L came downstairs the coffee was filtering, high clouds just visible from the window were showing a touch of pink, and I was deep in the newspaper.

'That coffee smells so delicious,' said L. 'It always gives me such a feeling of exhilaration when I'm up early on a cold morning, and everything is still, and the dawn is breaking and the coffee is steaming. It reminds me of frost and Alps and town squares with *Konditoreis* and steep little roofs and freshly baked *Kuchen*.' L was on a study tour in Central Europe a couple of years ago, and it had left a deep impression.

'I'm glad to have nourished your Heidi fantasies,' I replied, 'and if you'll give me a minute to slip out and milk Schmüdel and Strüdel, you too shall have a bowl of steaming goat's milk of your very own. Yes,' I said, 'it is a day of promise. On the one hand I don't see how events as scarring as those of yesterday could possibly repeat themselves, while on the other there is State of Origin fever and the very real possibility that tonight will see intruders in the *Big Brother* house. I hardly like to guess what feelings that may stir up among the housemates.'

'It doesn't bear thinking about,' said L, swigging her coffee as she looked for the car keys. 'I'll see you this evening, then – or sooner, if you're home.'

'This is the day I'm meeting Professor J,' I replied. 'I'm having lunch with him, so I'll probably be home late afternoon.'

'Bye bye, then,' said L, and gave me a kiss with a passion content nicely judged to last me till her return, plus a little extra just in case.

*

Professor J is a former colleague that I see from time to time; every six months or so he will ring up to suggest a meeting at some place of his choice, and we have lunch. I was looking forward to putting to him some of the ideas my researches had provoked. These were still inchoate, I had to admit, but a fresh mind might help clothe them with more substance.

Our designated meeting place was the Chinese Garden at Darling Harbour. This was a place that I had once visited regularly, but where I hadn't been for a few years now. The plantings would have grown up, I expected, and the whole place would have acquired a settled harmony which should be very agreeable. With the sense of renewing an often enjoyed but unaccountably neglected delight, I arrived early and walked slowly up the peripheral path. The curious black-stemmed bamboos had thickened since my last visit, and the tree on the pretending mountain had at last acclimatized, and was no longer covered with shadecloth. I walked to the edge of the cascade, and felt as before an unreasonable satisfaction at the way the water continually renewed itself, and poured and bubbled and splashed its way down to the improbably named Twin Pavilions of Pear Fragrance and Lychee Blossom. I picked my own way down the path to those pavilions and stood on the bridge. I looked at the carp.

All human life was here. Forest, mountain and stream for wild nature, the teahouse for civility, and, I reflected, the cash desk at the entrance to represent commerce. This was a world; the outer world that seemingly contained it held no more than these same elements tricked out in confusing and irrelevant detail. Synecdoche works both ways, I thought: when we say 'a decision is expected from Canberra' the figure of speech is not at all enriched by our knowledge that Canberra contains Garema Place with its sad drug dealers as well as the Federal Parliament in that peculiar bunker of theirs. God is not in the details: the details are in God. The wild creature that nestles inside the cardigan tells us all we have to know about Nora; the skinned and gutted carcase served up to society at large to feast on is Janet. She did that for them and they didn't even turn up, I thought. But then I caught sight of Professor J twinkling at me from the teahouse entrance. He was an unmistakeable figure – slight, with a rosy complexion and tufts of white hair above his ears – and was looking more and more like Yoda done in pink. We met and greeted one another and climbed the narrow stairs that lead to the refreshments.

For aesthetic reasons as much as for good fellowship we seated ourselves at adjacent sectors of the small table. I looked towards the north-east and the city, he towards the Maritime Museum and the Casino. The third sector we left empty for the teapot, and any other delicacy we might wish to share. Iron Buddha, it seemed to me, was what the moment required, and with his concurrence I ordered a pot.

From where I sat the central background was filled by an anonymous office tower. Its base was obscured by the mimic mountain of the garden, and from that in turn fell the ever-renewed cascade. I looked at this vista and looked at Professor J, and then looked from Professor J to the cascade again. Their conjunction seemed to have an obscure significance, and the subject of significance in turn brought my mind back to its recent preoccupation.

I advanced a few ideas in a tentative sort of way, getting as far as suggesting that there was something larger there, something revealed by each book only in part, much as a scatter of reefs might hint at the contours of an underlying seamount. As Professor J shook his head and frowned slightly at my words, he made me think of Yoda admonishing a refractory pupil.

'No,' said Professor J, 'I might grant you that the meaning of a text is an emergent property – though I'm not even convinced that that idea itself has any objective content – but if I understand you rightly you want to put forward some concept of a meaning that preexists the text and that the text draws on. It's sheer Platonism; I'm surprised that you can seriously suggest something like that in the 21st century.'

For Professor J, science and reductionism were twin sisters.

'Then where do you locate meaning?'

'The meaning of a text is its words, neither more nor less, and the meaning of the individual words is their context of other words.'

'You mean each word is the sum of its predicates? But that's just Fodor and Katz.* I didn't think anyone believed that any more. That's like saying a man is the sum of all the women he's ever slept with.'

'No, you mistake my meaning; it's saying that to understand who you are we should replace you with all the other men who have slept with the women you have slept with.'

'Let's not go down that road,' I said. 'Put it this way – to understand Brett Kimmorley, you must understand that he can be replaced by Andrew Johns or Scott Prince – is that what you're saying?'

'Yes, or Preston Campbell.'

'Campbell's a five eighth,' I said. 'You're shifting your ground.'

'No,' said Professor J, 'let me give you an analogy. Last month I was with a group in Hawaii.'

'You do get around,' I said. 'What were you doing there? Was this a conference?'

'We booked ourselves into the Grand Wailea Hotel,' he continued, 'and it really is the most extraordinary place. I would say that it had far and away the most extensive system of indoor water slides in the world.'*

Light dawned, for this venerable scholar was addicted to water sliding. Now I knew why he had selected this place for our meeting – a not too deeply repressed hankering to ride the cascade which even now was welling up and plunging down again in the background of our conversation.

'There is a whole network of slides and pools and grottoes,' he went on, 'Hawaiian gods and things like that – a bit like the River Caves in the old Luna Park – and then in the middle of it all there are bars and what have you. We spent a whole day climbing and sliding around, and barely would have visited the same spot twice.'

'And so, what is your point exactly?'

'That if you could construct a map of the meaning of a text, it would be rather like that sort of slide. Some words would be much closer than others, and the further they were apart the more ways there would be of getting from one to another.'

'You mean instead of getting schoolchildren to read *King Lear* you would take a school excursion to King Lear the theme park, and they would spend a whole day sliding around from scene to scene and concept to concept, and no doubt getting up to goodness knows what in the tunnels while the teachers weren't looking.'

'Well there is that,' said Professor J. 'It was a bit like sharing your bathwater with half of America, because for reasons of conservation alone, I suppose, the Grand Wailea would have to recycle the water.'

By now, though the enlightened one was unchanged in bodily form, its *chi* was in need of replenishment. I went over to the counter to order another pot and looked back across the tables to Professor J, silhouetted from this angle against the brightening western sky, and then in the other direction towards the cascade, flashing and sparkling now in the full sunlight of early afternoon. This endless game of snakes and ladders that Professor J had imagined as played out through the interstices of a classic text was like a more complex variation of the garden itself, with its intersecting paths. I was sure there was no single way that could take you through all of it — the path would have to double back and cross itself more than once. I thought again of Wally World and of King Lear the theme park; it would have a Luna Park-like entrance, I supposed, with chattering groups of schoolchildren filing through the open mouth of the demented monarch.

'Your remark about bathwater,' I said, carrying the fresh pot to the table, 'made me wonder if your so-called analogy was anything more than a projection of your own unconscious. Perhaps you watched *The Third Man* too often when you were young. Isn't your meaning park just a glamourized version of the sewers of Vienna, or even the intestinal tract of some creature with an advanced case of diverticulitis? What if you plunge down a slide and find yourself in a dead end, stuck in the animal's appendix?'

'Before you go any further in this rhetorical flight,' said Professor J, 'let me say that the word *unconscious* which you are using so freely is dangerously prescientific. You are mistaking words for things. The unconscious is nothing more than the spare capacity of the mind, what is not at present in use.'

'Aren't you just appealing to Chomsky's dichotomy of competence and performance* under another name? That's just sophistry if you won't let me have the unconscious.'

'On the contrary: your preconceptions keep making you miss the point. You will grant, for example, that there is a network of blood vessels at the back of the eye?'

'If you say so.'

'And yet you are unaware of them 99 per cent of the time. But if you stare fixedly at a bright light for a while, those blood vessels will be all you can see, because your eye is too dazzled to take in anything further away.'

'So the unconscious is what I am not occupied with at the time, is that what you are saying? Just as when I look at you sitting there I'm not actively aware of the Maritime Museum in the background.'

'Exactly.'

'But then what about the waterfall — because when I look at you, the waterfall is not in my field of vision at all. Are you drawing a distinction between significant absence and non-significant absence? Some philosophers would say the waterfall was not there if I wasn't looking at it.'

'Some philosophers talk a lot of nonsense,' said Professor J.

'Well take another example: you know that different languages differ in the number of colour words that they have, so that in some language there might be one word that covered the whole range of blue, green and grey.'

'Yes, that's so.'

'And if I was to go into a paint shop run by one of those people I would have great difficulty getting the colour I wanted.'

'I'm not sure I'm happy about where this argument is going, but continue.'

'Because until the person has the language they can't be said to have the concept.'

'You could always show them the colour patch on the chart.'

'Now suppose a bee came into my paint shop with a colour chart looking for ultraviolet paint. I could never learn to pick that out, because being a human I just don't have the perceptual apparatus to do it.'

'And yet we have the concept — the tin could be labelled 'ultraviolet' even though the colour patch on the chart looked like black to you.'

'So what you want to call an objective real-world category is only made available to us by the language. Doesn't that follow? Are you familiar with Green Lantern comics?'

'I must defer to your extensive knowledge of popular culture.'

'Green Lantern is a superhero who is only vulnerable to the colour infra-green.'

'You are reinforcing my prejudices about the writers of comic books.'

'On the contrary,' I said, 'while DC Comics such as Green Lantern are not my favourites, some of the creations of Stan 'the Man' Lee are not unworthy to stand beside the great figures of imaginative literature. The Human Torch and The Mighty Thor are up there with King Arthur and Tarzan of the Apes.'

'You devalue your argument by bringing in pulp book heroes like Tarzan,' said Professor J.

'My point was going to be that as imaginative creations of things inaccessible to the human senses, infra-green is on all fours with ultraviolet. If none us had ever seen that waterfall over there,' I continued, reinforcing my words with a sweeping gesture, 'or...'

I was obliged to cut off the flow of my argument at this point, because my sweeping gesture had upset Professor J's teacup. Most of the tea remained in the saucer, but a stream reached the edge of the table and was now dribbling onto his trousers.

'Or such a waterfall as I have just created,' I went on, taking advantage of the moment as he scrubbed at his trousers with a handkerchief, 'we could still say "waterfall" because our language makes it possible. If, instead of sliding round Hawaii like Duke Whatsisname, you were one of those Indians in the flatlands of the Amazon, you could still imagine *waterfall*, and if you paddled upstream for long enough you might find something that matched your imaginings. Or you could imagine *dragon* in the same way. Your waterfall and your dragon and your infra-green and your ultraviolet are inventions, not discoveries – what about "dark energy"?' I added, just to provoke him. 'Some of these things correspond to what you like to think of as real-world categories and some don't – which just goes to show that the real world is no more than a subset of the world of the imagination.'

'This sounds very like Aquinas's ontological argument for the existence of God,' said Professor J. 'Rhetoric pulling itself up by its own bootstraps.'

'I don't disdain the help of rhetoric,' I said, 'if by pulling at my bootstraps I can raise myself enough to stand on the shoulders of giants; a journey of ten thousand *li* must begin with a single step.'

This last sentiment I put in not so much because it was appropriate, but because it seemed so in harmony with the setting.

This seemed a suitable note to part on, which we did with many good wishes and promises of another meeting. I felt that tactical victory had been mine, though there was much that appealed in the professor's imagined waterslide. One thing we had not thought about, though, I reflected, as I made my homeward way along Sussex Street, was the question of directionality. However one bounced around from scene to scene, *King Lear* would inevitably bring you to the final curtain of Act V as surely as the cascades in the park flow downwards. However we perambulate the walks of the Chinese Garden, the time will come when they roll down the shutters and we have to leave. Does meaning, however we conceive of it, have a structure that compels us to some end? Is it a narrative from which all other narratives derive? Do these questions mean anything? I crossed to the eastern side of the street to make the most of the afternoon sun.

Though Chinatown was now well behind me, an Asian theme still lingered in my mind, and I resolved that for the evening's meal I would serve satay sauce poured over some strips of grilled chicken breast and salad vegetables. What remained of the lamb would be all the more welcome on another occasion. I bought the chicken and the peanuts — everything else I thought I already had. You might care to note that there is absolutely no need to shell the peanuts yourself: just buy a packet of unsalted nuts that are as fresh as possible. Almonds, yes: always buy the nuts fresh and shell and blanch them yourself before you start, but with peanuts I've never been able to see that it makes any difference. Some satay recipes tell you to use peanut butter, but if you were going to do that, why not just buy the satay sauce ready made, or better still cook something else? I pounded the peanuts to an agreeable consistency and fried the onion, garlic and ginger; if all this was prepared ahead of time, there would be plenty of opportunity to catch the latest developments in *Big Brother*. As the shadows began to draw in, L returned.

'Hello,' she said, 'I've picked up Billy; I thought we could just sit him down in front of the television till Gracie gets home.'

'How did the prospectus go over?'

'Everyone loved it. There are just a few details to tidy up.'

'They didn't pick up on a certain — intertextuality, shall we say?'

'Anyone that did would have felt they were being located in a tradition of educational excellence. Now be a darling, will you, and put on this Teletubbies video for Billy.'

I did so, and settled down to keep an eye on the child. Billy sat like a stuffed frog, with his knees up and his face propped between them, eyes never moving from the screen. Twinky-Winky, Po and company squeaked and gyrated in front of him.

'Do you think there is something wrong with Billy?' I asked L later. 'He seems to find the Teletubbies a riveting televisual experience.'

'Good concentration is the sign of a high intelligence,' said L.

'What about the critical faculty?'

'I've known grown men that can find nothing better to do than watch *Big Brother*.'

'Speaking of which,' I said, 'tonight is a special live intruders edition, so I would be grateful if we could have minimal interruptions, particularly plaintive appeals to watch something else.'

'Well you don't ask much,' said L. 'I suppose you will be allowed this once.'

*

It was already dark as L prepared to take Billy home.

'Would you like to come for the ride?' she asked. Billy, the attractions of the Teletubbies now at an end, was looking at a copy of the former Santa Sophia prospectus, which lay where L had discarded it on the floor in front of the television. He pointed to the three intertwined Ss of the school badge.

'Eff,' said Billy.

'Clever boy,' said L. 'Yes, that's s.'

'Like a fnake,' I said.

'Don't try to be smart,' said L. 'you're confusing the poor child. Come on, Billy; we're going home to Mummy now.'

'Mum-ma,' said Billy, brightening visibly. 'Mum-ma.'

We buckled him into his seat; I sat in the front; L drove.

Gracie lives in one of those inner-city suburbs that have all the appearance of a slum, and fifty years ago no one would have hesitated to call it one. In the evening you have all those bright young people of Generation Y or Z or whatever we are supposed to be up to crowding along the footpaths and jostling one another in the pubs and eating houses; in the day what you notice is the dirt and the rubbish and the shuffling schizophrenics with urine stains down the fronts of their trousers. Why do we say the area is being gentrified when people like Gracie move in? Isn't it rather that Gracie and her like are being dragged down? We stopped at the house. Till recently renovated for Gracie at huge expense, it had been a corner shop – most lately a pizzeria – with an awning over the street; earlier still there would have been a balcony above, with bevelled veranda posts at the edge of the footpath. You could have imagined a stone horse trough in between if you had cared to go that way, and carters leaning against the deep wooden counter as they swapped yarns with the shopkeeper. Now, however, what you had were two walls blank to their full height; in their angle a deeply recessed front door with heavy panels. The upstairs french windows which at one time had given onto the balcony had long been filled in, but something like windowsills had been inserted at chest height, above which window-sized recesses still displayed in their arches the skills of Victorian brickwork. On ground level, the spaces where the shop windows would latterly have been were also bricked up, but had been given recesses that matched the upper storey. The whole was painted in a yellow ochre which Gracie told us had been formulated to resist graffiti. The building's suggestion now was not quite so much of 19th and 20th century commerce as of an extremely small-scale Italian palazzo. Statues in the ground-floor niches, a few of them headless where the populace had shown their contempt for this broken-down ducal *famiglia*, would have completed the effect; here their role was played by a number of scribbled tags in places where the anti-graffiti treatment had not been entirely successful. We buzzed, and Gracie opened the door.

'I just can't thank you enough for dropping Billy off and picking him up today,' said Gracie. 'My secretary is giving birth, the temp they've sent me is hopeless, and I've had to put in goodness knows how many extra hours just making sure that everything will be ready when I need it.'

Once across Gracie's threshold you are no longer in Tuscany. I have mentioned that the front door is deeply recessed, and the reason for that quickly becomes apparent. Heritage constraints required the architect to preserve the outer walls: given that the most recent tenants of the shop may well have been Italian, the reshaping of those outer walls in the direction of 15th century Urbino was a nice acknowledgement of their heritage as well. Inside, however, a second skin enclosed a different structure altogether. Four steel posts supported the roof; on the side away from the busier street a living space opened to a small courtyard through doors in a double-height glass wall; opposite, on the street side, were rooms on two levels partly or fully enclosed in stainless steel. There was a stairway with open treads, a stainless steel handrail, and balusters threaded with stainless steel wire; an airy bridge of the same construction linked one of the upper areas to another. Billy paused to hug his mother's legs, and then picked his way upstairs, one hand steadying him against the wall.

'That's a good boy,' said Gracie. 'Time for bath, isn't it Billy?'

'He's so sensible,' L said admiringly. I knew what she was really thinking, for she had voiced her opinions to me often enough. 'It gives me the horrors to see him on those stairs,' she would say. 'When the poor child slips through and is hanging by his head, what will Gracie have to say then about her lovely modernist design?'

'He'd have to be a contortionist to get through those gaps,' I would reply. 'They're not nearly as wide as you think.'

'One of my uncles ran away to join the circus,' was L's reply, 'so the possibility isn't as remote as you like to make out.'

Meanwhile Billy had taken a wrong turn, and was headed for the bedroom.

'No, not the bedroom, Billy, it's bath time,' called Gracie. 'Go into the services pod, darling, and Mummy will be up in a second.'

'What was that expression that just soiled your lips?' I asked. 'You mean the bathroom, I take it.'

'There is the upper services pod, which holds the bathing and toileting arrangements, and the lower services pod, for cooking and washing. I can show you on the architect's plan if you like. I think children should be encouraged to call things by their proper names. The era of euphemisms is past, Dad.'

Knowing architects, I could easily believe that the name was on the plan – once, when I sketched a window for an extension we were thinking about, an architect friend of mine had said 'that's an overwrought little statement of fenestration.' I supposed Gracie could call parts of her own house whatever she liked, so I took another tack:

'By the way,' I said, 'it may be all very well for tough young modern women like yourself to use feminist jargon like "giving birth", but next thing your mother will be picking it up, and it would pain me if people thought less of her. "Having a baby" is what we say.'

'We lawyers are trained not to prejudge an issue,' said Gracie. 'She may produce a spotted hyena for all I know.'

It seemed time to leave, if only because I could sense *Big Brother* looming behind the horizon, like a full moon about to rise.

'Goodbye, Gracie, goodbye Billy,' we called, and a thin little voice from upstairs faintly called back: 'Bye gam-ma, bye gam-pa.'

'He is an exceptionally intelligent child,' said L, as we made our way up the approach to the Bridge. 'Fancy being able to understand an expression like *services pod* at his age.'

'Or does it just underline what I was saying about the critical faculty?' was my reply.

We drove on.

4

*E^3 – favour to a dead person**

By the time we got home, the *Big Brother* special was just starting. I settled in my favourite chair to watch. Unaware that this was to be the night for intruders, housemates were going about their usual activities: cutting one another's hair, lounging in the spa, pedalling an exercise bike with furious concentration. A casual observer might have thought them interchangeable – even indistinguishable – but here too, I thought, was directionality. However much remained of the prize, one of these young people was going to win it, and who that was to be was in some sense already written in the contours of their personalities. Each housemate's personality I knew to be amazing – I had their fellows' word for that – but among them was the piece of the jigsaw that was destined to be put in last. We spill the pieces out of the box, and the next step seems quite random, but just accept for a moment that we are guided, however subtly, in the order in which we construct the picture, and it is certain that only one piece will fit the last position.

For our choice in such things is not as unfettered as we like to think. When you entered the Chinese Garden, it would be quite wrongheaded to begin by turning right towards the two enamelled dragons of Guangdong and Sydney. No, you are guided towards the left, and whichever of the many paths you take, and however often you retrace your steps to look at some attraction as yet unvisited, you are going to finish near the teahouse, and finally refreshed you will leave your change in the wishing pool just before you reach the exit. And so it was with jigsaws – obvious first, then slow advance into unconquered territory until the last, most challenging move was made. It reminded me of the tactics of Santa Sophia in their quest for knowledge, and I pictured a neatly turned out girl in a Santa Sophia blazer with a line saying 'Jigsaw team 2003'.

When Gracie was at school, summer holidays had often been a time for jigsaw puzzles. The cottage up the coast where we gathered with other families or a crowd of Gracie's friends had a stock of them. The two thousand or five thousand pieces advertised on the box would be laid out on a table a little out of the way, and gradually picked at by returning swimmers, or by individual members of the party who were feeling a little less than sociable. Sometimes groups of three and four would ignore calls to meals and could be heard still murmuring as they shuffled the pieces around late, late into the night. At last there they were: the Banff Springs Hotel with its background of pine- and snow-covered mountains, the thatched cottage with cosy dormers and roses climbing above a flowery border, the New England woods overlapping splashes of red onto swathes of orange and yellow — all perhaps with a tiny lacuna or two where a piece had slipped between the floorboards or fallen victim to heedless vacuum cleaning.

Techniques differed. Some people attacked the edges straight away. Others began on an obvious feature of design — a chimney, say, or a window — and built out from there into areas that required a nicer attention to relative degrees of definition in slates or brickwork. But always the endgame lay in expanses of sky or foregrounds of dappled shadows for which nothing would do but exhaustive matching of shape and fit, until at last there was just the one distinctive lobed vacancy that remained, and that one piece that unequivocally matched it.*

'It's a shame to break it up,' someone would say then. 'Can't we leave it till we go home?' But it would probably be sooner rather than later that you disengaged the pieces and gathered them back into the box.

Apart from a couple of small jigsaws of abstract art that came with just a plastic sleeve, most puzzles I have owned or known are in boxes covered with the kind of representation that makes much of contrasts in colour, texture, and definition. They define a class of real-world scenes that you can almost believe were themselves inspired by jigsaw puzzles. And so did my current researches stir me that I realised at that moment with a flash of insight that just such a scene is the one that greets you as you walk through the gates on College Crescent and up the driveway towards Ormond College at the University of Melbourne. I could see it all: the bluestone masonry, the glimpse through a shadowed arch of a sunny internal courtyard, the gravel edged with bushy lavender whose countless flower heads reach up long curving stems towards the northern sun, and above all that mad grey spire in the French taste, its filigrees and finioles drawn with a crisp ink-line against a lustrous blue sky. And just a couple of centimetres higher up, you would come to the edge of the picture.

Ormond College was, of course, the scene of the events which were the starting point of Helen Garner's *The First Stone*. I had read that book when it first came out, and remembered the outlines of the story well enough, though I had not yet revisited the text as part of my current project – my only new information being Gracie's note that it contained no rabbits. *There are no snakes in Iceland*, I thought irrelevantly.

Garner tries in the book to make sense of how a couple of incidents at a drunken college party had the effects and ramifications that they did. The Master of Ormond was alleged to have groped one student and propositioned another. He lost his job: the nightmare outcome an academic can expect when alcohol meets fantasy. If among your students, for example, there should be a young woman you like to picture lying naked on a tiger-skin rug, it will be as well if you, she, alcohol and the rug are never together in the same place. I don't know whether there are any tiger skins at Ormond College: the Melbourne Club, resort of many an Ormond graduate, has more than one – evidence of the ascendancy of its members over wild nature as much as their fellow human. Had the mute surrender in those glass eyes ever seemed to invite a High Court judge to expect the same from an attractive chambermaid after one glass too many? Just so might the squire, flushed by the reckless consumption of gingerbread, seek to have his way with that rosy-cheeked kitchen girl.

But the sequence of events at Ormond College – so fortuitous and at the same time so inexorable as the book had presented it – seemed to demand more than a facetious explanation. If it was only by accident that no face-saving formula was offered to the offended students at a time when it might have been accepted, how was it that, even before the incident, Dr Shepherd appeared marked for destruction? The situation had its own structure and its own dynamic; nothing could deflect it. Or was this just hindsight?

With these and other reflections jostling in my mind, the daily episode of *Big Brother* flashed by, and we were just into the live intruders special at twenty five to eight when a timely commercial sent me out to the kitchen.

'I hate to strike a sour note when you are obviously enjoying yourself so much,' said L, 'but aren't you leaving the dinner a little late?'

'We are having chicken breast,' I replied, 'and I would venture to say that the chicken breast that can't be cooked in twenty minutes can't be cooked.'

'If you say so,' said L politely, though it didn't seem to me that as far as content went this was much of a step up from 'whatever you reckon'. It was more a matter of her demeanour. I lit the griller and put what was to become the satay sauce on a low gas: the next commercial would be an opportunity to add coconut cream, however much was desired, and lemon juice could wait till the last moment.

Things were getting exciting: I was so unwilling to miss a second of the drama that I nearly cannoned into L while running out to turn the chicken at ten to eight.

'Who's that girl?' asked L. 'I haven't seen her before.'

'That's one of the intruders.'

'She's rather pretty.'

'Yes, that blobby nose reminds me of Giulietta Massina in *La Strada*. I could go for someone like that – if my circumstances were other than they are, of course. Now, if you'll excuse me,' I said, as signs of a break flashed up, 'I must put the finishing touches to our dinner.'

'Do you mind if I have mine in front of the television?' asked L.

'So you have become a fan of *Big Brother*?'

'No, it's too futile for words – but I'd just like to see what happens.'

And with that she took my place in the chair and disposed herself comfortably.

*

The next few days passed in a rush of obligations and commitments. L has a truly extended family, and some of its more aged members need to be visited from time to time. Besides, before beginning my present project, I had begun to feel the weight of repeated suggestions that the railings on the terrace needed repainting. That this was so was obvious to the most casual observer, but the thought of scraping and sanding back so much peeling and blistered paint from so long a panel of iron railing had caused work to be deferred several times. I felt obliged now, as the weather remained fine, to try and do something about it. So the days passed, till by the following Wednesday evening I was able to feel that if my debt to the railings had not been discharged, at least I had met the minimum monthly payment. The capital would keep till another occasion.

L came home with news: 'It seems that Poppy will only have to wait another couple of weeks at the most. Mrs Smith told me today that one of the girls in Year 10 is pregnant, and as soon as the expulsion ceremony has been held, Poppy will be able to take her place.'

'Expulsion ceremony? Isn't that a bit harsh? I thought such people were just allowed to slip quietly away, like Emmeline squeezing between the palings in that illustration from *When We Were Very Young*. Though it could have been a tight squeeze for Emmeline if she had been pregnant, I suppose.'

'That just shows how far behind the times you are,' said L. 'No other school could possibly take a girl if she hadn't been properly expelled. People today "seek closure", you know. So they can move on.'

I pictured shadowy hosts of gravid girls, like the souls of the unburied in Book 6 of the *Aeneid*, denied passage to another school and driven back from the banks of Styx by heartless Charon in his dirty singlet. This in turn called up a picture of Alby, and seeing him now as an infernal deity, perched on his stilts and wearing his trademark blue singlet, I gave an involuntary chuckle.

'There's no need to snigger like that,' said L. 'It's a very sad situation, but it will be some consolation to the poor parents that the whole ceremony is conducted with a degree of dignity.'

Here, however, the thought of the headmistress's court of honour summoned to my mind an anecdote a colleague had told me about the Korean War: of a WAC court-martialled on the grounds that pregnancy counted as a self-inflicted wound. The chuckle turned into a splutter, and I had to retreat to the kitchen to avoid L's anger, which was likely to be terrible.

Later, by way of an overture of peace, I said: 'You will be pleased to know that the railings are now all ready for repainting. I think it will make a better job, though, if I leave them for a few days. Where I had to sand them back to bright metal it will be best to give that time to oxidise, which will make a better key for the paint.'

'It's wonderful how you know all these technical things,' said L.

'So,' I went on, 'tomorrow I intend to get *The First Stone* under my belt, and by the time I've done that I will have laid a certain platform for attacking *Joe Cinque's Consolation*. People have told me it's quite a controversial book, so I'd like to feel fully prepared before I approach it.'

'That sounds lovely,' said L. 'It's a shame you won't be able to do it. I take it you've forgotten that tomorrow we're going to Gerald's funeral.'

Forgotten, or at least repressed.

'Do we have to go?' I asked.

'You know the answer to that as well as I do,' said L, and the subject was closed. She is not a woman you defy.

*

Gerald was a local man with whom we had had a long acquaintance. Neither L nor I would have thought of him or his partner – and he did have a partner – as friends, but we were old associates. 'It's Gerald,' he would say in that soft Irish stage-whisper of his when you picked up the phone, and you knew you were in for distributing a few thousand leaflets in support of the current campaign, whether it was to save a threatened strip of foreshore, to clear the weeds from a bushland reserve, or to support some candidate for the local council. Some of his initiatives, such as the establishment of a network of bicycle paths, we naturally supported less enthusiastically than others, but in the course of many years' campaigning everyone was entitled to fire a few blanks. Sometimes I would close my eyes and try to visualize all the letterboxes in our suburb, and I must say that I could do a pretty good job, arcane though some of their locations were. We prided ourselves, L and I, on never missing a box, and I at least took a fierce joy in stuffing leaflets into boxes with provocative notices on them such as 'Australia Post mail only' or 'No junk mail'. If a box had 'Post' written on it, as some of them do, I would deface it, at least in my mind, and beam the owners a telepathic message to go back to where they came from. *Letters*, yes, *Mail*, yes, depending on whether you were thinking of them separately or in the mass, but *Post*, no − *post* is a verb. And if the lid fell off while I was depositing a leaflet, too bad.

Letterboxes are not what they were. Ours is just a small tin affair near the front gate, and most of the neighbours are much the same, though some of them will have those brass ones with a spring-loaded flap that take all your strength to open. The older flats and units tend to have die-cast metal affairs set into a brick wall that rattle and are not quite big enough to take a regular letter with ease. Where the place is rented there will typically be a lot of envelopes and advertising fliers hanging out of them and spilling down onto the footpath. I don't know what the tenants do for mail, but such as it is they certainly don't read it. The newer units have those chaste banks of pressed aluminium boxes in the foyer terminating in one labelled Strata Plan No. 12457. How they eat up the leaflets! In many areas not far from here you will get rid of a couple of hundred in half a block.

In my young day people were more fanciful, I think; they built their own letterboxes out of brick or stone, or had one in the shape of a house with a roof that came off to take the letters. And on their gateposts were little enamel plaques saying 'Hawkers and canvassers need not call'. And I dimly remember in a street near us a telegraph pole with a label on it saying 'This street helps to support an Australian Prisoner of War'. I can't visualise it — it's a purely linguistic memory, though I must in the nature of things have been very young at the time — but I do know it's my own memory and not something I was told, because no one else I've asked ever seems to have noticed it.

And now Gerald was no longer with us; someone else would have to galvanize the protests and organise the campaigns. I felt it probably wouldn't be me: I don't have enough free-floating indignation for the job. 'Relatives and friends are invited to mark Gerald's passing at a gathering in the North Chapel, Northern Suburbs Crematorium' — so read the funeral notice.

'What do they mean — *passing*?' I had asked L rhetorically, and we both huffed and puffed for a while. The word lending itself to being spat, we had accorded full justice to its synaesthetic properties. Now we were on our way, threading the curves down to the Lane Cove River, which as always lay flat beneath the bridge in a mute grease-green pool. Water that might have washed a very dirty singlet. The Styx itself. We swung up the hill.

It doesn't take long to get to the crematorium, I reflected sombrely, yet somehow it is always a bright, clear, pollution-free day. You can see for miles across suburbs where you probably wouldn't want to live, though they would be pleasant enough when you got there. The Spanish mission chimney trails a slender wisp of smoke, and the sunlight glints on the tiles and flattens the sky to a clean, uniform blue. It wouldn't make much of a jigsaw.

It would be hard to count the times I had been here through the years. The first time, perhaps, as a teenager, when I accompanied my grandmother to the funeral of a cousin — cousin's cousin? — who was beaten to death by police after a botched bank job. I had only met the young man two or three times — he was warm, witty, put you at your ease — perhaps, as it now seems to me, the first person I had known with that camp sensibility that brings out the ridiculous in the ordinary things of life. I remember him debating with my grandmother the weight he should give to her offer of flannelette sheets against the possibility that he would feel effeminate. His young wife, too, I remember, standing alone, unacknowledged, his family somehow nursing an obscure feeling that she must have been responsible. I can still see the wide brim of her hat against the sky as she stood outside the chapel, and its low round crown. I expect she is still alive, somewhere; quite likely a grandmother herself.

I had been here as a son and as a nephew; I had been here as a grandson and as a son-in-law; I had been here as the loutish mate and as the sober family friend; I had been here as neighbour and as colleague. In short, I had played every role you can play at a funeral except the corpse.

Quite a crowd had gathered outside the chapel by the time we arrived; L stopped to talk to some neighbours with whom we had shared in many of Gerald's campaigns, while I spotted a woman in the middle distance who had once lived next door but moved away many years ago. I went to say hello and she asked about Gracie, whom she had known growing up.

This was an opportunity. Self-aggrandisement may be a disreputable upstart, but boasting by proxy has a long and honourable pedigree; done by way of an adult child or grandchild, moreover, it is so much less brazen than the 'my baby is better than your baby' sort of thing which is so prevalent from maternity ward to kindergarten. I opened on an appropriate note of self-deprecation.

'I can't keep up with Gracie,' I said, in a gush a trifle embarrassing to look back on. 'She goes from strength to strength. She's earning three times what I ever did; she moved into a house not long ago that she's renovated within an inch of its life, and Billy, her little boy, is so advanced for his age, and not the least bit spoilt. He's a lovely child and he never gives her any trouble. We see quite a lot of them off and on.'

'And is there a Mr Gracie?'

'To tell you the truth,' I replied, 'the subject has never come up.'

Gracie was coming to the end of an eighteen month secondment to her firm's associates in London when we had a postcard from her one day. On one side was some *objet* from the Tate Modern – all resin and animal parts. On the other it said, 'Billy and I arrive Qantas 7.30 a.m. Saturday. xxx Gracie.' L and I were at the airport to meet her of course, and quite keen to see this intimated travelling companion. Then out came Gracie pushing her trolley with a baby in one of those papoose affairs. She slipped it off, handed it to L, and said, 'Just hold Billy for me, will you Mum? One of these cases seems to have slipped sideways.' That was it; the moment passed; no further information was ever volunteered.

Meanwhile the crowd had begun to move in. For a while I hung back, hoping to join up with L, but she was not to be seen, so at last, with all the seats already taken, I squeezed in to a standing position near the front. Now finally I did see her, still talking to our neighbour, near the further door.

You will have seen the words 'Funeral service' – probably even used them yourself without thinking too much about it. Well this one was strictly self-service. The coffin stood on a trolley near the front and someone, the most self-assertive of Gerald's friends, asked a couple of others for help to wrestle it onto the platform that would carry it towards the furnaces. It skewed round like Gracie's luggage, but eventually they got the job done between them, and the same man then delivered a long rambling monologue about the old days. Gerald was brought in now and again as straight man in these anecdotes to show the speaker's own wit and daring to greater advantage. His speech seemed endless. He was succeeded by a woman in a woolly hat that looked like a tea-cosy – the hat, that is. She was one of those people that think they don't need a microphone, and, deaf as I am, her words were mercifully lost on me. Gerald's partner spoke briefly and with feeling. For a moment I felt reconnected, but my cord was abruptly jerked out of its powerpoint again by another long self-congratulatory ramble. I started to look around. What length blocks do they book these places in, I wondered. Twenty minutes, half an hour? Surely some attendants will appear and start making shuffling motions, and this whole dispiriting mockery will have to end. Were they groping towards *some better, broader, freer, less rule-bound gathering of the tribe; a forum in which everything might be said, everybody listened to: where bursts of laughter and shouts of rage might not be outlawed: where if people agreed to take turns everyone might at last, at last be heard.'**

If so, how would you know when it had come to an end? With a quick prayer, a reference to 'our brother or sister here departed' — no need to mention names — and an *Amen* to follow, you know exactly where you are; Charon can push the boat out, and you can all say to one another, 'Well, at least that's over'. *Ubi solitudinem faciunt, pacem vocant*: the gap is there, but they don't know how to fill it: the marketplace does nothing for our communal lives. Whereupon two people stood up together. So much for taking turns, I thought, and began, for want of anything constructive to do, to look around.

Perhaps you have been to a school reunion. I went to a primary school one once, and it was amazing how those middle-aged faces changed back to six- and seven-year-olds when I knew their names. Yet if there are people you don't know, a curious cognitive dissonance can arise. I had been at a funeral here not so long ago — a friend of my youth that I saw from time to time — and so many of the people that turned up, grey-haired now, or bald, and slumping, soon took on the lineaments of lively young men and women I had once known. But now and again I would think, 'Why did you marry that old woman, my friend? You were popular enough with the young ones back then.' For the woman had no young chrysalis in my mind to emerge from. As I looked around now, more and more of the people in the chapel were beginning to take on an obscure familiarity; there was a sense I had known them once, somehow, though I couldn't yet say where.

Then it was that on the other side of the chapel, not far from where L was standing I noticed two young women. They were whispering to one another during the speeches, and certainly smiling, if not actually giggling, from time to time. What was their role, I wondered. No one among all this talk had seen fit to tell us how Gerald had died; were these two, perhaps, his executioners? They seemed to be taking an uncalled-for delight in the situation. I posited some grotesque *folie à* *deux*, some plot to destroy a good man, some murderous equivalent of the complainants of Ormond College.* History always repeats itself, first as tragedy, then as farce. It was like *Melinda and Melinda*, I thought – but which was which? The doings in *The First Stone*, if you believed everything claimed against Dr Shepherd, were at best a sour sort of a comedy, a *Measure for Measure*. Did that mean this would have been a sweet kind of a tragedy? The headline 'Prof Bashed in Love Nest' came to my mind as I dallied with the details of what such a tragedy might have involved. What would Woody Allen have done with it, and who would play the two murderous seductresses in the screen version? Come to think of it, the taller of the two was not unlike Meg Ryan.

Then identification was certain. They were of course none other than Elisabeth and Vicki, the rabbit girls, and having made one leap, I quickly made many, many more. For this whole congregation, and I employ the word purely in its etymological sense, were, I now realised, fringe members of the libertarians, that old Sydney push whose single-minded devotion to selfishness made some of them think they were at the cutting edge of social change fifty years ago. Not that Sydney had any monopoly. On your bike, Anaïs Nin, I thought, who needs you? There's more integrity in cooking up a communal feast out of a dumpster. Looking across at L, I rolled my eyes upwards in a sort of 'let's get out of here' gesture and she nodded slightly. She knew.

Thus we worked our way close to the front of the line to give the partner that perfunctory kiss and few words of consolation that convention requires, and quickly sidled away along the colonnade. Some acquaintance is best unrenewed.

'Did you happen to notice two blonde girls who were standing just along to your right?' I asked L when we had reached the shelter of our car.

'You mean the Lever sisters? I certainly did. If I'd had a programme I would have donged them with it to get them to be quiet. That's no way to behave yourself at a funeral.'

'In that case, they fitted in perfectly,' I said. 'I've never seen such a shambles. But who are they?'

'They're old Santa Sophians – clever girls, but both of them caused a bit of trouble in their time. Too fun-loving by half. I've got an idea they are some sort of nieces of Gerald's.'

'I wonder how you would get a surname like Lever?' I ruminated. 'It sounds like someone that could apply a lot of pressure.'

'I think it must be Scottish,' said L in a reprovingly sensible voice. 'Remember Lever Brothers, the soap people? Well these are the Lever sisters.'

'I expect they changed it from Le Lièvre.* There are a lot of ties between France and Scotland. Do you know that in Scotland they still call a leg of lamb a jiggot?'

So Vicki might be short for Victorine, I supposed – but in that case, wouldn't the French call her Vivi, or Toto? Maybe even Vovo, like the biscuit? I pictured Vicki with hair dyed strawberry blonde at the sides and a plum-coloured stripe down the middle.

'Speaking of jiggots,' said L, 'is there any of that Scotch broth left? After that performance I need something to settle my stomach.'

*

In my heart, if you will excuse the metaphor, I had pencilled in ratatouille for the evening meal, but L's late lunch from the remainder of the Scotch broth forced me to reconsider. Ratatouille after Scotch broth would make the day's menu altogether too blurry an experience – an overwrought little statement of gustation, as you might put it. We needed something crisp and clinical, astringent even, to reorient us, mildly yet firmly, to the elements of flavour – much like the brisk birching that is supposed to follow a sauna. That is a step they always seem to leave out in *Big Brother*, I thought, and pictured to myself one of the housemates as I had last seen her, making straight from sauna to bedroom, a fuzzy bit demurely placed across her chest like the right hand of the goddess in Botticelli's *Birth of Venus*. Venus. Of course – wiener schnitzel was just what we needed. One lightly fried slice of veal, a baked potato, a sprig of steamed broccoli. Moisten the meat with lemon, anoint the potato with butter, and you had it − simple flavours, understated, distinct. I shouldered my eco-bag and set forth in search of the ingredients.

The butcher, when I arrived, was at the back of the shop, engaged so far as I could tell in flensing a side of lamb. I watched curiously. The knife moved in deft, calculated strokes till each rib stood up distinct, and they began to cry in unison 'rack of lamb' rather than 'chest of sheep'.

'Sorry to keep you waiting, sir,' said the butcher. 'What'll it be?'

'It's a pleasure to watch an artist at work,' I replied. 'Could you do two nice slices of veal schnitzel for me?' There was probably a tautology in there somewhere, but if it's worth saying once, it has to be worth saying twice.

'No worries, mate,' said the butcher, selecting and wrapping the requested items. 'There you go, sir, seven bucks. Have a nice evening.'

'I was still planning on a nice afternoon,' I replied.

'I get ahead of myself, mate. Comes of getting up so early in the morning.'

'Rather you than me,' I said, ceding the moral authority. No skilled tradesman I − I am a mere drifter. It's not a good idea to get offside with shopkeepers. Some of those pieces he had been trimming off didn't look too savoury, and I wouldn't have wanted them to end up in my mince.

Now if I pre-prepared the veal, I thought, while proceeding to buy the broccoli and the lemon, there would still be time to make a start on *The First Stone* before seven o'clock should signal the start of my evening's viewing. Milk and flour and egg and breadcrumbs for the veal − it's a mistake to season the flour, because there's enough salt in the meat as it is, and don't forget that there will be salt in the butter. That is, there will be if you've bought proper Australian butter and not that insipid, unsalted, European-inspired apology for butter that you see in the shops. Unbranded butter is the best, because not only is it always salted, it's usually sour, the way butter is supposed to be if it hasn't been blandified to suit the childish tastes of Generation-somethings who wouldn't know a cow if they saw one. Which is probably why, I reflected, people give their children cows' names. There's a model you see on the television — Gracie remembers her older sister from school — and apparently the whole family have cows' names, like Clover, and Daisybelle. *Come up Whitefoot, come up Lightfoot.*

So in my reverie I prepared the schnitzels, ensuring that once fried their coats would take on that desired texture, like the softly wrinkled skin of a baby rabbit. I quartered a potato; I cut the florets from the broccoli and put them in the microwave, ready to steam. Now for *The First Stone.*

The library copy of this work was graffiti'd but sparingly. The title page had a tetchy two-line inscription in blue ballpoint that read: *Stick to fiction* and *this is a fiction book.* The inner pages were highlighted here and there in violet, though the force of the highlighting was rather lost because of the roughness of the paper; besides this, a number of passages, I noticed as I flicked over the pages, were marked with pencilled stars in the margin. Whether or not these two critical hands were the same I could not tell, though they seemed to be of similar mind. Ms Violet, for example, in the sentence

> *I think they felt that Shepherd, as a man, was part of the power clique, and that they were victims and vulnerable.**

had singled out the words *Shepherd, as a man, was part of the power clique* for highlighting, whereas Brenda Starr, as I silently named the second hand, had drawn the attention of the reader to *Sexual harassment is an abuse of power.**

Over the whole text as I began to re-read it brooded the presence of Ormond College: menacing, hierarchical, anachronistic — a gothick fantasy come to life. Here was the high school for Poppy. I could see her rubbing shoulders with Elizabeth Rosen or Nicole Stewart. 'An amazing place' someone had called it to Helen Garner's narrative persona, and amazing it was, not in its banality, the way the personalities of the *Big Brother* housemates were constantly referred to as amazing, but in the context of a meta-narrative that included the household of *Monkey Grip* and Sweetpea Mansions. It would have been no more appropriate for the students' complaints to be ventilated at a gathering of the tribe than for Ray to pursue Maxine for his misappropriated money through the Small Claims Tribunal. Or would it? For a leading theme of the book seemed to be the transformation of narrative into meta-narrative. A story of a dance and of a hand became a story of sexual harassment and of Woman with a generic singular and a capital W. 'Give us back our plurality,' Garner was calling: 'we are not Ws on stilts.'* If a knee in the groin was good enough for the pushy boyfriend in Sweetpea Mansions in the old days, it should be good enough for a drunken professor at Ormond College. It's not an anti-feminist tract, Brenda, I thought, it's a pro-anarchist tract; I've marched in many a demonstration behind the black and red banners of the anarchists. They stir the blood in just the same way as those green flags blazoned with the words of the Prophet that led the hosts of the Mahdi into battle. Are you too young to have seen *The Four Feathers*? You can get the same thrill whether or not you are in the front rank. Having your arm broken by a policeman, it seems to me, doesn't contribute to the downfall of capitalism so much as to reinforcing the cash nexus that corrupts the relationship of doctor and patient.

Odd that I should have been thinking of demonstrations, for at quarter to eight, just as I was beginning to heat up the oil, the phone rang.

'People are rude to ring when we are just about to have dinner,' I said to L.

'You can't blame them,' L replied. 'Most people would have no idea that we had dinner so late.'

'I suppose they have nursery tea,' I said irritably, 'and like to be tucked into bed at eight for a good early night. Try and buzz them off; if they're such rude people themselves, they're probably too insensitive to have their feelings hurt.'

'I'll do my best,' said L loyally, and went to answer the phone.

After a period in which most of the talking seemed to be at the other end, I heard L say, 'Yes, Erna; yes, certainly, I'll tell him. You can count on us.'

My heart sank, for Erna – Erna O'Malley – was none other than the partner of Gerald, deceased. I had thought we were safe from campaigns for the time being. Now it seemed that Gerald's passing, the word we had been so quick to mock, was more of a passing in the Andrew Johns sense, and Erna had caught the ball and was running with it.

L came back into the room just as I laid our plates on the table.

'That was Erna,' she said.

'I heard.'

'She said that Gerald's last wish had been that everyone who was kind enough to come to the funeral should be asked to contribute to the campaign he was working on.'

I felt we could hardly refuse, as they had asked on ecological grounds for no flowers to be sent.

'So how much are we up for?'

'They don't want money; but there's an action on tonight, and I said you would go.'

'What sort of action? I'll tell you here and now that I point blank refuse to be associated with street theatre in any shape or form. If people want to strut round in Uncle Sam masks they can do it without my help.'

'I shouldn't think there's anything like that involved. She said it was for Angry Penguins, and to meet at Cabbage Tree Bay at midnight.'

I groaned. I had read something about this campaign in the local paper. Cabbage Tree Bay was a small indentation in one of the inner harbour bays not far from here. There was a miniscule beach, about the width of a regular house block, and passing it in the ferry I had noticed pilings from a long-vanished wharf and some dressed stones that could have been part of a 19th century harbour pool. There are sites like that all around the harbour. Now someone, I think the owner of a nearby marina, was proposing to put down a concrete slab and install some sort of apparatus for lifting yachts out of the water. A routine harbourside development in other words – you would expect opposition from homeowners close to the site, talk about excess traffic in residential streets, and on the other side a lot of rhetoric about nimbys and the working harbour etc, etc.

But what gave this situation its special significance was that the beach — if it was this beach — had been mentioned in a journal dating from the 1790s, Watkin Tench or one of those people, as a haunt of the little penguin. No one as far as I knew had sighted a little penguin west of Cremorne Point in the last hundred and fifty years, but close on council approval of this development had come a report that a little penguin had come ashore and looked as if it was going to nest in Cabbage Tree Bay. How you would divine a penguin's intentions, I wasn't too sure, but that didn't stop Gerald — he had founded a group to liberate the beach from commerce and return it to the penguins, a campaign on which he had been working right up till his death. I communicated these facts to L.

'Little penguins?' she asked. 'Is that the same as fairy penguins?'

'I believe so,' I said, 'but there's a lot of prejudice about activities on harbour beaches. Someone probably thought it would be better to change the name in case neighbouring householders should object.'

'I'm sorry I can't drive you,' said L, 'but I have a working breakfast on tomorrow, so I must be in bed by ten. Will you be all right?'

'See these shoulders?' I asked.

*

I looked in the wardrobe for my warmest jacket. It had a zipper and an outer flap with press-studs that closed over the front, and padding inside the lining. I hadn't had occasion to wear this jacket for quite a while, though surely I must have had it on more recently than the father-and-daughter camp memorialized by a sachet I found in one of the pockets containing some white powder that turned into orange cordial when you mixed it with water. Perhaps I should fill an envelope with this stuff and mail it to our would-be developer. That would teach him to respect our penguins!

Soon after 11 I set out. Cabbage Tree Bay was not far from Rita's, so I walked, following the same general route. I don't like to drive at night, there was no convenient public transport for this cross-country journey, and it went against the grain to take a cab — you don't catch a taxi to a demonstration. Some parts of the way were very ill-lit; I stumbled more than once where a block of the footpath had risen or sunk out of the level. Up the steps past the Sydney Water hunting lodge it was completely dark, and I had to rely entirely on the regularity of the steps and on the handrail for guidance. A sort of clanking noise that seemed to be coming out of the bushes to the right of the path would have set you running for your life if you had been that sort of person.

On the road above Cabbage Tree Bay a small group of people were hanging around waiting for something to happen. Some of them were wearing sweatshirts with a plagiarized Penguin Books logo and the words 'Angry Penguins' underneath. They didn't look very angry. I joined them. The upper edge of the site was marked by a high white plywood fence mottled here and there with splotches that probably would have said 'Bill Posters Prosecuted' if it hadn't been too dark to read. *Hawkers and Canvassers Need Not Call.* The fence blocked all sight of the water, but at one end were high gates of the same material, and through the gap between these it was just possible to make out, close to the waterfront, the dark outline of a crane, silhouetted by the streamers of light that fluttered across the water from Millers Point. Of penguins there was no sign.

An old station wagon came round the corner then, and Erna was in our midst. A large woman with a bush of grey hair, she was now dressed in a crocheted caftan which showed shades of red and brown in the headlights. We gathered round her.

'First of all,' she said, in a brogue at least as compelling as Gerald's, 'we will all join hands while we acknowledge the Eora people who were the traditional custodians of this site.' We joined hands. Erna intoned a number of syllables in a language which was certainly foreign to me, though I was prepared to bet that she had no more idea of the Eora word for little penguin than I did. Perhaps it was Irish Gaelic she was talking in. At any rate, our sense of ceremony satisfied, we could feel that police or no police, the *genius loci* was on our side.

My job, and that of many of the others, was to be chalking. Erna opened the back of the station wagon and handed out those thick sticks of chalk that you make up out of plaster of paris and pigment. All the access roads were to be chalked with slogans to a considerable distance. Erna put us into teams to go off in different directions and work back towards the building site. I was white captain in our team, and you will realise that when we're talking penguins, white is an important colour. The road surface would do for the black. Actually, I thought later, little penguins are coloured more like a kookaburra as far as I could remember, but we weren't aiming to be veridical. The night wore on.

About an hour and a half later, my knees so sore from the asphalt and so stiff that standing had become hardly more tolerable than kneeling, we were back at the bay. We had been working down the slope, and naturally had been travelling backwards for the most part, but in any case the curvature of the streets would have obscured whatever was happening at base camp. Now, close to home and judging that the surface of this road was adequately embellished, we turned to face the water. The gradient was quite steep, and it was possible to see over the boundary fence and down to the shoreline. The crane was still there, but against its latticed silhouette there seemed to be a dark bulk that cut off the light from the water. I watched. The bulk moved. I watched again. From out of the bulk came a shower of sparks. Someone had climbed up the crane and was cutting through the boom of it with an oxy torch or whatever you used for that sort of job. Let's hope the ancestral penguin man is on the job, I thought, we may be needing his help before the night is over. Another shower of sparks shone out against the water, brighter and more dynamic than any of the reflections. As to the identity of the saboteur, he or she was much too far away, and whatever light was cast back by the sparks revealed only the Ned Kelly-like aspect of a welding mask.

The view was also obscured by the illumination of the foreground. The lights of two or three cars were shining on the white plywood fence. That is to say, it had been a white plywood fence. It was now decorated from end to end. At each extremity of the design was a penguin, whose over-large eyes and threatening aspect showed close observation of the manga tradition. This artist was no *Hello Kitty* dilettante – these skills had been honed on much darker matter. In between the two creatures were the words 'Penguins before Profits' executed in a stylised and baroque script whose calligraphy betrayed the practised hand of a master. This person was even now spraying in the finishing touches of the design. At the artist's feet was what we used to call an airline bag in the days when airlines gave you free things; no doubt it contained a battery of spray cans in various colours. A final flourish. Then, the design apparently finished to the artist's satisfaction, the lights went out. No sense making yourself too obvious.

But in that short interval, I had seen all that I needed to see. There was something about the slender, not quite stick-like figure of the artist, something about those movements of the head and the shoulders that had guided the spray, something about the fall of the dark hair that left me in no doubt at all. Poppy had joined the Angry Penguins. Skills which had flowered, perhaps, on Melbourne's tramcars were now the possession of our fair city. The world as I knew it would be a more decorative place. And then I knew, of course, who it was inside the Ned Kelly suit on the crane. It had to be Dave.

5

G^2 – the hero rides, is carried*

I was becoming depressingly familiar with the six o'clock alarm; at least today, I thought, as L, like an over-ambitious salmon tackling Niagara Falls, jerked herself upright with a twitch that ran the whole length of her body, I could resubmerge until kindly Nature should awaken me, at perhaps half past nine. Fortunately there had been a fellow activist living in our direction to give me a lift home; on the downside, environmental considerations forbade her to turn on the heating in her car, and I felt like one of those Antarctic pioneers of a hundred years ago when I fumbled the key into our front door, fingers numb and cold clinging to my clothes. That had been after two – now it was just six. I lost consciousness. Five minutes later, it seemed, L was shaking me.

'Wake up,' she said. 'Wake up. You're looking after Billy today.'

'What?' I said thickly. 'It's all right. Gracie can bring Billy. He won't mind if I'm in my pyjamas. I'll wake up then.'

'You're looking after Billy at Gracie's house,' said L slowly and firmly. 'Gracie just rang. Apparently Billy has a streaming cold, she said, and she can't take him to child care. The poor little thing was up half the night, and Gracie thinks it will be best if he just potters round at home today.'

'I know just how he feels,' I said.

'If you're quick I can drop you off on my way out to breakfast.'

I swung my legs down to the floor and made for the bathroom. You have probably noticed how in films, particularly English films, characters will just pull on their clothes without any hint of ablution. At the beginning of *Four Weddings and a Funeral*, for instance, Hugh Grant is in bed with some woman, and he gets straight up and puts his clothes on and rushes off to a wedding. No shower or anything. As a race of people, the English are not committed to personal hygiene. Mind you, that whole story is predicated on the idea that Andie McDowell is wildly attractive, so it's not exactly *cinéma vérité*.

With these and similar thoughts in mind I gave myself a brief and inefficient shave, abrading the surface layer in a few places round the corners of my mouth and the lower aspect of my chin, and soon, showered and dressed, I joined L downstairs.

'That was quick,' said L.

'The shower that can't be concluded in three minutes can't be concluded,' I replied sententiously. L has a different attitude. For her the shower is a form of meditation, and I sometimes think she would stay under it all day if other considerations didn't supervene. Occasionally, if I get irritated with this, or even if I'd just like to talk to her for a change, I will put on a load of washing or fill a kettle to give her a sudden jolt from a jet of cold water and return her to the real world.

On the way to Gracie's I gave L a sketch of the night before. She had unashamedly turned the heater on full blast when we got into the car, and now we were feeling snug and cocooned.

'If the engine is creating all that heat anyway,' said L, 'I don't see that it's worse to warm ourselves than to let it all out into the environment.'

'Your logic is impeccable,' I replied, 'and does credit to the girl who topped Philosophy I all those forty whatever it is years ago.'

'I'll thank you not to be too specific,' said L. 'It's only because I look ten years younger than my age that the clients still give so much credence.'

'You can't give credence intransitively any more than you can give birth,' I put in.

'*Give so much credence to what I suggest to them,* I was starting to say before you interrupted,' went on L, 'and here we are. Out you get, and don't go teaching Billy to interrupt and answer back. He's a dear little boy, and he doesn't need to learn cheeky habits from his grandfather.'

'Not when he has a grandmother to instruct him in repartee,' I answered, bending down to kiss her left hand which was resting on the gearstick.

'OK, Prince Charming,' said L, 'that's enough. You'll have to restrain yourself till this evening.'

'If I can,' I replied, 'but a hot-blooded person such as myself could hardly be blamed if his eyes were to stray elsewhere under the stress of intolerable deprivation. If Gracie runs to a rosy-cheeked kitchen girl, she might need to be on her toes.'

'You wish,' said L's expression, though her actual words were: 'I wouldn't have put on the heater if I'd known you were going to get over-excited. Now off you go.' And she pulled the door shut and drove away.

*

Gracie was full of thanks when she opened the door.

'It's so good of you to come at short notice, Dad,' she said. 'Billy was crying and snuffling all night, and it wouldn't have been fair to leave him among other children like that.'

'As long as I can work off a bit of my sentence,' I replied.

'You're surely not suggesting that looking after Billy is a punishment?' said Gracie with mock severity. 'Now this is what he has for lunch,' she went on, pointing to a jar of anonymous cream-coloured glop that was standing on the bench next to a two-litre container of apple and cranberry juice, 'and you can give him some of this later in his cup. I usually break it down half and half with water — they're too little for their kidneys to cope with pure fruit juice, you know. And there are plenty of nappies over there,' she rattled on. 'Just see that he stays warm, don't take him outside, and I'll try to leave work early and be back here by five.'

Billy was sitting on the floor, looking rather limp and sucking on a bottle. Gracie had dressed him in a sort of one-piece white towelling tracksuit, with the feet all in one and pink binding round the neck and cuffs. I had to assume there would be some way of getting it off.

'Clothes like these send out very confusing messages,' I said to Gracie. 'It's hard enough for people in the street to tell whether a baby is a boy or a girl without doing up a little boy in pink ribbon like this.'

'I'm hoping my little boy will be in touch with his feminine side,' said Gracie. 'The time is past when it was acceptable for a male to be some kind of emotional cripple. Honestly, when I look at your generation of men, some of them are so contorted and twisted in their attitudes they remind me of the Hunchback of Notre Dame.'

'Well call me Quasimodo if you like,' I said, 'but ever since I was a young man I've found it was a good idea to outsource my feminine side. It means I can get in touch with it in a less spiritual way than you have in mind.'

'Don't be disgusting,' said Gracie, wiping the streaming mucus from Billy's upper lip. 'Now have a lovely play with Grandpa, Billy, and Mummy will see you tonight.'

She kissed him and made for the door.

'Mum-ma,' said Billy hopelessly, but made no move to follow. He must have been feeling out of sorts.

The twin facades of Gracie's house had been in shadow when we arrived. This meant of course that the high glass wall that faced north was beginning to take the morning sun, and a beam slanted across the upper verge of the western wall. Soon it would strike the services pod. Billy remained seated, as content as he could reasonably be in the circumstances, and, the floor being heated from below in some fashion, I supposed he might just as well stay there. I turned my mind towards breakfast. Our departure from the house had been much too hurried for anything of the sort, and L was eating out, in any case. I began to prospect in Gracie's cupboards.

Coffee would be no problem — I found a mini-plunger that would hold a cup or two, and soon had some of that on the go. Food, however, was another matter. There were a couple of packets of those cereals that women in the advertisements tuck into when they come back from jogging — full of protein and fibre and 97% fat-free. These, needless to say, I ruled out immediately. Then there was some sliced white bread in the freezer, and the fridge afforded some individual slices of processed cheese which I assumed were for Billy, a few assorted spreads, and that was about it. The makings of a gentleman's breakfast appeared to be in lamentably short supply. But then I opened a high round tin that I found in one of the overhead cupboards, and inspiration struck.

For there are some times, everyone will agree, particularly when you are a bit too tired or just generally jaded with the world, when only Vegemite will do. The sliced bread would have been an unworthy vehicle for that king among spreads, but the tin contained grissini. Now we were in business! To Gracie's designer table I carried the coffee plunger, a mug, a plate, the tin of grissini, and the medium sized jar of Vegemite I had seen among the spreads in Gracie's refrigerator. I pulled out one of the designer cane-backed chairs and sat down. This might not be my own terrace, but it was the next best thing. I uncapped the Vegemite, dipped into it with one of the grissini and drew it out. The end of the bread stick was coated with a thick swirl of the life-giving substance. It was like a torch – like the Statue of Liberty done as a negative. 'Vegemite enlightening the world,' I thought, and crunched off the end of the grissini – or grissino, perhaps – and dipped it in again. This was about as good as it got – except, I reflected, that my choice of beverage needed adjusting. Black coffee was my usual breakfast drink, but the thought of teaming Vegemite with black coffee somehow didn't appeal. The flavours would neither clash nor complement each other: just sit uneasily side by side like teenagers at a Year 9 dance. What I needed, I now realised, was a cappuccino, and though such a thing was not to be had, I topped up the coffee with milk and added a couple of teaspoons of sugar.

Billy had been watching me, first listlessly, then with more animation. At last he spoke.

'Billy eye-ceam,' said Billy.

Seeing what he had in mind, I rather doubtfully broke a grissini stick in half, swirled it in the Vegemite, and put it in Billy's hand. He started to suck on it, and brown stuff ran down his chin and onto the white tracksuit. I did my best to reach round and wipe both chin and clothing with the kitchen sponge, but it didn't seem to make much impression. Then he pushed the clean-licked bread stick towards me.

'More,' said Billy.

By the time we had finished half the jar between us, Billy seemed a lot happier. I cleaned him up as best I could, though I baulked at changing the tracksuit — it looked far too complicated. Then we sat on the stairs and built things with blocks. Gracie's perfectly flat designer floor and the perfectly flat wooden treads of her designer stairs were ideal surfaces for building with blocks, and we put together quite ambitious structures between us — ones that rose up from stair to stair in vertiginous pinnacles, with towers and arches and cantilevers. Billy contributed when he could, and at other times simply knocked the buildings down, and there was much laughing as the blocks scattered down between the open treads or skidded across the polished boards.

The blocks were made of some dense modern foam material designed to ensure that you would not be at the mercy of your litigious neighbour when your child hit their child over the head with them. They were a good size, there were plenty of them, and all six primary and secondary colours were represented: with these materials architecture could proceed very satisfyingly. We made some of the smaller ones into cars and boats, and pushed them across the shiny sea. It was lots of fun. Billy laughed; eleven o'clock came and went; only another six hours, I was thinking. And then there was a knock on the door.

I scrambled to my feet. I hadn't been kneeling much because of the bruising of the night before, but had been sitting sideways most of the time with my legs tucked around. Now I felt the soreness in my knees again, and momentarily had to catch at the stairs for support. The stainless steel wires were not comforting to the touch, and I was limping as I opened the door.

Dave was standing outside.

'Hello, Dave,' I said. 'What brings you here?'

'Your wife told me I'd find you here, mate,' said Dave. 'I went round to your place this morning, and there was no one there, but I found one of those yellow notes stuck to the door with her mobile number on it.

So I gave her a ring, and here I am.'

'How extraordinary that she should leave you her number,' I said. 'Was she expecting you?'

'No, mate, it wasn't for me. It said "Erna, if I'm not home, leave it in the porch, or if that doesn't suit, I'll be at this number" and it had her name underneath.'

It? What was L up to, I wondered, but there was not likely to be any light Dave could shed on that question.

'So what can I do for you, Dave?' I asked. 'Is everything all right? The police haven't caught up with you after last night?'

'Were you there too?' said Dave. 'No, mate — it's something I'd like to show you.'

'Have you got it there?'

'No, it's back at the workshop,' said Dave, 'but we can go on the bike.'

He made a sideways movement with his head, and looking along the street I saw the Harley-Davidson propped on the footpath. Inside Gracie's house you were never aware of much traffic noise, and the double walls had stopped me hearing his no doubt thunderous approach. Standing beside the bike was a figure I took to be Poppy, though as she was wearing one of those motorcycle helmets with a visor that goes all the way round, positive identification was impossible.

'But I'm looking after Billy, Dave,' I said, jerking my head in turn to indicate where Billy was pushing a block boat across the floor with fierce concentration.

'Kids love motorbikes,' said Dave. 'We can bring him along.'

'Gracie told me he wasn't to go outside,' I protested, backing into the house, but Dave was having none of that.

'What she doesn't know won't hurt her,' said Dave. 'We'll be back before she knows we've gone.' With these words Dave walked past me, and seemingly in a single movement had zipped Billy inside his leather jacket and buttoned up the front. The effect was not quite that of a baby rabbit cradled inside a cardigan, for the feet of Billy's tracksuit dangled helplessly below the front of the jacket while his head emerged from Dave's chest like the joey of some strange marsupial. I supposed that Billy should have had his nappy changed by now, but if it wasn't worrying Dave it wasn't worrying me, and it certainly didn't seem to be worrying Billy.

When we reached the bike Dave opened one of the panniers and pulled out another helmet, which he offered to me. Then we took our positions. Dave naturally sat in front, and I suppose Billy's legs accommodated themselves to the saddle somehow. Poppy sat immediately behind Dave. She was one of those girls who are terribly thin from front to back, so her presence didn't make much difference, though I found I had to bow my legs outwards to go over the panniers, because I was a long way further to the rear than the designers of the bike had had in mind.

'Is this legal, Dave?' I asked.

'Look, mate,' said Dave, 'if this is the worst thing you ever do, you won't be doing too badly.'

Poppy hung on around Dave's waist, and I rested my hands on the corners of Poppy's pelvis, which projected far enough to give quite a good hold. Off we went — Uncle Tom Cobleigh and all, I thought, and hoped we would meet a more kindly fate than those luckless adventurers.

Our destination, it turned out, was one of those back lanes in Glebe, only a short walk from The Courser's Arms where my tutor friend had sought sanctuary from Rita all those years ago. To return here with Rita's daughter seemed to be closing some kind of a loop. Dave chose his route carefully to avoid travelling along any main roads, and my fears that we might attract unfriendly or censorious attention were somewhat allayed. He pulled up beside a gate in a paling fence, just like all the other gates in all the other fences round about.

'Here we are,' said Dave. We dismounted, and Dave opened the other saddlebag, the one that hadn't contained the spare helmet. This was completely full of a heavy galvanized chain, one end of which was apparently attached to the frame of the bike. He wound the free end a couple of times round the shaft of a No Standing sign. The unused length lay in the gutter, coils glistening dully, a fit serpent to guard this mechanical treasure. Dave secured the chain with a padlock.

'Can't be too careful when you've got a bike like this,' he said, and removed his helmet. I followed suit. Poppy apparently preferred to keep hers on, and in fact continued to wear it for the rest of the proceedings, looking remarkably like that ad for cold sore cream that you have probably seen on the television. Billy's eyes were bright, and he said 'Ra-ra' to himself in a dreamy voice from time to time.

Dave pushed open the gate and we went in, stooping to avoid the lowest branch of a lemon tree heavy with shining yellow fruit. Then he used a key to unlock a door in a corrugated iron shed that took up about half the backyard of whatever building it was that fronted the major street. There was a driveway leading away in that direction, and a roller shutter in the distal end of the shed made it likely that it had been constructed as a garage for the main building. What its present function might be remained to be seen.

These odd little spaces, adapted to all kinds of semi-industrial purposes, are as common as lemon trees in the inner suburbs. Not far from here was a bookbinder that L had searched out for me – you went in through just such a gate, along a side passage you had to share with a stained innerspring mattress propped against the fence, and found yourself in a workshop that smelt of glue and dust and leather; you could fancy it might have stood there unchanged since the days of Dickens.

The space now revealed to us had nothing of tradition. There was a free-standing machine whose purpose I could hardly guess at: it seemed to combine elements from a drill press, a pantograph, and one of those things they have in a dentist's surgery. Then there was a computer. For a moment I wondered whether Billy and I had perhaps been lured into an interrogation facility belonging to some organization like Al Qaeda: the machine would be used to inflict unspeakable tortures, and the computer, from which, as I now saw, hung a number of trailing leads, would no doubt record our responses by way of cuffs strapped to our limbs and probes inserted into our persons. They were not likely to get much out of Billy.

Then, as I noticed a couple of books on the table that supported the computer, further disturbing possibilities came to mind. The uppermost book had a plain blue library binding with a call number stamped on the spine. Its title was *The Bulletin Reciter.** Poppy, I now saw — if it was Poppy inside the helmet, for its anonymity now took on a more sinister aspect — would wield the needles or apply the thumbscrews, or whatever else they had in mind for us, while Dave would read aloud relentlessly from Banjo Patterson, making us the more ready to break down and confess all. On the other hand, if this was no more than paranoid fantasy, could it be that Dave had stolen the book from the Mitchell Library, and in the process destroyed all my present and future credibility with that institution? I had seen Dave's cavalier way with the traffic laws, and his work on the crane suggested he held little respect for private property.

But my fears on this score were dispelled as soon as had I reached for the book and opened it. The title page carried the impression of a rubber stamp of that familiar kind which has two concentric rings with lettering between. In the upper semicircle were the words 'State of Victoria', in the lower, 'Dept of Corrective Services'. Dave probably had assisted the book to regain its freedom, I thought, but at least he had not liberated it from the custody of the State Library of New South Wales.

'Top book,' said Dave. 'Now look at this.'

He switched on the computer and dimmed the bank of fluorescent lights that had been creating a bright glow inside the shed. Then he pulled down a screen which was set up to show a larger image of whatever was on the computer. I had seen my younger colleagues doing this sort of thing in their lectures, and I was sure that L's presentations to her clients would be full of such gimmicks, but it was a technology of which I was happily ignorant.

Then Dave opened a file, and there appeared on the screen a large circular device crammed with emblematic content. You may have seen one of those medieval maps of the world that have everything in them and get everything wrong at the same time. The Borgia map is one of my favourites: it's a 15th century production, and about as highly-wrought as those things got before people started to find out what the world was really like. The Mediterranean is in the middle, with Italy featuring very large and quite the wrong shape. Africa is at top right, with mountains and villages and Prester John and little pictures of elephants. Asia runs round from top to bottom left, and has little figures like those *Chineses* that Milton said *drive their light and airy wagonets of cane*. Then there are fire-worshippers with their altars and the Land of Women with Amazons shooting bows, and you come round to a fantastically distorted Britain and two literally minded Pillars of Hercules at the far right, while dotted all around are dense little blocks of information in Latin, all of it wrong, and the Ocean runs round the outside.

Dave's diagram was divided in half horizontally, the background of the lower semicircle predominantly light, the upper dark. To the extreme left of the lower semicircle were what seemed to be allegorical images of the States, taken perhaps from a late 19th century pamphlet or adapted from the pediment of a real or projected public building. New South Wales and Victoria wore mural crowns, and while one carried a fleece, the other rested her hand on some piece of gold-mining apparatus. Tasmania bore a horn of plenty, out of which spilt apples and ears of grain. Western Australia was got up like the Queen of Sheba, with ropes of pearls around her neck, while Queensland was a barefooted, somewhat Tahitian-looking maiden cradling a pineapple in the crook of one arm and a sheaf of cane in the other. I had to assume by elimination that the sixth maiden was South Australia, for in this case the artist's fancy deserted him: she was seated on a bale of straw with a peewee perched on one hand like a poor imitation of Athena. Below these appeared the Fathers of Federation — Deakin and Barton addressing respectful crowds, and beyond them stately public buildings and works of engineering. Then at the bottom of this semicircle were lines of troops, whose smart turnout and spiked helmets suggested they were about to embark for the Sudan War.

Lower right of the centre were at first images of bushfire and flood, and then what appeared to be some confrontation between troopers and aborigines, rifles being levelled on the one hand and spears on the other. Then came a swagman, a mob of sheep being driven by a figure on a horse with dogs nipping at the stragglers, and finally, at the right extremity of the lower semicircle what could have been, and very likely was, a picture drawn to accompany Lawson's 'The Teams' in one of the illustrated papers. The bullocks, the wagon, this one loaded with huge logs, the road, the dust, and the bullocky with the greenhide goad that was making it all happen.

The upper semicircle, as I have said, was on a darker background. Beginning at the right we had shearers, their work finished, sitting on the steps of the shed in their sweat-stained Jacky Howes and with hats pushed back on their heads. There was a creek in the background, and some men were setting up a keg on an improvised stand.

Further round, two lovers, Dave and Mabel as it might have been, talked to one another over a split-rail gate. The selector's cottage stood in the background, a cow grazing beside it, and through the open door you glimpsed a woman bent over a kitchen table in some domestic task. Close to the circumference at the centre of this upper right-hand quadrant the full moon threw dark shadows from trees and isolated huts, and at upper centre was a simple homestead silhouetted against the night sky. The left upper quadrant was substantially empty: there was a starry sky, and most of the way to the left a church and some gravestones, though these did not appear to be associated with the structure. The isolated graves of settlers, I thought, or of Boake's dead men: they stood out against a background now mostly grey. The topmost part of the church steeple, though, had just begun to take the first rays of the sun – which brought us round to the beginning. Dave had certainly assembled a representative range of images, I reflected, and apparently from all kinds of sources – a panorama of Australian life at the close of the 19th century. Perhaps this was what he had been doing in the Mitchell Library. The skills that had qualified him to teach Computer Studies and Industrial Design were clear to see; I hoped Dave was employing these powers for good. For the moment, his purpose in making the collage remained obscure.

Still peeping out of Dave's jacket, Billy seemed reasonably appreciative of the display: if he was disappointed that it wasn't Thomas the Tank Engine, he didn't show it.

'That's just the black and white,' said Dave. 'I'm working on bringing some colour into it, but it needs a bit of thought. That's for the future. Now watch this.'

He rested the base of his right palm on the edge of the table and typed some code in that nonchalant way that computer people have. The results of this manoeuvre were as striking as they were unsettling. All the images — statesmen, stockmen, beasts and buildings alike — began to flow and mutate and bulge and twist in unexpected ways until they came together in a totally new and colourful arrangement. Billy looked disturbed, seemed likely to cry, and burrowed his head inside Dave's jacket. For a moment the surprise of the new display made it seem abstract, but then I realized that far from consisting of mere juxtaposed shapes and planes of colour, these new things were words, and words rendered with the accomplished freedom of an inspired *graffitista*: in short, Poppy.

The words around the periphery of the circle were on the whole larger, and eight of these stood out more boldly again, not because of their size but through a deft use of shadowing and colour contrast. Beginning at centre left and reading anti-clockwise, these were BIRTH, POWER, MAN, FIGHT, DEATH, BREAST, DREAM and WOMAN. Between these and inside them were other words — for example, between BIRTH and POWER where the maiden emblems of the states and the images of the founding fathers had been were the words *state* and *nation*. The word *fight* was in the same space that had held the shameful image of troopers and aborigines; *sweetheart* stood in the place of Dave and Mabel; DREAM replaced the previous darkened homestead. If the correspondence with the preceding view sometimes seemed less exact, a less prominent word might give the clue: the shearers having a blow, for instance, had coincided not with

DEATH but with *rest* which appeared in smaller characters and partly obscured by the more prominent word. I've made this account of the image as it struck me as clear as I can, but you might like to get a piece of paper and draw it out for yourself if you find it hard to follow.

Billy was quicker on the uptake than I had been, for as soon as he gathered the courage to peep out again from Dave's jacket he said 'lettuh' quite distinctly, seeming reassured that the momentary chaos had been succeeded by something so well-known. I reflected that he was no stranger to graffiti: every outing in the pram around Gracie's part of the world would have introduced him to new and striking examples, and here in Dave's workshop he was finding the comfort of familiarity.

Dave now tapped the keyboard to bring about another transmutation. This time the words did not move or flow, but the whole picture was replaced by a single striking image. In inspiration it may have owed something to the tarot, though the whole handling of the lines, together with the androgyny of the central figure, suggested a much greater debt to Hideaki Anno.* It looked as if Poppy's original had been in charcoal or some such medium, and Dave had scanned it into the system without as yet modifying it or integrating it with the other displays. The image was of a tree, its twisted branches and foliage taking up much of the upper semicircle which had been darkened in the first display Dave had shown us. Though treated in manga fashion, it was unmistakeably an angophora. From a branch close to the trunk on the right hand side hung the body of a man. The shadow of his feet, beginning about halfway between the centre of the circle and where the word FIGHT had been, ran up diagonally as if cast by the morning sun, and intersected the circle at the centre of its right hand margin. Here, instead of DEATH, was now written 3.5.1892. At least, I thought, this will go over Billy's head.

'I'm a bit lost,' Dave,' I said. 'Perhaps you could take me through it.'

'Well you probably guessed the words came first,' said Dave, 'but I wanted to find graphics to suit them; I got the last few from the Mitchell, and full marks to you, mate, for coming to the party.'

'Any time, Dave,' I said. 'Yes, I got as far as that, but where do the words come from and why are they set out the way they are?'

'It's all in here,' said Dave, slapping *The Bulletin Reciter*, 'but the way of doing it I got out of this other book.'

Here he showed me the second of the books in the pile. At the point when I had been still afraid we had been taken hostage or worse, I had not got as far as this. Now I looked at it. It was Cecil Day Lewis's translation of the *Aeneid*: not, in my opinion, the most inspired of renderings. Did the laying out of a new nation, as it had greeted me in the first set of images Dave had put up, owe something to Dido proudly showing the shipwrecked Trojans around the foundations of Carthage? She had always made me think of Rhoda, a girl of Lebanese family I once taught, whose father had a construction business in the British Virgin Islands. At least it was registered in the British Virgin Islands, but I would be willing to bet they never constructed anything there. Why would the British Virgin Islands need a lot of buildings, or a lot of anything, if it came to that? Where were the British Virgin Islands, anyway? I'm sure it was a tax dodge. But whenever I read Book 1 of the *Aeneid*, I pictured Rhoda with her big shining dark eyes and spiky hair wearing a hard hat and leading Aeneas round to show him the new international terminal and all the other unwanted facilities her father had under construction. This strictly private fantasy, though, was unlikely to have motivated Dave, and I was briefly at a loss.

But then the book itself came to my help, falling open at what was clearly a much-loved passage.

> *The fleets are converging at full speed,* I read, *the sea is all churned and*
> *   foaming*
> *As the oarsmen take their long strokes and the trident bows drive on.*
> *They manoeuvre for sea-room: you'd think the Cyclades isles were unmoored*
> *And afloat, or mountains were charging at mountains, to see those massive*
> *Galleys on one side attacking the turreted ships of the other.*
> *Volleys of flaming material and iron missiles fly thick*
>
> *And fast; a strange new slaughter reddens the plains of Neptune.**

and so on. The shield of Aeneas – and that was just the central panel.

Al Gore may have invented the Internet, I thought, but Virgil invented the web-site; what couldn't Vulcan have done with the shield if he had had the kind of resources that were available to Dave?

'I see where you're coming from, Dave,' I said, 'but I'm still a bit vague on how to get to where you've ended up.'

'When I was a younger bloke,' said Dave, 'I spent a bit of time in the slammer for reasons that we needn't go into, and that's where I first read this book,' and he shook his right hand, in which he was still holding *The Bulletin Reciter*, in earnest affirmation. I murmured a sort of assent, as much as to say that while this news of Dave's antecedents was not wholly unanticipated, it in no way diminished my opinion of him.

Dave continued. 'It gave me some values, mate,' he said. '"Out where the dead men lie" − that would've been me if I'd kept on the way I was going. So I got an education. They have these courses you can do, and I've always been good with my hands, and fixing things and that, so I did a design course and I did all right, and so then I did a CAD course, and then I really got into computers in a big way, and to cut a long story short, I thought it was time to give something back.'

This was a praiseworthy sentiment, but not knowing who Dave had injured or done down − apart from the prison library, that is − I didn't yet see where it was leading.

'You see, when I was reading these poems,' said Dave, 'I kept noticing that the blokes writing round about the same time, and it didn't matter who they were, would be always using the same sort of words, and I thought "there's something in this".'

Dave was on my territory now; I looked at him eagerly.

'So when I had the knowledge behind me,' said Dave, 'I ran all this stuff through the computer, and this is what came out.'

'The words that you put up?'

'That's right, mate: you can run all the way round from *birth* to *death* and back again, and all the way you will find these groups of words that hang together.'

Birth of a nation, I thought, yes, that makes sense.

'You remember the first one I showed you,' said Dave, 'the one with black at the top?'

I nodded assent.

'I laid it out as a sundial,' said Dave, and flashed it up again on the screen to the excitement of Billy, who had quickly tired of the hanged man. Of course. Put the top to the north and a stick in the middle, and the shadow would move around the lighter half of the dial from left to right. A clock would have the lighter side at the top.

'The yin and the yang,' said Dave. 'Shadow and sunlight, you see.' Kuan Yin, I thought, Iron Buddha, I could do with a cup of you right now. He flicked over to the next display. Billy squirmed as he recognised the change that had upset him before, but with pleasurable anticipation, like a child who is expecting to be tickled. Then I saw that the bold words would mark the hours, the eight boldest of them set at three-hourly intervals.* BIRTH was at 6 a.m., DEATH was at 6 p.m. At high noon we marched off to war in splendid array, at midnight it was the time to DREAM.

'You could sell it as a sundial,' said Dave, ' though I see it more as a clock, with LEDs lighting up around the rim to show the time, and on the hour the whole thing would morph from pictures to words and back again.'

'And maybe it would recite a poem for you while that was going on.'

'The sky's the limit, mate,' said Dave, 'and I think I owe it to those blokes to get some of these things out into the community. People don't know the old poets these days. It's heritage, mate, that's what it is, and they reckon that if you don't honour your heritage, you don't deserve to repeat it.' This seemed to have as much truth in it as most sayings, so I let it go.

'And what about the hanged man?'

'Something I was thinking of to combine with the clock. It would make a good memorial to Barcroft Boake; the council could fund one on the site. Ten to one they'd jump at it when they saw the style of drawing, because a lot of Japanese families live around that area now.'

'Cowra would be another possibility,' I said. 'But honestly, Dave, this set-up must have cost you a packet. Heritage or not, do you think you're going to sell enough of these clocks to get your money back?' It was certainly a striking product, and I could see Dave might find buyers for one or two; what I couldn't see was Dave's *Bulletin* poets conceptual timepiece as a thing that would sweep the country.

'Well, there's something I haven't told you, mate,' said Dave, tapping his nose. 'Which is why Rita agreed to bankroll the project. If you can keep it to yourself, I might just give you a hint over an ice-cold you know what. I don't know about you, mate, but right now I'm as dry as Warragamba.'

Whereupon Dave switched off the computer and the lights and locked up the shed, and the four of us made our way towards The Courser's Arms. Billy had been decanted from his long-time perch, and was now walking happily along holding Dave's hand.

'If we're going to the pub,' I said, 'what about Billy?'

'He doesn't have to shout,' said Dave, 'and what he drinks won't break us.'

On that note we entered The Courser's Arms.

*

The hotel in question was of a refreshingly unregenerate kind. Tiles up to dado height and black sheet vinyl with a white fleck in it on the floor. You could hose or mop it out quite quickly, and that had not long been done when we arrived. Poppy, Billy and I took positions next to a large plate-glass window that looked towards the dog track; the stools were backless, and I steadied Billy with one hand as he leant forward and steered coasters around for boats on this mini-ocean of tabletop. Slick trails on its surface were witness to a recent quick wipedown.

Dave returned with the drinks, holding all four glasses between his large hands. Schooners for Dave and me, a small lemon squash for Billy, and for Poppy something pinkish that I trusted was non-alcoholic.

'Cheers, mate,' said Dave, taking the top centimetre off his glass with a quick gulp and wiping his mouth with the back of his hand. I would have responded, but I now needed both hands for Billy: one to support his back and one to keep his glass from tipping as he alternately sucked and blew through the straw. This was great fun for him: I could see that the stocks of the 'ra-ra man', as Billy began to call him, stood high above those of a grandfather as a provider of entertainment. Poppy had somehow inserted the straw up inside her helmet, and now rested her elbow on the table and held her glass high enough to take a sip whenever she felt moved.

'You read Alan Kohler,* mate?' asked Dave now, in a new conversational initiative.

'I try to keep up.'

'A few weeks ago, he was writing about the Reserve Bank and the interest rates, and he reckoned they knew where the economy was at, but they didn't know where it was going.'

'I seem to remember the column,' I said guardedly.

'Now follow me here, mate — if a bloke had known what the Reserve didn't know, he could have done OK for himself.'

'I'll give you that.'

'Now let's say you had a clock face with no numbers, and your hour hand is on the left and pointing up about thirty degrees off the vertical.'

'I'd say it was 11 o'clock, Dave.'

'You would,' said Dave, 'and so would most blokes, but it all depends whether it is working like a clock or like a sundial, because they go round opposite ways.'

'But who ever heard of a clock that worked like a sundial?'

'Those old Roman blokes for a start, mate, if you go into the history of it.'*

Billy now asked to be put down; he had spotted on the floor a cigarette packet that had escaped the cleaners, and probably saw that its boat possibilities were as superior to a coaster's as a half-cabin was to a raft. I helped him off the stool and he sank to a sitting position and grabbed for the packet. Now I was able to broach my beer, which anticipation had made all the more welcome. The head may have relaxed into the appearance of tidal scum, but energetic trails of creamy bubbles were still rising profusely from invisible flaws in the glass.

'Now,' said Dave, 'what would you reckon it is that makes a poet a poet?'

'That's a big question, Dave.'

'I'll tell you what it is, mate – they're more sensitive than the rest of us.'

'I don't think Pope would agree with you, Dave,' I replied. 'What about

What oft was thought, but ne'er so well expressed?'

'The Pope's entitled to his opinion,' said Dave, 'though if you ask me, it was a while since the old one had been on the ball for the full 80 minutes. This new bloke would have to be an improvement.'

There was little doubt, I thought to myself, that the former Cardinal Ratzinger would be gratified by this unsolicited tribute.

'But I reckon,' went on Dave, 'that if you can't say it, you never thought it in the first place, so it boils down to the same thing in the end.'

Coming from Dave, this *Big Brother*-like dissolution of the *signifié*, which in my mouth might have seemed a mere debating point, carried the more conviction. I yielded, though I didn't necessarily see that the argument followed.

'If they're more sensitive, then, where does that take us?'

'Well, they're like canaries, you see; they sniff what's going on, and if a bloke keeps his eye on the canary he can be out of the mine before the whole thing blows. Here,' said Dave, moving his glass from the coaster, 'got a pen on you, mate?'

'Yes, for sure. Use this one, Dave.' I always carry a pen in my inside pocket.

'This is your yin and your yang,' said Dave, cross-hatching one half of the coaster with a few rough strokes. 'And you see what I found out was that the words that belong in your daylight hours, those were the words the poets were using all the time when the country was booming, back at the end of the '80s.'

I began to see where this exposition was leading.

'So if they're all writing about *man* and *battle*,' I said, 'you know you're at twelve midday, and things are going to get worse.'

'Got it in one, mate,' said Dave, now bisecting the coaster in the other direction and cross-hatching half of this new division with lines that ran at right angles to the ones he had drawn at first. 'And that's what the Reserve Bank doesn't know. They may know it's good, but it's a 50-50 bet which way it's going. So if you could monitor what people were writing, you see, mate, you could get a jump on the stockmarket and make yourself a killing.'

Billy had now settled himself at the entrance to the toilets. Constant foot traffic here had worn away the overlying vinyl, exposing an older layer of pink and grey tiles arranged in a 30 centimetre check. A residue of detergent and beer slops had accumulated in this hollow, and Billy was happily sailing his boat around in it.

> *high above*
> *clouds coloured as ash of vanished fires*
> *flies the galah, pink and grey**

I thought – what might not the Jindyworobaks have taught us about the economic crises of the 1930s?

'And I suppose Barcroft Boake fits into this, does he?'

'That's right, mate,' said Dave. 'Second of May, 1892, that's when he went missing. Just when the collapse was happening fastest. *Death*, that's the word they were all writing. There was death in the air, and the poets could smell it. A sensitive bloke like Boake was, no wonder he topped himself.'

Yes, I thought, Boake had chosen his moment. At 6 p.m. on a 24-hour dial you would be going straight down – in free fall. What might any of us do if we knew, not only where we were, but where we were going? My mind went back from Barcroft Boake to the painting and to Rita's apartment, and to the apartment it had been, and to the wavering light, and the shining walls, and my own crisis with K. The trouble was that mostly you did know where you were going; you just didn't dare to admit it.

'I can see a few problems, Dave,' I said, draining the last mouthful from my glass.

'Well hold on to them for a few minutes, mate,' said Dave, 'because I reckon we could use a refill.'

Looking now at the inscrutable Poppy and now at Billy pushing his cigarette packet round and around on the chequered sea, I began to arrange my thoughts. Like any of those get-rich-quick schemes that seem to be exposed daily on the current affairs shows, Dave's ideas had a superficial seductiveness about them. *Pensioner Fleeced of Life's Savings,* I thought; *Police Powerless to Act* – but mightn't there be a few considerations that Dave hadn't thought of?

6

*I^2 – victory or superiority in a contest**

Dave soon returned. First he brought two hamburgers, and having used both hands to tear one of these in half, he pushed the plate with the other one towards me. Poppy put down her glass, still more than half full, and divining, or perhaps just used to, Dave's intentions, began to break off crumbs of bread and meat from one of the severed halves and introduce them with her fingertips to the interior of the helmet. I held out to Billy half of my meat pattie, and he swallowed it in a couple of bites without either removing his right hand from the cigarette packet or his left from the floor. It was like pushing something into the tube of a food processor. So then I gave him the other half. Vegemite and hamburgers, I thought, and mild-mannered Billy is transformed into The Umami Kid; I could only hope it wouldn't weaken his links with his feminine side. In any case, the bread roll and the salad would do me. I picked up some rather messy fingerfuls of onion and a slice of beetroot, that prince among vegetables. That is, if you count it as a vegetable; I was quite an age before I realised it wasn't called 'beet-fruit', which is how I referred to it when I was young. By now Dave had returned with two more schooners.

'OK,' said Dave. 'First of all, just so we know where we are, that can be yours and Poppy's shout. Ten bucks will about cover your share of it. Now shoot.'

I held out a note and Dave pushed it into his back pocket.

'Now, Dave,' I said, 'what you've uncovered is very interesting, but if you want to do the same today and make some money out of it, I think you need to realise that in the 1880s and 90s poetry was a popular medium, hence of course things like *The Bulletin Reciter*, but these days it isn't, so you're going to have to find something to look at which is the modern cultural equivalent of that poetry.'

'I've been thinking about that,' said Dave.

'And then,' I continued, 'even if we can locate the cultural equivalent and set up your matrix of words, it's the places where the words fit in your scheme that you need to look at, not the words themselves.'

'How do you mean?' said Dave.

'Well, look at what you've got,' I said, pulling the decorated coaster towards me. 'This side is your yang, and the words you had there seemed to belong to stereotyped male roles: one end there are your thinkers and planners, in the middle your soldiers, and down at the far end your bushmen and bullockies and what not — so you could say it's inner against outer: men that work with their brains against men that work with their hands, if you like, and you've got that word *man* right square in the middle.'

'OK.'

'Then on the other side, at the overt end you had your woman at the kitchen table, and the word *breast* in the middle, whereas in the other quadrant you've got the word *woman* up there with *God* — things that are hard for a man to think about: a bit of a mystery. To boil it right down to basics, Dave, on the yang side you've got the minds and the hands, on the yin side you've got what men would like to get their minds around and what they'd like to get their hands around. The whole thing is a projection of a male fantasy, and I'd say that's because most of your poets, or all of them, were men. Now one, you can't assume men these days are exactly the same as they were a hundred years ago, and two, whatever you're looking at these days, it's much more likely to have been produced by a woman. So what you need to look for are not the items that fill the categories, but the categories themselves.'

Poppy had been gradually stiffening during this speech, and was now sitting at attention; I had an inspiration, and turned over the coaster. Reclaiming the pen from where Dave had left it on the table, I drew two lines to divide the coaster into quarters.

'Now, Dave,' I said, writing the names as I rotated the coaster, 'let's call this quadrant — the one with *nation* and the founding fathers in it — Ray, and this next one with the fighting and the bushmen we'll call

Alby, and this third one Janet and this one Maxine, just for the sake of convenience. Now you've got a Maxine, and I've got a Maxine and Poppy's got a Maxine, and so has Billy, I suppose, if we grant him the status of a rational human being. But you can't start out by assuming there's any overlap between my Maxine and Poppy's.'

'But, mate,' said Dave, 'you've given two of your quadrants boys' names and two of them girls' names, so in my book we're still talking areas of meaning – and words have to be just little areas of meaning, don't they, mate? And if Maxine is like a box with different stuff in it for me from what it has for Poppy, say, or even you, how come we can all read the poem and get some charge out of it?'

'These, Dave, are questions,' was my reply, and I went on to tell him and Poppy, who had gradually relaxed once more, something about my reading of Helen Garner, so far as it had gone. That is, I assumed Poppy was listening: it was hard to tell inside the helmet. I wondered whether the four eponymous categories I had just plucked out of the air for the sake of instructing Dave would take me further in my understanding of those works. Time wore on, the way it does in pubs.

At last Dave said: 'Time for Billy's shout.'

'I thought we were going to excuse Billy,' I said. 'If we're going to have another, let's make it a scotchman's. And mine had better be a light,' I added, 'because I wouldn't want Gracie to figure out what I've been up to.'

'You really like to walk on the wild side, don't you, mate,' said Dave.

*

I walked back to Gracie's, having declined Dave's offer of a lift: it wouldn't have been more than three or four kilometres, and I didn't want to push my luck. Billy walked at first, and we made slow progress indeed, but then he got tired and wanted to be carried. He seemed to be damp all over, partly, no doubt, from the floor, and partly from his still-unchanged nappy. My advance, at least, was brisker now, but I needed frequent stops to put Billy down for a moment on top of a wall, or change him from one hip to the other. A man's hip is not made for a baby to sit on, I reflected, and remembered how when Gracie was little L had seemingly held her effortlessly in that position all day; Poppy's hips, if it came to that, bade fair to evolve from handholds for the pillion passenger to infant seats if given the chance. I thought about the day and about my recent conversations in that disconnected way you do when you are walking. The Maxine is the anima, I thought; no doubt for Billy it would be Mummy that filled that role. Perhaps for Dave, Poppy was the anima — nothing I had yet seen went either to confirm or deny that possibility. But Poppy would have an animus, which brought me back to Jung's difficulty with that category — but then I suddenly saw that of course Poppy would not have an animus, she would have an *anime*. The sun seemed to shine a little bit more brightly, and it was with a smile on my face and a spring in my step that I approached Gracie's door.

It still lacked a good hour of five o'clock. With some difficulty I wrestled the suit off Billy and dropped it into a bucket in the lower services pod which seemed adapted for such a purpose. I changed his nappy and put him into what appeared to be pyjamas. I wiped his face. Finally I turned on the television and sat him in front it. We had missed all but the last minute or two of *Play School*, but hoping the low-budget cartoons that followed would hold him for a while, I went to make myself some more coffee. Billy sat looking glazed, and by the time I had made the coffee he was asleep. I carried him up to his designer cot.

True to her word, Gracie was back on the dot of five.

'How did you manage with Billy?' she asked.

'We had a lovely day just playing around the house,' I said, 'but the poor little thing went to sleep just after four. I think the cold has really taken it out of him.'

'Well thankyou so much for stepping in,' said Gracie. 'There was no-one else I could have asked today, but I didn't know whether you'd be up to it.'

'Notice anything about these shoulders?' I asked. 'Now, I'm sorry to be dashing away, but as you no doubt realise, tonight is *Big Brother* live Friday night games, and I want to have time to make something for your mother's dinner.'

'It's beyond belief,' said Gracie, 'how you and Mum can sit and watch that sort of trash.'

'Don't include your mother in this blanket condemnation,' I said, 'to be fair to her, she does sit, but she says she isn't watching. And for my part, I have had a very intellectually taxing day and feel entitled to some mindless relaxation.'

'Whatever,' said Gracie. Little did she know, and I hoped it would stay that way.

*

As it happened, Gracie rang early in the morning.

'You dashed off so quickly last night,' she said, 'I just want to say a proper thankyou. Billy slept right through like an angel, and this morning he hasn't got a trace of a cold. It just shows how right I was to want him to stay inside.'

'Mothers have an instinctive feeling for these things,' I said.

'I don't know what you did to his poor little jumpsuit,' said Gracie. 'It was practically black, and if I didn't know better I'd say that it smelt of beer.'

'We had a lot of Vegemite,' I said. 'Vitamin B is the best thing for a cold. And they make it out of yeast, you know, so that would account for the smell.'

'He keeps saying "Ra-ra man",' persisted Gracie. 'What was that all about?'

'We had a lot of games on the floor with cars,' I said, 'and I'm sorry to say that I let him get a little overexcited. That's probably what he's thinking of.'

I was thankful Gracie didn't have access to Al Qaeda's interrogation unit.

'Well, whatever you got up to, it seems to have done the trick,' said Gracie, and to my great relief let me go.

'She's a hard nut, that daughter of yours,' I said to L when I had got off the phone. 'To the extent that she is a nut at all, that is.'

'I'm not sure I quite follow the metaphor,' said L, 'but I do agree that in another age she would have made a good Grand Inquisitor. So what have you been hiding from her?'

I gave L an account of the doings of the previous day. Perhaps my exposition was unclear, but as so often happens, she fastened on an insignificant detail.

'It was pretty bad of Dave to steal that book,' said L. 'I always thought he was up to no good.'

'All property is theft,' I replied. 'I don't see that it's so different from plagiarizing another school's prospectus.'

'That's another thing altogether,' said L. 'It's more like telling the parents a well-loved story. The other day I found a lovely book of Goldilocks and the Three Bears for Billy, with the same story we all know retold with new illustrations. Gracie said he absolutely loved it. Would you call that plagiarism?'

'I'd call it giving him a strong feminine role model,' I said. 'Gracie will be pleased. And what Dave is doing is no more than retelling the bush balladists with his own take on what they were saying – and how can he do that without a text? Now if you can do without me,' I said, 'I think I'll go for a walk. I have a lot to think about.'

This was true. I had woken that morning at about the middle of Maxine, as I was beginning to think of the interval between midnight and daybreak, and found myself worrying away at Dave's ideas and the apparatus that Dave had constructed, the way you sometimes will at that hour of the morning. Perhaps my sleeplessness owed something to the quick meal of which I had spoken to Gracie: I had served boiled vegetables with aioli, and, though a favourite of mine, it doesn't always promote sound sleep. Perhaps it's the oil that lies heavy on the stomach. I find a cup of oil and two egg yolks is about right, and say four cloves of garlic for a quantity that serves two people. Add just enough salt to take the rawness off the mayonnaise, but don't overdo it. A small pinch rolled between your finger and thumb as a Provençal peasant might do. What you must remember is to make the mayonnaise in a round-bottomed bowl — otherwise it will take you forever — but if you've been boiling a mix of vegetables while you were stirring the mayonnaise — say potato, kumera, carrots, peas — the whole thing can be ready in half an hour from when you first put on the water to boil. But then as I say, sometimes ease in the preparation is paid for with difficulty in the digestion, and so I woke up in the middle of Maxine and started to think.

There was obviously something in Dave's ideas — but what? I wondered how they would work for other eras of history; for my own lifetime, indeed. My earliest memories were of the war — not war as such, but the consciousness that it was going on. I remember my father reading something out of the paper about the Red Army, and it made a vivid if imprecise picture in my mind. My father often read things out of the paper. He would sit at breakfast with the paper held up in front of him, and pick out for our benefit any items that struck him particularly; my mother had to make do with the racing supplement. In our house, I pass L the news because she is more serious-minded than I am. I sort of remember Pearl Harbour, even though my parents always told me that couldn't be right, and I wouldn't have been much more sentient at the time than Billy was now. Probably someone said the words 'Pearl Harbour' some time, and they stuck in my mind.

But though I suppose it was grim enough at the time, after the war the stories you heard made it seem that our troops were a lot of freewheeling Albys. There were always teachers you could rely on to fill up a lesson with tall tales from the army, and I remember a neighbour of ours, a sober bank manager, telling me once how he had been one of a detachment of Australian troops and Americans in New Guinea when they came under fire from Japanese ships. The Americans headed for the hills, he said, while the Australians looted the American camp. They even made off with the commanding officer's bedstead. *Hogan's Heroes* sort of stuff, or do I mean *McHale's Navy?* — the sort of story all that genre was based on.

And then in the 50s it was Janet. Domestic values, suburban values, mowing the lawn or washing the car for a bit of excitement values. I thought of Betty Friedan — how women were pushed back into the kitchen in the Eisenhower years, and poor Mame having to put up with the world's worst hairstyle. Yin years. Australia slept through Menzies, America dreamt. JFK was Maxine with bells on. Camelot and all that — fantasy land. And then we had LBJ — the Great Society. He would be like the founding fathers — we're back in Ray territory now. Johnson would have been a great peacetime president — but we get round to the images of battle again. Vietnam was more like troopers against aborigines — and so we've come all the way round, back to Alby. How to fit in other things? The Beatles, swinging London, all that carnivalesque stuff, that was in the yin years, but what about the hippies? Were they forerunners or leftovers? After all, Vietnam didn't fall apart because the larrikins couldn't fight, but because not enough people believed in it. Whitlam thought he was Ray, behaved like Alby, but was actually Maxine. Fraser was Ray, Hawke and Keating and their silly Gulf War flag-waving were Ray turning into Alby, which would have to mean that Howard was probably Janet. Of course. Janette Howard! No wonder he wanted women back in the kitchen.

This was one of those deep insights you have in the middle of the night, and I rolled over and went back to sleep, vowing to pursue it in the morning to the utmost of my powers.

Now, in the light of day, some of these ideas seemed less convincing than others. In my night time historical sketch, we had rolled around a little more than two cycles in about sixty years, give or take. That sort of made sense if you thought of it in generations — but then surely generations were longer now. What kinds of culture were popular enough to tell us about these drifts in social attitude? Dave believed that artists had the antennae to sense the social mood, but which artists to look to? Song lyrics? Comics? The classic Marvel comics belonged to the sixties — the word *marvel* told its own story. *Birth* was the liminal word then — Kennedy the last of the night,

Johnson the first of the morning. Was it George W. who said we had a culture of death now, or was that the Pope? *Death* and *rest* fell together in Dave's diagram. *Give us long rest or death*, wrote Tennyson – he was tuned in. So if Johnny Storm in the Marvel era could shout 'Flame on!' and metamorphose into The Human Torch, was Terri Schiavo the superhero for our times? Cry 'Veg out!' and be transformed into The Human Vegetable? And then have someone cut you off at the roots like a bunch of spinach.

Though it was a cold and cloudy morning, and the sight of grey water, ruffled or roughened as the case might be, held little attraction, I made towards Cabbage Tree Bay. I was curious to see Poppy's handiwork in the light of day; I wondered too about the outcome of Dave's efforts with the crane. The artwork at least did not disappoint. It was even more splendid than the headlights had shown, the colours more vivid, the penguins angrier. Poppy must have been pleased. Dave's work, though, was harder to evaluate, for as I was trying to peer over the fence for a better look, I was accosted by a security guard. He could have been Dave's evil twin, which was saying something, given that Dave at first glance looked like an evil twin himself.

'Got a problem, mate?' asked the guard.

I assured him that I had nothing of the sort, and turned to go in as carefree a way as I could manage. Not before noticing, however, that a plate with some wording on it had been newly fixed to one of the gates. It said: 'Cabbage Tree Bay Marina Facility – an Initiative of van Tromp Inc.'

*

This opened up a new line of thought. On the one hand, it was obvious that it was the English language, not just the penguins, that stood to be murdered if this thing went ahead. On the other, if Rita, or Rita's money, was behind the marina, why was Poppy among the ranks of the Angry Penguins? Then I saw a way of integrating these facts with the insights that had come to me when I had been deep within Maxine, so to speak. For Rita would be much of an age with L and me. If you reckoned on a generational turnover of about thirty years, we were around thirty when we had Gracie, and now Gracie herself was around thirty in her turn. We and our child and Billy, in other words, had all entered the cycle at about the same point, and so our take on things might be supposed to be similar. Perhaps that accounted for Gracie's ability to see through us so easily. How wise is Nature, I reflected, in thus ensuring that the very way in which society propagates itself simultaneously makes for social cohesion! In one of our primary school geography books, at a time when it seemed not only quite permissible, but even obligatory, to look down on other civilizations, I had been gripped by an image of screaming votaries hurling themselves beneath the wheels of the idol of Juggernaut. Now I could see the nuclear family — mum and dad and the little baby clapping its hands in glee — riding high in just such a contraption over the twisted bodies of single mothers and same-sex couples and anyone else whose sole aim was to drag our way of life into the gutter. Well, perhaps. But what I did see was that Poppy was about half Gracie's age, which meant, surely, that she was half a generation out of step with Rita. When Rita wanted to march into battle, Poppy would want to dream. Etc.

I had reached the heights above Lavender Bay at this point, and would soon make my descent past Sydney Water's sylvan folly. Just then, the edges of one of the ragged north-easterly clouds was lit up by the hidden sun, as will sometimes happen, and the cloud loomed darker still against that glowing edge. Looking at it, I seemed to see, written on the heaven itself in letters of fire, two portentous words: BABY BOOMERS.

That was why John Howard and co. hated the Baby Boomers so much: because they were half a generation out of step. When one lot wanted to make war, the other wanted to make love, and so it went on. That was why Rumsfeld and his cronies still nursed their *Dolchstosstheorie*. They had tried to send Baby Boomers to war, but the boomers either evaded the draft, or else got to Vietnam and smoked themselves silly on pot or fragged their officers. In the normal way of things, I thought, children would be born every day, or so you would assume, and so you had a balance, a mix of different attitudes, but a phenomenon like the Baby Boom upset the whole show: one cohort was so numerous that its concerns could preempt the concerns of society at large. I pictured a young John Howard sitting gloomily in a corner at some hippy party he had been dragged along to against his better judgement, glowering from under an ill-fitting headband at the presumptively loose women in their undoubtedly loose Indian dresses, and the roll-your-owns that he darkly suspected would contain drugs.

The story of the 1890s would be much the same. *The price of wool was falling in 1891*, I knew, and when the boom was crashing around you, and your friends found themselves begging or living on the street, you didn't have to have the sensitivity of a poet to feel that there was death in the air. If you did have that sensitivity, or if the spirit of the times coincided with some crisis in your personal life, no doubt it could force you over the edge. But such things, sudden economic just as much as sudden demographic change, could force a dominant *récit* upon society at large. Which was why, I reflected sadly, Dave's device, like all attempts at fortune-telling, wouldn't work. I was sad for Dave, that is – I hadn't ever seen myself as a potential investor. For Dave had not, as he believed, invented a kind of *Zeitgeist*-ometer which would tell you the thoughts of the poets, the health of the economy and the names of your sister's unborn children all in one hit, but rather a good way of characterising how the dominant mood of a society at one point in time was reflected in its art. If you wanted to outguess the Reserve Bank, it seemed to me, the way to do it was to collect better statistics. Even if the heights of women's hemlines seem to tell you the way the economy is moving, they are unlikely to do so consistently enough and over a long enough period of time to make money out of it.

On the other hand, I reflected, by now as good as home again in my journey, there is nothing in the demography or the economy that would place all those words just where Dave had put them, or which would tell you which way to move between them. That was Dave's discovery

— that his poems moved through a field of meanings as surely as a planet will navigate its way among the stars. It might take external forces to determine how long the focus of poetry lingered in one place, or how quickly it moved upon its way, but the geography of those poets' meaning had been Dave's discovery. You come to the Chinese garden as a tourist, or for a meeting, or as a visitor with an hour to fill in, but the forces that send you there did not build the pavilions, did not fill the lake with luminous and hungry *koi*, and did not direct your path at last through or past the teahouse to the exit, with maybe a curry puff consumed along the way. Dave's methods, whatever they were, might help me clarify the meanings that belonged to Helen Garner. And perhaps her field of meanings and Dave's, if not the same, might yet turn out to be contiguous. These were things to explore.

*

I tried to explain this to L.

'The metaphor has its own integrity,' I said, 'which is quite separate from its referent. So it is legitimate to explore the world of the metaphor without bringing the referent into it at all.'

'How do you mean?' asked L. 'Sometimes I get the feeling that you just like to string words together for their own sake.'

'Take this, for example,' I said, seeing in my mind's eye a picture of Billy in his soiled white tracksuit with its soiled pink binding blending chameleon-like into the pink and grey tiles of The Courser's Arms. In my presentation, though, I would have to disguise this picture somewhat, for in the account of the day I had given L I had necessarily glossed over some things, lest the information should fall into unfriendly hands. 'I am thinking of someone in a Sydney Swans jersey,' I said.

'I think they call them jumpers in Melbourne,' said L.

I ignored this interruption.

'I am in a pub,' I said, 'and there's a Swans supporter who is harassing a young woman.'

'So far, it's believable,' said L.

'And I say to the young woman: "Is this galah annoying you?"'

'I can't believe you would do that,' said L. 'The next thing that happened, he would beat you to a pulp. But anyway, what's the point – did I miss something?'

'The point is that I called him a galah in reference to his pink and grey jersey, but in using the word *galah*,' I said, 'I simultaneously expressed contempt for his thoughtless behaviour.'

'But the Swans' colours aren't pink and grey,' said L, 'which rather robs the story of its point.'

'This is a very old, very dirty Swans jersey. Anyway, I couldn't think of any football club with pink and grey for its colours.'

'There wouldn't be one,' said L. 'A combination like that would make them look too silly. And if you meant red and white and wanted to make him a typical footy supporter, why pick a boutique outfit like the Swans? You could have said St George just as well.'

'Your vocabulary has taken a racy turn,' I replied, '"Boutique outfit", forsooth. Let me just say that if, as you believe, the fan's likely response would have been to beat me up, don't forget that Ross "The Skull" May is a number one St George supporter, and he's not someone I would choose to be in a fight with. But however that may be,' I continued, 'the point I was trying to illustrate was that there is no necessary connection between the colouring of the galah and its proverbial association with oafishness. That belongs to the word *galah*, not to the person wearing the jersey. Indeed, historically speaking,' I went on, 'I believe it derives from a play on the similarity of the aboriginal word *galah* and the word *galoot*, which I wouldn't be surprised to find was Irish. In fact it's never seemed to me that galahs, objectively speaking, are any more thoughtless than other birds.'

'But I thought this person wearing the jersey was behaving oafishly?' said L. 'Wasn't that what you were trying to convey?'

The conversation didn't seem to be getting very far, but continuance was prevented by the telephone, which rang at this point.

L went to answer it; if she had really been interested in the discussion, she would have let it go through to the answering machine as we usually do.

'It's for you,' she said, coming back. 'It sounded like Dave.'

'G'day, mate,' said Dave when I picked up the phone.

'What's the story?'

'I'm ringing from the cop shop,' said Dave. 'They seem to have got the idea I was mixed up in something, so I was wondering if you could come up and help me out.'

'I'm there, Dave,' I said, running over the various offences, from carnal knowledge of a minor to larceny and drink driving, of which I knew or suspected him to be guilty. Perhaps I could do something to ease his situation, if only to pledge my credit. I went back to L.

'Dave wants me to perjure myself for him,' I said, 'so I'd better get going.'

'Tell them he's a metaphor for the ugly side of our society,' said L, 'and try not to get yourself into any trouble.'

*

I had done quite a bit of work with the police over the years – it's amazing how communications theory, properly applied, can point out the holes in a story or show the most fruitful direction for an investigation – and now and then I'd been asked to address a police training seminar or something of the sort. In other words, the inside of a police station held no terrors for me, and, though it may seem naive to say so, I had rarely met a police officer that I hadn't liked. So it was in a spirit of curiosity rather than apprehension that I entered our local police station.

This resembled more than anything else the reception area of the sort of place where you go to hire a car – I suppose they're trying to convey a sort of accessible, can-do atmosphere. Not so long ago, they were in an annexe of the local courthouse, which gave a much grimmer, Newgate-like cast to the whole experience. I mentioned Dave's name, and a detective came out to talk to me.

'One of our constables pulled this man over this morning,' he said, 'for riding an unregistered bike. But then he recognized him as someone that was caught on a security camera the other night in the course of an illegal entry to the Cabbage Tree Bay Marina site. He seems to think you might have something to say as a character witness. Just at the moment we're inclined to hold him without bail.'

This didn't look too good. As I was thinking my way around it, another officer happened to come to the counter. I recognized him as Detective Fergus C, with whom I had spent many hours a few years ago in an attempt to track down a would-be extortionist by analysing his style. I greeted him.

'G'day Fergus,' I said.

'G'day Prof,' he replied with apparent pleasure. 'What brings you here?'

'Seems you've got a friend of mine locked up.'

'A friend of yours? Doesn't seem likely. What's the problem? Must be some sort of misunderstanding.'

This line seemed promising.

'He's suspected of breaking into the Cabbage Tree Marina,' I said, 'but I think if the officer knew all the facts, he'd have to say it was all most unlikely.'

'So what are the facts?'

'Well, Fergus, the way I see it,' I said, 'Cabbage Tree Marina is an initiative of van Tromp Inc. as you probably know, and Dave, this man that you've detained, is actually heading up another initiative van Tromp Inc. is establishing right now. He was showing me over their plant only yesterday. Add to that the fact that he's been staying with Mrs van Tromp in her apartment,' and here I did that nose-tapping gesture in the hope that it might convey some sort of imputation.

'In fact, Fergus,' I said, 'your reasonable man would probably conclude that if Dave was at the marina, he was there to keep an eye on Mrs van Tromp's investments. If he left his bike while he was doing that and there are no plates on it now, your reasonable man might conclude they'd been ripped off by the demonstrators.'

'Makes sense to me, Prof,' said Fergus. 'You've got a great way with a narrative, and ten to one you've hit on it.' He went out to the back. 'Come on, mate,' I heard him say, 'the prof's sprung you.'

Dave came out, looking as sheepish as Dave could look, which wasn't very.

'Can I go?' he asked.

'Look mate,' said Fergus, 'if the prof says you're OK, you're OK in my book.'

'I owe you one,' said Dave, as we walked away.

'Don't forget that, Dave,' I replied, 'I intend to make sure that you regret those words.'

And we went our separate ways.

*

'Professor J would be proud of me,' I said to L when I got home. 'Reductionism is a powerful weapon; much can be achieved by using it to sculpt people's view of the world.'

'I can see that you need to rationalize helping that criminal friend of yours,' said L, 'but there's no need to make a philosophical principle out of it.'

'They laughed at Galileo,' I said, 'but where are the sceptics now?'

'But Galileo was right,' said L.

'On the contrary,' I replied. 'The Ptolemaic system is not less correct, it's just more complicated. It's a matter of your frame of reference: rightness doesn't come into it. '

'Well rightness certainly doesn't come into it with Dave,' said L.

'Don't they say it's better for ten guilty men to go free than for one innocent person to be punished?' I asked. 'And in a world where fun-loving Aussie teens are clapped into foreign jails in their hundreds on trumped-up drug mule charges, I think it's up to us to set an example.'

'Perhaps a prisoner exchange with Indonesia would have been the way to go,' said L, but I could tell she knew I had got the better of her for the time being. Her usual strategy at this point is to launch an attack from another direction, in the hope of throwing me off balance. This she now proceeded to do.

'Don't tell me you went up to the police station in your ugs,' she said. 'It's a wonder they didn't throw you into jail as well.'

'If a man does not respect his own feet, what will he respect?' I replied. 'Your police officer is trained to look beyond superficial appearances. If I was to put on a suit and tie and slick my hair down, I might as well write "shyster" on a placard and hang it round my neck. If they give heed to my opinions, and I am happy to say that they do, it is precisely because I don't pretend to be anything other than a typical Aussie battler.'

'I'm surprised that you didn't put on a blue singlet to complete the picture,' said L, 'it would have shown off that manly physique of yours to advantage.'

I would not have been surprised if this last speech had been delivered derisively: instead, I seemed to detect a subtle shift in her tone. I waited to hear what might be coming next.

'Now promise me you won't be cross,' said L. I groaned inwardly, though ever since the intercepted note that had enabled Dave to find me at Gracie's, I had known that L was up to something.

'What have you let me in for now?' I asked.

'I wish you wouldn't say it in that flat, unenthusiastic voice,' said L. 'It makes me feel terrible. It's just something I promised Erna, and I knew you wouldn't really mind.'

'Speaking of Erna and her campaigns,' I said, 'did you know that the person behind the Cabbage Tree Marina is none other than Rita van Tromp? There's a new notice on the fence that I saw when I was over there this morning.'

'Oh dear,' said L, 'that may make things a little awkward. I rather wish now that I hadn't promised Erna what I did, but you know how it is when people put you on the spot. But I thought we owed it to her after you dragged me away from Gerald's funeral like that. It must have seemed terribly rude.'

'It's amazing,' I said, 'the way your memory has had an extreme makeover in so short a time. I thought the neurosurgeons would have had you locked away in a Hollywood hotel for six weeks, and you would re-enter down a staircase while we all said "oh my God". But apparently I'm behind the times.'

'Well sarcasm aside,' said L, 'I promised you would do it – and knowing how broad your shoulders are – ' and here she rubbed her hands around the extremities in question and did lascivious things with her eyes.

'Whatever it is that Erna wants must be pretty bad,' I said, 'if you're prepared to go to these lengths. Perhaps I could whisper a few things you might do if I am prepared to fall in with your wishes.'

'I will be putty in your hands,' said L, dropping her voice to a husky tone as used by Lauren Bacall. 'I will make myself a plaything to your every whim.'

'I'll hold you to that in due course,' I said, kissing her fondly on the nose. Then I spun her round and kissed her again on the back of the neck.

'Right at this moment,' I said, pushing her away and making an effort to slip out into the next room, 'I'm afraid I have to fulfil a long-standing engagement with a rosy-cheeked kitchen girl.'

'Not so fast,' said L. 'What's the point of me screwing myself up to tell you something if you're just going to run away? I have to show you what Erna wants. She brought this round earlier on this morning, while you were out on your walk.'

Here L indicated a carton that sat on the floor, firmly sealed with tape. It had that crisp, new-cardboard look that showed it probably hadn't been recycled, and it bore the name of a well-known theatrical costumier.

'There are two points I would like to make, Madam Chair,' I said. 'The first is, that I seem to recall saying that I refuse to be involved in street theatre in any shape or form, and the name on this box strongly suggests that that is what Erna has in mind. My second point is that, for a grassroots organization, Angry Penguins must really have struck it rich if they can afford the sort of money these people charge. Whatever is in the box, it wouldn't have come cheap.'

'Wouldn't it be better to open the box,' asked L, 'before you started forming theories about the purpose and the price of what's inside?'

'The untheorized packet is not worth opening,' I said, but in response to L's suggestion I found a sharp knife and slit the tape holding the flaps together. Inside was a heavy-duty polythene bag of the sort that are used to suffocate young children. This was sealed in its turn with staples, but it wasn't necessary to open the bag to realise what was in it. There, folded with the professional touch that is so impossible to duplicate when you try to re-do it yourself, was a life-size penguin costume.

When I say life-size, I don't intend you to take away the wrong idea. A little penguin that grew to 50 centimetres would be a Gulliver among little penguins. This suit, as I found when I had scissored away the staples and pulled it out of the bag, was at least five times the life size of a penguin. The body was rectangular like a sack, the two lower corners terminating in feet like rubber swim flippers which I supposed you must push your own feet into from inside. The head was quite lifelike, and joined to the body by a neck of some stretch material. The body was finished in fake fleece or fur or whatever the appropriate word is for a penguin's bodily covering, and it opened down the front by way of a full-length velcro flap of the sort I understand is favoured by habitual streakers. If you had it in mind to bare all, it would be a lot quicker to get out of than a plastic raincoat.

'Put it on,' said L. 'Let's see how it looks.'

I complied. The feet were rather cold, but fitted quite nicely. Perhaps in a later model they could learn something from ug boot technology, if there was going to be a lot of winter work to be done. Also, the way the bottom of the suit tied your ankles together made walking an ungainly affair — quite realistic for a penguin, of course, but in human terms it imposed a motion that seemed rather like a sack race. I went to look at myself in a mirror.

'I must say, I make a fine figure of a penguin,' I said, smoothing the velcro strip so that it lay as flat as possible. There were eyeholes in the front edges of the penguin's eyes, and I could get quite a good look at myself. I turned from side to side, and waved the flippers that encased my arms up and down, and lifted my head and made various crowing noises. The effect in the mirror was not unpleasing.

'Better stop now,' said L, 'if you don't want to attract sex-crazed female penguins from miles around. Remember what happened in *The Birds*.'

'I don't recall any penguins in *The Birds*,' I replied, 'but I wouldn't be surprised if the effect of such an outfit, worn by a virile man in the prime of life, on a rosy-cheeked kitchen girl could be quite devastating.'

'Perhaps it's as well that you'll never have the opportunity to find out,' said L.

'If I am to wear this thing, and I stress the word *if*,' I said, 'I wonder if someone would be good enough to tell me what Erna has in mind.'

'I think the idea is to add a bit of theatre to the demonstrations,' said L. 'In fact, I think I may have given her the idea. I was telling her that you really have to have some kind of gimmick if you want to make it onto the television, and it's not till you get these things on the nightly news that you can hope to have mass support.'

'In speaking of theatre,' I said, 'you have employed the very word which it is not permitted to utter, and in consequence have transformed me from a handsome penguin into an ugly old frog again.' And suiting the action to the word I tore open the velcro, pulled my head out of the helmet and shook my feet out of the flippers.

'See what you have done?' I said, pulling down the corners of my mouth into a suitably frog-like aspect.

'I knew it was too good to last,' said L.

'But tell me,' I resumed, once I had rearranged my clothing and put my ug boots back on, 'where did the money come from?'

'It came from Sarah Lever,' said L. 'I suggested to Erna that she ought to try her. Seeing the girls at the funeral put it into my mind. She has stacks of money her husband left her, and her house is right on Cabbage Tree Bay, and almost next to the marina. I don't suppose she'd want people on yachts roistering under her windows half the night.'

'Oh, are they those Levers?' I said. 'The newspaper ones? They should certainly be good for a few bob. But it sounds as if a fight between her and Rita would be a battle of the titans.'

'Let's hope it doesn't come to that,' said L, 'but if I'd known the whole story I never would have got involved, or got you into it either.'

'Think nothing of it,' I replied. 'What sort of a husband would a man be who refused to impersonate a penguin at his wife's request, even if it meant he had to die in the attempt?'

'You're too good to me,' said L. 'Sometimes I wonder if I deserve such a lovely husband.' What I wasn't telling L was that if anyone was going to wear that penguin suit, I intended it should be a certain ponytailed bikie of my acquaintance who owed me a large debt of gratitude. Even if L was present on whatever occasion Erna was meditating, she would never know the difference under the suit. She might claim to know me inside and out, but she didn't have x-ray eyes. You may think I could have confessed my intention, but it's always wise in married life to keep something up your sleeve; you never know when you are going to need it. So all I said was: 'It's very sweet of you to say so – in fact, it does you credit,' and I went out to the kitchen, because I had planned a pizza for the evening meal and I wanted to get the crust on the go.

You've probably seen that show where Jamie Oliver makes a pizza from scratch in the time it takes to get a take-away one delivered, and you are wondering why I wanted to start my preparations so early in the piece. The point is, of course, that I wasn't intending to make Jamie's sort of pizza with the thin Neapolitan crust, but something with a bit of body and bounce to it, as supplied, for example, by the organisation to which Herr Heydenreich was the erstwhile fictive courier. And if you then were inclined to object that the Neapolitans invented pizza, I would say two things: first, spread something on bread dough and put it in the oven – big invention! Pussy could have done it. Secondly, I would say, just because the Neapolitans thought of multi-coloured ice cream, why should that give them the right to lord it over the rest of us? When I make a pizza, I make it my way.

*KF² – the object of a search is pointed out, etc.**

There being no *Big Brother* to watch on a Saturday night, L and I had our meal at the dining table in gentleperson-like fashion. Then L settled in front of the television for a sixth or seventh go at *Notting Hill*, a film of which she is inordinately fond.

'If they ever run short of crocodiles in Kakadu,' I said, 'they'll know where to look. That woman must have at least three times the normal number of teeth.'

'Don't be absurd,' said L. 'Julia Roberts is lovely. And Hugh Grant has so much boyish charm about him.'

'There's an ugly word for women of your age who slobber over little boys,' I said, 'or if there isn't there ought to be. Who do you think you are, Germaine Greer? I can't be wasting time watching this sort of stuff: I've got serious reading to do.'

'Please yourself,' said L absently, 'but thankyou for that pizza tonight – it was really lovely. And you know how much I always adore that ally-oley you made yesterday.'

'The word is *aioli*,' I said. 'Four syllables: a-i-o-li.'

'That's what I said,' replied L. 'Ally-oley – don't tell me that's not four syllables.'

'Your command of arithmetic is second to none. Now if you can spare me, I want to have another look at *The First Stone* before I get too sleepy.'

I went to search out the book, wherever I had left it, and find a suitable place for comfortable reading. At times when the terrace is not an option, sprawled on the floor in front of the television is one of my favourite locations – I've often contended television gives us so little to occupy the mind that a good book is a useful accompaniment – but *Notting Hill* wasn't the sort of background I had in mind. I didn't want to be shut in a small room with vengeful feminists, an unwashed Englishman and a human crocodile. The next best choice was the breakfast room, where I would be able to prop my feet on L's chair while stretching them out towards the heater. Professor J had counselled me that if I wanted to explore meaning I should look at the words, and Dave had shown me that words alone, ripped away from the contexts that had nurtured them like so many spinach plants sliced off at the roots, still had much to tell. I wondered about a good method of reading Helen Garner's words without being distracted by the way in which they built towards a larger whole. Would holding the book upside-down be feasible, or reading from the back, or choosing random pages? In the end it seemed best to sample the book here and there, and to flick back and forth in the hope that recurrent threads and parallelisms would reveal themselves. After all, I had read the book through twice, I knew what was going on, and I felt that I had a keener appreciation of the background since realising that Poppy was a natural inmate of Ormond College. While Poppy's powers and abilities may not have been far beyond those of ordinary mortals, I knew that in some respects − the creation of graffiti art and the execution of striking pieces in the manga style, for example − they were far beyond mine. But apart from that, in all three of our meetings to date she had been not so much *in esse* as *in posse*: a brooding and inscrutable potential. Much like Ormond College. Besides all of which, I reflected that if you reshuffled a lot of the episodes in *The First Stone*, it wouldn't have too much effect on the narrative.

The narrative − that was one thing. I supposed Helen Garner's dialogue was all made up, but ever since the invention of the English novel, a lot of the load has been carried by dialogue. Dialogue, action, description. *The First Stone* was a novel because it used the techniques of a novel. I didn't agree with whatever disparaging imputation was intended by the author of those words 'This is a fiction book' on the flyleaf of the library copy − how could it possibly matter? Recently, I seemed to remember, one woman who wouldn't talk to Helen Garner at the time had later complained that in the book she had been split into two or three different people. So? The implicit claim of a novel is not to be truthful but to be veridical. If I wanted to find out the facts as they are publicly known I would look up the files of *The Age*.

What I am working around to here is my conviction that the primary meaning of *The First Stone* was to be the sort of thing that it was. Dave would have found the same thing as he looked at his poems: apart from the differences in vocabulary that he had plotted as the poems changed in sympathy with the travails of the world, they all had a common purpose – to be poems – which carried with it a kind of expression and a kind of vocabulary you mightn't have met as you walked up Pitt Street in 1890.

Then there was the trajectory I had already identified: the trajectory that led from the raw facts that were the starting point of the Shepherd affair to the labelled and docketed occurrences with which it ended. From drunken grope to culpable sexual harassment. From *signifiant* to *signifié*. And Helen Garner was saying: there is no *signifié* – go home Bronislaw.* We don't play out social roles or realize moral principles, we just stumble around like poor hopeless human beings, and if we can manage to do what seems to be right at the time, we'll be doing well. And if we're too hopeless to assert ourselves, perhaps we just have to live with it. If when we are students we want the right to walk in on our tutors in nothing but a plastic raincoat – and I think if we're Helen Garner we probably do – we can't complain too loudly if they seduce us and abandon us in return. I couldn't foresee what Poppy might do when she finally got to Ormond: I didn't see her as a prim and humourless Nicole Stewart, nor did I see her trashing her room like Elizabeth Rosen, but I was sure that whatever the college's future alumna had in store for it would probably be an outrage of some kind. But all she and any of us could hope was that whatever we did, whatever was done to us, in the end it might have taught us something along the way. Learning, I thought, moving along the syntagmatic axis, shifting our one personal bead in the cosmic abacus, that was the thing. To draw a result from all these chaotic experiences. If in my young ignorance I flap my butterfly wings in the Amazon jungle, or, and a happy thought struck me at this point, my penguin wings in the wastes of Antarctica, this random and insignificant action, properly understood, may bring about a vast and beneficial change in the future.

At this point I stood up and did a bit of a penguin shuffle round the room, flapping my arms and crowing as I went.

'Are you all right?' called L. 'You're not having some sort of fit?'

'No,' I replied. 'Just trying a few moves that might come in useful when Erna summons me into battle,' and I tried a more stylised shuffle, swinging one shoulder forward as far as it would go in synchrony with advancing the opposite foot, the way they taught us in high school dancing classes. It was all in the hips, I remembered, taking a while to get the timing right as I tried to put this movement together with the flapping and crowing. It was reassuring to find that the skills honed under the tutelage of Miss W, as I'll call her, short for Whatever-her-name-was, had remained with me even if her identity hadn't. I could still see the scene as if it had been yesterday – polished boards, girls in velvet supper dresses with lace collars, Miss W's offsider at the piano. I had nurtured a brief, unreciprocated, infatuation for a tall, thin girl who showed she was on the cutting edge by wearing a fetching light blue (linen?) outfit rather than the velvet fall-back option the school prescribed. In fact I wrote her a number of poems, and I would reproduce one here were it not for two things: it could be of no possible interest to a third party, and it would be terminally embarrassing to myself. Tall thin girls – such as L herself as a young person – had tended to be my thing, I reflected, though there was certainly the odd shorter dumpier one included in my list of all-time greats. Picturing one of these last, I conceived the idea of working out a song along the lines of 'I am a little penguin, short and stout,' to include in the routine, but somehow the rhymes wouldn't come so I just shuffled in to show L anyway.

'Would you mind getting away from in front of the television?' said L. 'This is one of my favourite bits.'

'Many people consider live entertainment far superior to the prepackaged commercial product,' I said.

'Call me superficial,' said L, 'but in that case I'll have the McDonald's version every time.'

Then too, I thought as I walked back to the breakfast room, for shuffling had lost some of its appeal just for the moment, there was a third thread: the facts, whatever they may have been, and Helen Garner's pursuit of them. Text and metatext. I picked up the book again; then my eyes stopped focusing, and I realised I was too spent for further effort.

'I'm going to bed,' I said to L. 'Exercising the avian side of my personality has overtaxed my powers for the time being. Goodnight.'

'Goodnight,' said L. 'This is almost over; I'll join you shortly.'

L's idea of shortly is an elastic concept; I knew that when watching television she could be waylaid by almost anything. All I know is that I had been fast asleep for some time when she did come to bed.

'Goodnight, love,' I said sleepily, rolling over as I felt her hit the bed beside me, and shut my eyes again. L lay still for a little, but then began to launch into one of her seafood impressions. Flip, flop, flap.

'Whatever's the matter?' I asked.

'I'm thinking of Sarah and Rita,' said L. 'I never should have said you would help Erna. It was so disloyal of me; I don't know what I was thinking of.'

'These things have a way of working themselves out,' I replied.

'But I've been doing everything I can to get Poppy a place at Santa Sophia, and Rita has promised quite a big donation if they take her. Now what will happen when she finds out I've been scheming against her?'

'Isn't that rather dramatising things?' I asked. 'After all, you had no way of knowing that Rita was behind the marina.'

'It's all very well for you,' said L. 'It's not your livelihood. I'm worried sick about the whole business. I think I'll go and watch television again for a while – it might settle me down.'

'With any luck they might be showing *Waterloo Bridge*,' I said. 'That's the sort of thing you get at this hour.'

'Well, in the mood I'm in, a good cry may be just what I need,' said

L, and left the room. I turned over and went heedlessly back to sleep again.

*

In the morning I woke slowly. It was one of those cold, cloudy days when bed is unutterably pleasant and a final definitive waking can be postponed. L had reinserted herself at my side at some unknown point during the night, and was sleeping heavily. The late-night television, whatever its bounty may have been, had worked its magic. I let her sleep till about nine, and then woke her to let her know there was porridge freshly made.

'Oh you are a darling,' said L. 'Porridge! Just give me a moment,' and soon we were together at the breakfast table, me enjoying a final cup of strong dark coffee while L eagerly spooned up the lifegiving substance.

'So you got to sleep all right,' I said. 'What did you watch?'

'I didn't watch anything,' said L. 'When I came down I saw your book lying there and I thought I might read a bit and picked it up, and before I knew where I was I had read it right through.'

'You've read it before haven't you?'

'Oh yes, I read it back then when everyone was reading it, but that doesn't really count,' said L. 'That was just so I could keep my end up in conversation.'

'So what did you make of it?'

'I couldn't help seeing it as a sort of play,' said L.

'You don't think it's just your worries about the disruptive effects of street theatre playing on your mind?'

'Perhaps it was,' said L, ' but as I was reading I kept labelling things as dialogue or action or set. It seemed to make sense.'

'Forgive my lack of enthusiasm,' I said, 'but it's hardly an insight that a play has dialogue and action and a set. Mind you, you wouldn't need many sets if you wanted to put it on the stage. I could see it as a sort of Globe Theatre production. For the college, inside and out, you'd probably just manage with the big generic front stage that could do for the dinner and the dance and the quadrangle, and a college study could be the inner part. Put in a sofa and that could double for the room where the young Helen Garner sleeps with the tutor: it would make a good parallel for when Shepherd propositions Rosen,' and here I explained to L my thoughts about *signifiant* and *signifié* and about text and metatext. 'I think, by the way, you'd dump that girl that the supervisor tried to get off with, and you'd need a domestic interior for the various houses where Garner goes to interview people – that could be "within" too – and I see a sort of movable grandstand on the front stage to represent a lecture theatre slash courtroom: I'm seeing a parallel scene where the feminists sit in judgement on Shepherd.'

'Hold on,' said L, 'that's not in the book.'

'Not explicitly perhaps.'

'I wasn't thinking so much about actually putting it on stage,' said L, 'as of the sort of elements you've got there. When I said *dialogue*, for example, I meant a general wordy element, not just conversation: there's a pamphlet, and graffiti, and Helen Garner keeps ringing people up and writing letters, which is all the same kind of thing.'

'Pinero has someone write a letter on stage,' I said, 'while the other characters talk about him. I think it's in *The Second Mrs Tanqueray*.' Once I had taken a tall thin girl to a Pinero play, and it turned out she hadn't even heard of Pinero before. I was shocked. Mildly shocked perhaps, but shocked all the same.

'Then there's the stage set,' said L, 'which is obviously the college, but also the whole apparatus of students and tutors and the college council and the various judges and the Melbourne establishment, etc. And that isn't reality, any more than a stage set is reality – it's just what Helen Garner wants to show us for the sake of the book.'

'So you're saying that the wordy element sort of puts a form onto people's thoughts, internal things, while the setting puts a form onto external things?' I couldn't help thinking of the categories that had come up in my discussions with Dave.

'I suppose you could say that if you wanted to.'

'And when you have action, like dancing, or breast-grabbing, or whatever it is, this is like the internal, the mind, impinging on the external. So you have the internal, the external, and the formal.'

'That's not even reductionism,' said L. 'I started out with three categories, and you've rearranged them and you've still got three.'

'But what if your three were green, orange and purple while mine were red, blue and yellow?' I said. 'I'm looking for an underlying simplicity – wouldn't that be an improvement?'

'I thought,' said L, 'you were telling me that this kind of simplification was exactly what Helen Garner was arguing against.'

Further pursuit of the topic was made difficult in the short term by the roar of a motorcycle close at hand. This was followed by a sharp diminuendo as the rider cut the motor. Evidently Dave was coming to call. I went to the door. Dave was on the mat, dressed as in our last encounter, this time sans Billy peeping out from his chest.

'I wanted to tell you, mate,' he said, 'that picture of Rita's – I followed it up in the Mitchell, and they put me onto an artist bloke up the coast who reckons I'm spot on with the poetry. He says you see the same thing going on in the art. Stands to reason, I suppose, with their sensitivity and all that. So me and Poppy are off to pay him a visit.'

The by now not unexpected figure of Poppy manifested itself in the background, still astride the bike. I waved, and rather to my surprise, Poppy waved back.

'Like to come with us, mate?' said Dave.

'Thanks all the same, Dave,' I replied. Travelling to an unspecified destination – hundreds of kilometres perhaps – as second pillion on what was probably still an unregistered bike seemed a bit too much like defying the lightning. But remembering the penguin suit, I added, 'Suppose I want to get in touch, Dave, how would I contact you?'

'Poppy's got a mobile,' said Dave. 'If you've got something to write with, I'll give you the number.'

This was soon fixed. Then, just as he was leaving, Dave produced a package from somewhere, much as he had the bunch of flowers at our first meeting.

'Poppy's video,' he said, pushing it into my hand, and with these enigmatic words made his departure.

*

'What do you suppose this might be?' I said to L, as I came back holding the cassette.

'I expect it's Poppy's video,' said L brightly. 'Didn't I tell you about that?'

'Any more of this,' I said, 'and I may become a very angry penguin indeed.'

'Apparently Year 10 at Santa Sophia have an assessment to hand in soon, and the school suggested to Rita that Poppy should make a start on it, and Rita asked me if you would look at it and perhaps give the girl a few pointers, so naturally I said you would be only too happy.'

This whole breathless sequence as L articulated it had the sort of specious plausibility people that work in promotions are so good at creating, so I contented myself with a token protest.

'What do I know about videos?' I asked.

'Don't tell me,' said L, 'that you don't know a hundred times more about anything than a fifteen-year-old girl.'

'On the contrary,' I replied, 'this fifteen-year-old knows far more than I do about all sorts of things, ranging from the art of the modern Japanese masters to the wholesomeness or otherwise of the intentions of Dave, which remains a mystery as far as I am concerned.'

'Well I think it's most unwholesome,' said L, 'the way she seems to hang around with that frightful Dave every tick of the clock.'

'So long as they both stay on the bike,' I said, 'I wouldn't worry too much. There are limits to what the human body is capable of.'

Poppy and Dave were on their own *Winterreise* now, in quest of the artist of the death tree and his peers. I pictured the furrowed sandstone wake of the bike, dark with exhaust, as they swooped down towards the Hawkesbury. I followed them over ridges of scrubby tickbush and between stiff files of Gymea lilies. I roared with them over the Hunter,

I coasted with them into Kempsey, I swept in a huge right-hand curve past the Big Banana. How far was 'up the coast'? Endless kilometres of head-high cane scrolled past the stationary bike as if on rollers while the elusive tree shimmered ahead of them in the mirage above the bitumen: Dave's Holy Grail. A bike trip up the coast: was Poppy then turning into Nora? That was how *Monkey Grip* started. And once you were Nora you were launched on the path that would turn you into Janet, for the scene of *Monkey Grip* was recognizably that of *Cosmo Cosmolino*, just twenty years less jaded:

> In the old brown house on the corner, a mile from the middle of the city, we ate bacon for breakfast every morning of our lives. There were never enough chairs for us all to sit up at the meal table; one or two of us always sat on the floor or on the kitchen step, plate on knee. It never occurred to us to teach the children to eat with a knife and fork. It was hunger and all sheer function: the noise, and clashing of plates, and people chewing with their mouths open, and talking, and laughing. Oh, I was happy then.*

All it lacked was Alby and a pair of stilts. Nora was swept away up the coast, then to Tasmania – where we had the rabbits – and then to all sorts of other places, for Javo was always going somewhere, always making a fresh start – and always going to give up the heroin. Did I see Dave as Javo? Somehow Dave's substantial frame was a comfort: no emaciated junkie there. On the other hand Nora, like Poppy, seemed to have little aptitude for verbal communication. If I was going to generalise from L's dialogue/setting/action model, I would have to say that if letters and the phone were wordy elements for the narrator of *The First Stone*, sex had much the same role for Nora. Poor old Javo, I thought, to the extent that he was rational he would have liked something more:

> He wanted us to communicate on some intellectual level where we didn't usually function together.*

And how did Nora respond on that occasion? By talking him through an article about Buñuel, written in French, of all things. I ask you. The meeting of minds, day by day and year by year, as you plagiarize a prospectus together or discuss a bunch of spinach, turns passion into love, and for Nora and Javo that never took place. There's a lot of sex in the book, there's laughing and there's smiling that does for dialogue, but precious little talking. Take off that helmet, Poppy, I said to myself, I don't want you to waste years on a junkie boyfriend; *Monkey Grip* would be a tragedy if we cared about the characters.

I wound back the road trip in my mind. I had Dave stop the bike at the Big Banana and chain it to one of those treated green pine logs in the carpark there. I had them get off, and point and laugh and walk into the cafe hand in hand. I put their heads together, and Dave talked and Poppy talked and waved her white hands, and then Dave rocked back in his chair and Poppy leant across the table and stabbed with a thin white finger as she made her points, and Dave shrugged and talked and Poppy talked again. Now I was happier for them. Swap that black helmet for a white hard hat, Poppy, and talk Dave around the foundations of your life together, like Rhoda on the site of Carthage. It worked for Dido. Big, founding, words – big-sounding words – on the overt side of your relationship, and big, magical, unspeakable things on the hidden side. Let Ray be seen and Maxine be hidden.

Clarity and muddle, I thought, that's one of the things that's going on in *Monkey Grip*, and part of the muddle is the idea that something as muddled and muddling as sex will do for a signifier. Nora has to let go of muddle. It was much the same in *The First Stone*: the precipitating action assigned a clarity that it just didn't have – as a result everyone was a loser. Didn't *breast* belong in Dave's evening quadrant? Rest, relaxation, a yarn on the steps of the shed, a keg set up on a stand, drinks and no doubt cups. *You have to cup a breast in order to squeeze it,** I thought. Come to think of it, weren't breast sizes measured in cups?

'I'm beginning to see a sort of pattern here,' I called out to L, who was now busy with some work of her own. 'There's a contrast between something that's clear, structured, organized, sensible, and a bit hard-edged maybe, and things that are warmer and softer and dumber and hopelesser, as Patrick White might say; Helen Garner is all about putting them in the right places; keeping the baby rabbits safe in the cardigan. Sydney is hard and cruel. In *The Children's Bach* when Athena goes to Sydney, she says: *I was walking through Martin Place and I said good morning to an old woman who was selling flowers. She looked at me coldly and when I got past her she laughed.* In *Monkey Grip* Nora says *a hard-faced clerk inspected the ceiling* when she's trying to buy a train ticket back to Melbourne. You see the pattern? Melbourne is fuzzy and kind. It's like AFL and Rugby League – in AFL no one has a clue what's going on, but in a proper game you're either up this end or up the other end. The baby rabbit stays in the cardigan, the big rabbit runs free on the road to the airport; then ten to one it hops on a plane to Sydney, and George Piggins signs it up to a six figure contract.'

'Go the Bunnies!' said L. 'But what about the rabbit in the pie?'

'At least it's cosy and warm,' I said. 'The truth is, I haven't completely integrated it into my thinking yet. Perhaps the idea is that it's all stewed and muddled together, so that in the end you can't tell if you're chewing on a rabbit bone or if it's the core of a parsnip. But what Helen Garner is saying is that if you have something as uncalculated as a drunken grope, you can't put a hard-edged label on it like sexual harassment; if all you've got is something as vague as sex and passion, you need to get to Sydney to clear your head. See, both Nora and Athena come to their senses in Sydney. Philip has to put some words onto what he feels for Athena, and as soon as he does that she knows he's faking. If they'd stayed put, the fog never would have lifted.'

'It's very interesting,' said L. 'I'm so glad you're getting somewhere. Now I'm just trying to work on this press release about Rita and Santa Sophia, so if you'll give me a little while I'd be very grateful.'

'Don't tell me it's all fixed up at last,' I said.

'Yes, we're hoping it will all happen in the next few days,' said L. 'Poppy's admission ceremony will be a good opportunity for Rita to present her cheque to the school, and I'm hoping we can get a bit in some of the papers. There are just a few things to iron out; Rita's trying to work on the dyed hair and the piercings.'

'Why shouldn't Poppy become a Muslim?' I asked. 'They couldn't object if she wore a burqa in the school colours. Then the hair and the stud wouldn't be a problem.'

'It may come to that,' said L. 'But I do know that the headmistress is having a rehearsal of the admission tomorrow.'

'Why do people rehearse things?' I asked. 'It's like weddings – it's not as though the priest or whoever you have in charge is going to lose control of the ceremony and the couple end up exorcized instead of married.'

'You may laugh,' said L, 'but let me tell you: the first suspicion that something at a school is a shambles, and the girls will be leaving in droves. Parents don't pay that sort of money to be messed around.'

'I'm beginning to form a mental picture,' I said. 'I suppose in the expulsion ceremony they have the girls going "sss, sss, sss" en masse, hissing the poor expellee out and taunting her with the initials of Santa Sophia School, and so in the admission ceremony they would suck her in,' and here I gave a triple intake of breath, whistling sharply through my rounded lips. 'And the expellee will catch the faintest murmur of it borne on the wind,' I continued, 'as the angel with the flaming sword drives her from the garden. She will look back clutching the figleaf with which she vainly endeavours to conceal her advancing pregnancy, and she will console herself by allowing her lips to frame the words "Sucked in".'

'I wish you wouldn't use vulgar expressions,' said L. 'Apparently you're at a loose end. Why don't you go and sweep the terrace?'

*

The day was still dark and windy; the terrace was liberally strewn with the last of the frangipani leaves, some still flaccid, others already crumbling underfoot, and the paving was pasted with vine leaves. I took a yard broom and began to assault the leaves, first using quick stabbing motions to dislodge the vine leaves from the paving, then sweeping them briskly into a heap. I worked in from both of the longer edges towards the middle. It was quite satisfying to clear the outer edge of the terrace by sweeping such leaves as lay there down onto cars in the street below, but it would probably excite adverse comment to dispose of the whole heap that way. The rest now lay in a long cigar-shaped mound along the middle of the paving. Only a few strokes with the broom, and the whole was shaped into the likeness of a penguin. Then a couple of clearing jabs, and what had been the penguin's beak and tail became the leading and trailing ends of a dollar sign. *You would profit from our penguins, would you, Rita?* I swept the dollar sign back into a penguin again. *But the spirit of the penguin dreaming will rise up and destroy you.* It was as good as Dave's anamorphic sundial, and twice as interactive. I swept the leaves together, all into one pile, and picking up a big armful, dumped it under the frangipani.

It occurred to me then to sweep the rest into a flat circle, and through the circle with one corner of the broom I raked out a clear Y-shaped track, to make it like a peace sign. Three divisions — scene, action and dialogue: structure imposed on concrete form, concrete form given to mental impulses, structure given to mental impulses. Like rock, paper and scissors, but transitive. Concrete form wraps mental impulse, structure wraps concrete form. The three bars of the Y would represent my three elemental quantities, mental, concrete and structural, the sectors between them the factors in the text to which L had called my attention. Then I scrubbed this out and divided the circle of leaves four ways à la Dave. Were these two different strategies reconcilable? I didn't know, so just while I was thinking about it I picked up another big armful and dumped it under the frangipani on top of the previous pile.

A few more armfuls of diminishing size, then double handfuls, and there wasn't much left on the terrace apart from a heap of dust which I briskly broomed over the edge and into the street.

'Hey, watch what you're doing up there,' came a voice from below. I looked over. Erna was standing beside her station wagon in the street, the grey bush of her hair powdered with leaf dust like an 18th century wig.

'Just checking that you got the costume,' she shouted.

'I love it, Erna,' I replied.

'So easy to get in and out of,' shouted Erna. 'We will strike without warning and then swim away among the peasantry like fish in the sea. Do you have a mobile?'

'I'm sorry, Erna,' I replied, 'the stationary telephone already gives me as much accessibility as I can handle.'

'Wait for the code word *fairy*,' said Erna. 'You'll be told the time and place. The weight of us angry penguins is going to sink this marina to the bottom of the harbour.'

'How many penguins do you expect to have?'

'There's you and me,' shouted Erna, 'and two lovely student girls who are very keen. But the suits are just for the shock troops. There will be lots of people with placards.'

'I'll be sitting by the phone,' I said, congratulating myself that I had already organised a stand-in. No need to bother Erna with the details, but she would have her angry penguin, while L would be freed from guilt by association. Considering what a mess reality is, I reflected, it's always gratifying to be able to arrange these win-win situations. Erna's station wagon chugged away up the street, trailing a plume of smoke that quickly merged with the grey light of the afternoon. If everyone's car put out as much smoke as Erna's, global warming could be postponed indefinitely. I went to find L.

Interrupting her, I could see, was more likely than not to lead to a further invitation to perform some unwanted duty. To read, then, or to cook? *Joe Cinque's Consolation* called to me from this side; from the other I heard the warning that if I didn't get things ready ahead of time there was the risk of missing some of *Big Brother Live Evictions*, which would have to be the highlight of anyone's Sunday night viewing. So cooking it was.

The day, though cold, was far from freezing — any of the larger kinds of penguin might well have found it unpleasantly warm. Something genial seemed to be required, but not necessarily comfort food with a capital *kuh*. A curry of koftas in a tomatoey sauce, I thought, was just about what the coming evening would require. Soon I was grating onions and ginger, squashing garlic, measuring out a nicely judged quantity of garam masala – no, I don't grind it myself; even for me there is a limit to how much I can be bothered – and rolling the meat and the flavourings into nice little koftas the size of a rather large marble. Do little boys still play marbles? Not Billy obviously, but boys of eight and nine? That was about the age when I played a lot: I seemed to remember having a stock of very nice-looking marbles, though I have no idea where they came from. There was one, I remembered, that was actually like marble, white with a red streak through it. I suppose it was made of china. Boys used to play marbles and girls played knucklebones – with real knucklebones too, that they painted or stained with ink. There were all sorts of progressions to it: picking up and catching one, and two, and three, and so on, and then holding some while you picked up others, etc, etc. If you ever joined in, the girls could make you look pretty silly. The only boy I ever knew that could really play knucklebones grew up to be gay, but as with Boake and the stockwhip, I don't think being gay made it easier. It was just that he was good at it because he spent so much time playing with girls.

Now for the sauce: onions and garlic and ginger again and some tomatoes. If you're not going to start from fresh, buy the generic tinned ones – they're usually about half the price. But you'll probably need to add some sugar. The more expensive ones don't need it, but then fifty cents or so is a lot to pay for a teaspoon of sugar. If you do use fresh tomatoes, don't bother to skin them, just chop them roughly. We're aiming at peasant-style cuisine here, and what does your Umbrian peasant care about a fragment of tomato skin? That's not the attitude that kept him in touch with the good earth and the wine and the cheese and the oil while his over-fastidious brothers took off for the New World and became billionaire Mafia dons. And, I thought, reflecting that this dish was to be a curry, the same goes for your Indian peasant. You wouldn't get round the block in Uttar Pradesh if you had nothing better to do than pick the bits of tomato skin out from between your koftas. The locals would be doubled up in derision. If you've ever watched *The Amazing Race* you'll know how pathetic it looks when the competitors won't eat stuff. Not to mention *Big Brother*. I saw a segment where the housemates had to eat fish eyeballs, and though they wouldn't be my first choice, I don't imagine they could taste of anything much worse than gristle and salt water. Much like a seafood pie I bought once in a cafe up the north coast. Take a tip from me, Dave, I thought – if you happen to be passing through Lismore, go easy on the seafood pies, or Poppy won't remember you with much affection.

And now for salt. Perhaps my proudest moment as a parent came to me a couple of years ago when Gracie said I had taught her the meaning of the word 'insipid'. I knew then that my time on this earth had not been wasted. You don't want things to taste salty – you want them to taste tasty. Cooking is all thinking and sensation: you think about what goes in: you taste, you react. On the one hand Ray, on the other Alby. Sweet cooking needs more thought, savoury more tasting. You can teach a child to bake a cake, but it takes a freewheeler to make a stew.

> *...great crocks and tureens of it, coarse with garlic and beans, weird salads hacked to chaff, onions, brown rice, the occasional sausage, vegetable curry that burnt your mouth when you gulped it,**

I remembered. Have you ever had that sort of food cooked by someone that didn't work by taste? I have, and I'm not keen to repeat the experience. Sweet is Ray, salt is Alby, sour is Janet, bitter is Maxine. When you stop off at the Big Banana, buy Poppy a smoothie, Dave, and a hamburger for yourself. Like with like. Homeopathy in practice. And order up some mushrooms if you happen to break your umbrella.

Unfortunately this final witticism coincided with a big spoonful of chilli-laden sauce, and the combination sent me reeling around the kitchen in an explosive burst of coughing. The sauce would have to do: the book beckoned.

Joe Cinque's Consolation, I soon found, was *The First Stone 2 – The Second Stone*, if you like – with the formula turned inside out. So much I could make out even without the helpful highlighting, underlining and marginal notes I would have got in a library copy. In her first treatment of the story, Helen Garner writes from the point of view of Melbourne about two vengeful Albys destroying a wayward, bumbling Janet; in the second, from the point of view of Sydney, she writes about two deranged Maxines destroying a harmless, geeky Ray. He was even an engineer, for heaven's sake – how much more Ray can you get? In his hard hat, showing Aeneas round the foundations of Carthage. But as we know, in that situation it's the one under the hard hat that gets the rough end of the pineapple. I hope Rhoda is OK, I thought, I'd hate anything to happen to that spiky head of hair, and if you get as far as the Big Pineapple, Poppy, forget what I said before – take off the hard hat and put the bike helmet back on. Then from another perspective, I thought, you could say there are two polar tragic texts, and *Cosmo Cosmolino* retells the first as a comedy, with Janet and Alby playing the Nora/Javo roles, and foreshadows the second as a comedy as well, Maxine a ludicrous prefigurement of Joe Cinque's malevolent succubus.

Why *succubus*, I wondered then, shouldn't that be feminine? I went looking for my *Lewis & Short.** The answer, as in so many puzzling situations, turned out to be simple: there is no such word as *succubus* in Latin – the word is *succuba*, which Messrs Lewis & co. define as *a lecher or strumpet*. A fine term, *strumpet! The Oxford Dictionary of English Etymology* calls its origin 'unknown': I like to think it comes from the German *Strumpf*, and refers to fishnet stockings, as so often worn by British Cabinet Ministers – and probably unwashed English actors too, if truth be told. But would even that affect L's opinion of them?

Then I thought again: Nora is no Janet, I realised – she is an ur-Maxine, and Javo is a would-be Ray, as we can gather from his desire for intelligent conversation. *Monkey Grip* and *Joe Cinque*, then, are Maxine/Ray stories, while *The Children's Bach* and *The First Stone* are Alby/Janet stories. The women take the irrational roles, in Jung's terms, the men the rational ones. One member of each of these pairs of texts is essentially true, one is fictional. The real story has some elements of tragedy, the fictional one is neutral. *Cosmo Cosmolino* incorporates both kinds, but as comedy. And yet formally, *The Children's Bach* is a reprise of *Monkey Grip* and *Joe Cinque* of *The First Stone*.

I read on, revolving these ideas in my mind. Then, just before *Big Brother* was due to start, I let out a shout.

'Darling!' I called.

'Yes, love, what is it?'

'Listen to this,' I said. I went to find L, and read out the following sentence:

> The food – pasta with ragu, rabbit, polpette, a salad, a platter of fresh fruit, and heart-shaped Abruzzese waffles filled with creamy chocolate and vanilla – repaid in full the severe concentration that the young man brought to its ingestion.*

'Sounds delicious,' said L. 'What about it? Are you planning a menu?'

'Didn't you notice?' I said. '*The rabbit is back.*'

'Does that mean something?' asked L.

'I'm sure it foreshadows a full-scale reappearance. The rabbit was last seen in a stew, remember – a symbol of dissolution – and now it comes back in ravioli or something. A sort of egg. A promise of new life. I see it as a sign of hope for the Cinques: the rabbit comes full circle. And look at this,' I said. 'Do you mind if I write on this?'

I picked up a glossy pamphlet on L's desk with a picture nicely calculated to attract a parent – four eager girls, heads together, looked into a computer screen in the foreground, none smiling so widely as to suggest levity, but each enough to make clear they were united in the joy of intellectual discovery. Over the shoulder of one of the girls – and here L's genius showed itself – you glimpsed the rest of the room: just enough of it to reassure your parent that the reason the girls were crowding together wasn't because the school only had one computer. Now I quickly adapted the picture to my use.

'This girl at the top left,' I said, 'the one that looks as if she's from an Indian family, I'll call Maxine. The one with the moustache is Ray, and the one with the beard is Alby. The other one, at bottom left, is Janet.'

'There isn't any girl with a moustache or beard in the picture,' said L.

'There is now,' I replied, looking at my work with some approval. 'Now we have four texts – I'm leaving out *Cosmo Cosmolino* for the time being, because it's sort of in the middle, like earth in the Chinese elements.'

'Whatever you say,' said L.

'And these texts are represented by four girls, who are in two pairs – two top ones and two bottom ones, and I've made the two on the right into men. Now the top two are one kind of text – a fact/fiction pair to be precise – and the bottom two are another kind of text, ditto; each kind has one or two women up against a man, or vice versa.'

'Hang on,' said L. 'I think I lost the thread with that last statement.'

'Each sort of text has a male and a female in it.'

'I can see that from the facial hair,' said L.

'No, that's not how it works: in both the fictional and the factual treatment Maxine exploits Ray and Alby exploits Janet. But get this – Alby is always played by a woman: Nicole Stewart and Elizabeth Rosen in *The First Stone,* and Athena in *The Children's Bach,* while Janet is always played by a man.'

'Then why on earth didn't you draw the beard on the one you called Janet,' asked L, 'and leave Alby alone?'

'Why would I have called her Janet if she had a beard?' I replied. 'I think you're missing the point. And,' I went on, 'each text is in sympathy with a different one of the characters. *Monkey Grip* and *Joe Cinque* are both Maxine/Ray texts, but *Monkey Grip* is in sympathy with Nora and *Joe Cinque* with Joe, so we could call *Monkey Grip* Maxine for short, and *Joe Cinque* Ray. Similarly with *The First Stone* and *The Children's Bach.*'

'Just tell me again,' said L, 'where do all these Maxines and Rays and so on come from?'

'They're names out of *Cosmo Cosmolino.*'

'I thought you said a moment ago that you were leaving out *Cosmo Cosmolino*,' said L. 'It all seems very confusing to me.'

'Exactly: I think that may well be the point of it,' I said. 'The books that are based on real stories are totally confusing. You never find out why Dr Shepherd really got sacked, and in *Joe Cinque's Consolation* you have the two young women who clearly did the murder, but though everyone knows that, they don't end up getting properly punished. But then *Monkey Grip* is all about muddle as well. You could say *Monkey Grip* and *The First Stone* are about how muddled the causes of things are, and *Monkey Grip* and *Joe Cinque* are all about how muddled the outcomes of things are.'

'So all these books are about unknowability, you think?' said L.

'I suppose so, though in *The Children's Bach* Athena seems to end up knowing something; I guess that's unknowability in a negative sense. *Joe Cinque* would have the most, and *The Children's Bach* the least.'

'On the whole, then,' said L, 'the more Helen Garner writes, the less she knows — is that it?'

'I suppose that as she goes on she gets to know more about herself,' I replied, 'and perhaps as a result she is more conscious of how little she knows about the "something something deep down things", as Hopkins puts it.'

'That Hopkins certainly had a way with words,' said L.

'Many people have thought so,' I said, 'but however that may be, it is time for us to leave these topics and turn our minds to *Big Brother Live Evictions.*'

'I hope you've voted,' said L. 'I do think it's important to send a signal about what you think of their behaviour. It's a bit much when girls not much older than Poppy are taking their clothes off on national television.'

'Speaking in general,' I said, 'you would do well to bear in mind whose daughter Poppy is, and then ask yourself what the mothers of these other girls may be like. In particular, however, I must say that Poppy has never shown the slightest inclination towards ecdysiasm – quite the reverse, if anything. But fascinating as this topic is,' I continued, 'I must dash out now to get our rice on the go, and make sure the dinner is properly warmed through.'

'I saw what you were making,' said L. 'I do so love that kofta curry – specially with the garasamolata you put in it. Or is that the Greek fish stuff?'

'Something like that,' I replied, and went out to the kitchen.

*

L and I had enjoyed our curry, and finished our analysis of the reasons for the latest *Big Brother* eviction. Then L said: 'Is there anything else on?' She knew that by 'anything' I would understand any show about doctors, lawyers, police or airports, or any film starring Julia Roberts.

'Nothing that you'd want to watch.' I was rather hoping for some cricket, but cricket with L is a very sometime taste.

'Will you let me see *The Guide?*'

L is always anxious that my own taste might be leading me to try and conceal from her that another re-run of *Runaway Bride* is just about to start – and I won't deny that I could be guilty of such impulses – but tonight even she had to admit that the television was barren.

'Well, let's watch Poppy's video,' she said, opening her face and letting her eyes sparkle in that faux-enthusiastic way she has.

'I will watch it without prejudice,' I replied, 'but nothing I do or say is to be construed as an agreement to help Poppy with her school assignment in any way.'

'That is very ungenerous of you,' said L. 'People who are fortunate enough to have gifts such as yours have a duty to help others.'

'Whatever you reckon,' I replied. L's response was to purse her lips with just a little distaste as she put the cassette into the machine.

First of all there were titles, on a mostly black background, generically, if not perhaps genetically, related to the homepage of *Buffy the Vampire Slayer*. Luridly coloured letters in Poppy's now familiar style moved around, assembling and re-assembling to spell out the title sequences. The whole was set to a driving heavy metal beat from a source I didn't recognize, but the synchronization of the letters' movement with the music bore witness to virtually unlimited quantities of ingenuity misapplied to it on somebody's part. From these preliminaries we gathered that the presentation was to be about the tarot.

Next we saw a spinning disc, which slowed down as if, its race now done, it was passing the baton to its descendants, while smaller discs in four of its segments began to spin in turn.

'This looks like a dramatization of some of the wilder parts of Ezekiel,' I said to L. 'You did say, didn't you, that Poppy had been to a high school – not one of those jumped-up holy roller academies?'

'Just sit down and watch,' said L. 'I think it's very clever.'

By this time the smaller discs had settled, and one saw that in their non-rotating form they were not discs at all, but four symbols.

'Aha,' I said, 'Reading clockwise, if I am not mistaken, we have sceptres, swords, cups and pentacles.'

'And?' said L.

'They are the four suits of the tarot pack. Ancestral to our modern suits. Each has its own particular virtue. Sceptres, for example, stand for civil rule and organization.' Here I stopped, not because I didn't have more to say, but because a particular thought had just struck me.

'In fact, I do believe,' I said to L, 'that the categories we have here are the very same as the yin and yang categories that Dave set up.'

'You've lost me,' said L. 'I know that thing on the Korean flag, but how do you get to the tarot from there?'

'The yang,' I began to explain, 'is often considered the cosmic male principle.'

'This wasn't made up by a man, by any chance?' said L. 'Taking masculinity and calling it a cosmic principle?'

'Had you waited rather than interrupting,' I replied, 'I was about to explain that the basic meanings of yang and yin are usually taken to be light and shade respectively, and that the association with masculine and feminine is a secondary cultural phenomenon. Now Dave, for reasons which we needn't go into,' I continued, 'associates certain kinds of image and certain sorts of words with the daylight hours, and for that reason he calls those images and words yang items, while the words and images associated with the night hours he calls yin. That's all: it's just a convenient classification. We don't have to argue about what it's based on.'

'I'm with you so far,' said L.

'With his daylight hours,' I resumed, 'Dave finds the sector from dawn to midday goes with all kinds of lofty sentiment – ideas like nation-building, glory, you name it – while the sector from midday to dusk is associated with strife and physical exertion. Now it seems to me,' I said, 'that the sceptre would be an appropriate symbol for the first of these sectors, and the sword for the second.'

'Skiting and fighting, in other words,' said L. 'Perhaps the idea that this is the male principle has something to be said for it.'

'*Mock on, mock on, Voltaire, Rousseau*,' I replied. 'And now you will appreciate why I associate the cup with the evening, which is the time for home and rest and relaxation, and the pentacle with the dead of night, the time of mystery. Or alternatively, you could say the four sectors were Ray, Alby, Janet and Maxine respectively.'

'Don't start on those people again,' said L. 'They mess with my head, as the *Big Brother* housemates say.'

'Perhaps you'd prefer me to call them mind, strength, heart and soul,' I said, 'or use Jung's terms: thinking, sensation, feeling and intuition. Though Jung cross-classifies them of course, in a way we wouldn't necessarily want to: thinking and feeling are grouped together as rational functions, while sensation and intuition are non-rational.'

'Wait a minute,' said L, 'you gave the men's names, Ray and Alby, to the thinking and sensation types – the ones you say Dave calls yang – but you told me that in the books the men play the rational roles

– Ray and Janet. So do you want yang, or do you want rational? Or are names classified one way and people the other?'

'Well from Dave's point of view, the black suits are yang,' I mused, my mind still on the tarot and its derivatives, 'while the rational would be hearts and clubs – the ones that are red and major or non-red and non-major.'

'Stop trying to confuse me with analogies,' said L. 'It seems clear enough to me. Weren't you saying earlier on that the books you were looking at could be placed on a sort of scale of muddle?'

'That is so.'

'And *The Children's Bach* was at one end, with the issues seeming reasonably clear, and *Joe Cinque's Consolation* was at the other.'

'Indeed.'

'Now I put it to you,' said L, her deep study of legal shows having given her a mastery of the techniques of cross-examination, 'I put it to you that in your own terms *The Children's Bach* is a fictional Alby-focused text, and that in your terms again, Alby stands for the unthinking man – the man of action.'

'It would be futile to deny it.'

'And I'd remind you that you were playing around with the terms real and conceptual and structural before, when we were talking about *The First Stone*. Why don't you just take the first two terms and do away with the structural? Then if I was to say that the real was the most mysterious category, followed by the conceptual, wouldn't that square with the way you've arranged the texts in order of the problems of understanding that they raise? You would begin with *The Children's Bach*, which is fictional and non-conceptual – that's Alby; then you would have *Monkey Grip:* fictional and conceptual – Maxine; then *The First Stone:* factual and non-conceptual – Janet; and finally *Joe Cinque.*'

'That would certainly fit.'

'The Crown rests, then,' said L, 'and speaking of rest, I've had enough of Poppy's video, clever though it may be. It's really not the sort of thing I enjoy. I think I'll have some hot milk and get to bed early. But I think you'll find that I've synthesized everything you've been struggling with.'

'You're certainly not just a pretty face, are you?' I said.

'You're very kind,' said L, 'but if I don't get to bed soon there will be too many people tomorrow thinking I'm not even a pretty face. All this planning for the school has taken a lot out of me.'

'Goodnight then, darling,' I said, 'and thankyou very much. You have given me a lot to think about.'

L was just like Sir Percival's sister, I thought – one of those maidens, or damsels, if there is a difference, that appear out of nowhere and tell knights all about the Holy Grail when the knights themselves have spent years looking for it and still haven't got a clue. I pictured her, Percival's sister that is, as a tall thin girl with long red hair and that kind of skin that looks blue because it's so incredibly fair you can see all the veins showing through. Her hair wouldn't be all bushed out, though, like that picture of the Lady of Shalott* – I think it would be very smooth on the top of her head and caught into one of those medieval ponytails that have ribbon threaded through them somehow. 'The Lady of Shalott', by the way, while a ridiculous name, is very typical of Tennyson. He's such a risk-taker of a poet, always trying to see what you will let him get away with. I wouldn't be surprised if when he recited *The Charge of the Light Brigade* he said 'volleyed and chundered,' just to see if anyone in the audience would notice.

Left to myself, I now rewound the tape and looked again at Poppy's video, in particular the part which had been playing in the background during our conversation, for naturally enough, neither of us had it given much attention. I saw a tower rising and falling as it swept around the periphery of the circle, for all the world like a Mexican wave at Aussie Stadium. I saw images of the trumps – the hanged man repeated from Dave's presentation, and others in the manga mode – and I saw these images take their place in the circle and rotate around and among each other there. I saw them stretch out their hands to one another, and the disc resolve itself into a pattern of a myriad interlaced hands like a fantastical snowflake, and I saw this vanish in a puff of smoke. I thought to myself, it's not only your face that you like to hide, Poppy — you are a girl of hidden depths; I didn't know that anyone read Charles Williams these days.* Are you on Dave's bike, Poppy, I asked myself, or is Dave on yours? Certainly, it looked as if Poppy would realise the futility of Dave's project, even if she had been complicit in getting her mother to finance it.

That's the trouble with reality, I thought, it's always asking you to take a punt. I had told L that *Monkey Grip* wasn't as unclear a text as *Joe Cinque*, but that was on the grounds that it was fiction. It was easy to say what you would have done if you had been the fictional Nora, but what if, as people said, the book was a *roman à clef?* What if you were the real Nora? Would you have done any better? On which note, in due course, I took myself to bed.

8

U neg — false hero or villain pardoned*

It was a bright morning — that is, as bright as a winter morning can be at about 6.30 — when I got up. The sky glimpsed from the kitchen window was paling to a bluish grey, and it wasn't too long till the sun, still below the horizon, had painted a gilded blush on the terracotta of some neighbouring chimney pots. I made porridge. By the time L joined me, it should be at Baby-Bear temperature. Then I collected the paper and brewed myself some coffee.

'You are a darling,' said L as I put the porridge in front of her, but she waved away the proffered paper.

'Thankyou,' she said, 'but I'm in a bit of a rush this morning. You enjoy the paper — I'll read it when I get home.'

'Just spare me a moment,' I replied, 'and confirm something that arose out of our discussions of last night. You suggested a meaning-space, I seem to recall, with two co-ordinates: the real against the non-real and the conceptual against the non-conceptual.'

'It was all off the top of my head,' replied L, 'so if you're going to turn it against me in some way I don't see that I can be bound by it.'

'Paranoia may be an ugly word,' I said, 'but it's an ugly thing — particularly in a person whose husband has got out of bed before dawn on a 12 degree morning just to ensure no whim of hers remains unsatisfied.'

'I'm an ungrateful wretch,' said L happily, 'but what was it you wanted to ask?'

'Just this,' I replied. 'We also established that this was a vector space, with a gradation from clarity to muddle, or from muddle to clarity, whichever you like — but that's the question: which is the preferred direction?'

'I can only say the answer's in front of you,' said L.

'What do you mean?'

'In the newspaper: *dog bites man* isn't news, is it?' said L. 'And it's not a narrative either. You have to move from the known to the unknown.'

'Hang on a minute,' I said. 'I see in this paper that Shane Warne is involved in some new sleaze scandal. What's unexpected about that?'

'I wasn't speaking about the actual newspaper,' said L. 'The real newspaper, as you would want to call it, would only print a story when Shane Warne wasn't sending lewd text messages.' And with that she said goodbye, leaving me to ponder her words on narrative order.

L's suggestions of the night before had certainly been plausible, but they weren't really satisfying. Dave's clock went round in a circle, the way a clock ought to do, but L had taken the same elements and arranged them in a figure 8. And then there was the question of *Cosmo Cosmolino*. If you were to take it that Ray makes claims on Alby, that would complete a circle much like Dave's. For Maxine always makes claims on Ray, Alby always makes claims on Janet, Janet pays the supreme price, while Maxine takes from all the others in the end. *Das ewig weibliches* etc.

And then there were the rabbits. If *Monkey Grip* was Maxine and *The Children's Bach* was Alby, the growth from baby to mature rabbit would run parallel to an increase in perspicuity, whereas the step from no rabbit at all in *The First Stone* to rabbit's egg in *Joe Cinque* seemed to move in the opposite direction to the texts. Clarity-wise. It was all very puzzling.

While I had decided to spend some time today making pasta, it would be tagliatelle probably, not *ravioli di coniglio* – I'd leave them to Mrs Cinque. Rabbit as a meat has never inspired me with much enthusiasm. I put it in the same sort of category as venison and hazelnuts: if they were edible, why wouldn't people have made a bigger thing of them over the years? The market may be imperfect, but would you go to the trouble to domesticate large animals like cattle with horns that can rip you to pieces when every little patch of scrub was full of deer? If deer was any good, that is? I think not. I'd be willing to bet that Robin Hood wouldn't have been so keen on poaching the king's deer if he could have afforded a few cows. And the same goes for kangaroos. I thoroughly enjoy a bit of kangaroo myself, but if 200 years of familiarity haven't taught Australians to like it, there must be something it doesn't have going for it. Some Aboriginal friends once told me they were off to hunt kangaroo. 'Kangaroo with horns', one of them put in, and everyone collapsed with laughter at the thought of liberating a meal from a nearby cattle property. And it wasn't as if there weren't plenty of kangaroos around. Who says aboriginal culture hasn't changed in 40,000 years? Say what you like about indigenous Australians, they're not silly.

My next step, you are probably thinking, would be to take the pasta machine out of the kitchen cupboard. Well, you'd be wrong; I don't have a pasta machine. The once or twice that I've used one, the result has been less than impressive, so I think I'm better off to hand over to my inner Umbrian peasant, and let him do it the old-fashioned way. Neither L nor I, as a matter of fact, are very at home with machines of any kind. Every so often Gracie comes over and shows us all over again how to work the video, and we just struggle along in between times.

No doubt you have watched pasta being made by Jamie Oliver and people like that. They construct a caldera of flour on their wide and spotlessly clean kitchen bench, and they break eggs and drizzle oil into the middle of it and work it all together with a spatula, keeping up a flow of chatter to the cameras at the same time. This is not my way. For a start, my kitchen is much less well-equipped. I begin in a bowl, and then transfer the dough to my probably not-too-clean kitchen table, which I have covered with fresh plastic. I suppose I could have employed some local *contadina* to scrub the table clean in the Umbrian fashion, but that wouldn't have eliminated gaps between the boards which would stump even the most rosy-cheeked of kitchen girls. The plastic, though, covered them all nicely, and if using new plastic seems an extravagance, bear in mind that we have a huge roll of the stuff, printed with little reindeer. It was left over from a Christmas-time promotion L was involved in some years ago, so the plastic essentially comes free. If you are making pasta, you will have to make equivalent arrangements of your own. Unless you'd like to come over here and get some plastic, that is.

The idea is to keep rolling out the dough until you can see the reindeer through it. Or the grain of your kitchen table, as the case may be. But it occurred to me, as I had extended my original compact lump into a wide flat circle, that the reindeer are still there whether you can see them or not. In the clarity of the afternoon light, as L had expounded it, you may think you can see the 10,000 things, and you may docket them and ticket them into a myriad fictive categories, but step outside your real door in deepest Maxine and see how long it takes before you fall over the gutter. The meaning of the real and the conceptual and the yin is like Poppy wants you to think her — brooding, dark, inaccessible, but with lots inside. It reminded me of an Arthur Machen* story I read in my youth, about a man who wanted to explore the continent you couldn't see because Africa was on top of it.

By now I had reduced the dough to a uniform Albyness, so I cut it into tagliatelle and hung the strands to dry over an old wooden clothes horse we keep in the laundry. Don't use string, or the pasta will cut itself under its own weight and you will end up with an unredeemable lump of dough lying on the floor. Perhaps the clothes horse wasn't quite as pristine as it might have been, but the pasta, after all, would be going into boiling water, so you couldn't be too fastidious. At this point the phone began to ring.

The first to call was Erna. '*Fairy*,' I heard her raucous voice bark into the answering machine, so I picked up the phone.

'Hello, Erna.'

'It's on for tomorrow,' she said. 'The word has just come through that Rita van Tromp will be making a public appearance at Santa Sophia School at 11 tomorrow morning, and Angry Penguins will be confronting her. I expect I can count on you?'

'One penguin suit at your service,' I said, using a form of words I judged suitably equivocal.

'We'll take them in over our arms like raincoats,' said Erna. 'That way we have the element of surprise. Then at my signal we strike.'

'So what are we supposed to do?' I asked.

'It will be quite clear,' said Erna. 'Just follow my lead and do what I do.'

'Won't the suits look a bit obvious over our arms?' I asked. 'After all, who ever heard of a raincoat with a penguin head and big rubber flippers?'

'You're not getting cold feet are you?' said Erna. 'Don't worry, no one will notice. All the attention will be on the people chanting and waving placards.'

'Whatever you say, Erna,' I replied.

'See you tomorrow then,' said Erna, and hung up.

It was obviously going to be necessary to make quick contact with Dave. What if he were in Murwillumbah or somewhere, I wondered, or lounging beneath the shadow of the Big Prawn? But I needn't have worried.

'Dave here,' was the response when I dialled Poppy's number.

'Where are you, Dave?' I asked.

'I'm round at Rita's, mate; where did you think I'd be?'

'I thought you were going up the coast.'

'We did, but we only went to Gosford, mate. We were back last night.'

'That's good news, Dave,' I said, 'because I wanted to ask you to do something for me.'

'Well, I reckon I owe you one, mate,' said Dave.

How good it was to hear those words again, to be assured that the weight of the penguin suit was to be borne by shoulders other than mine! Not that there was anything inadequate about my own shoulders, you understand — it was just that while I was willing for the demonstration to go ahead I was quite keen for it to do so without embarrassing either L or myself.

'There's a demo on tomorrow,' I said.

'Yeah, I know about it, mate,' said Dave.

'The thing is, I was wondering if I could ask you to wear a penguin suit for me, Dave.'

'Sure thing, mate,' said Dave. 'I'll drop round and pick it up. Lucky for me actually that you called, because I promised someone I'd be there, mate, but I don't want to get Rita offside. And now she'll never know me in the suit. It's a win-win, mate.'

'See you later, then, Dave,' I said, but then, recollecting myself, I added, 'By the way, Dave, tell Poppy I was really impressed with that video.'

'I reckon she'll be pleased, mate,' said Dave. 'Poppy's heavily into fantasy.'

More heavily than you know, Dave, I thought to myself as I put down the receiver. Who is milking Rita of funds on Dave's behalf and organising him to demonstrate against Rita at the same time? *A quoi bon?*, and if it came to that, *cherchez la femme!*

But that was not my concern; at least I had invoked the sacred code of mateship, and it had not failed me. One up to the *Bulletin* bards!

All the time I had been talking to Dave the phone had been making that sort of dut-dut-dutting noise that tells you someone else is trying to ring. I hadn't done anything about it, if only because I could never remember how. In fact, we would have disconnected the facility entirely, if either L or I had been able to follow the instructions. Now, it seemed, the frustrated caller was trying again. The phone rang. I would have let it go to the answering machine, but I reflected that it might not be a third party at all, but Dave wanting to change his mind, and I didn't want that to happen without knowing about it.

'Hello?' I said tentatively.

'Hello, Prof,' said the caller. I recognised the voice of Detective Fergus C.

'Hello, Fergus,' I said. 'Before you go any further, you know I've retired, don't you?'

'For sure, Prof,' said Fergus. 'No, the thing is, I just wanted to warn you about that bloke you were with the other day.'

'You mean Dave?' I said.

'Big bloke with a ponytail,' said Fergus, 'that's the one. No, we were just double-checking his record, you know, and you wouldn't think it to look at him, but he's been charged a couple of times with computer fraud.'

'And convicted?' I asked.

'No Prof,' said Fergus. 'It was women. Wouldn't give evidence. But you know what goes on as well as I do.'

I did indeed. People who come under the notice of the police have generally done something, even if it's not what they're charged with. But so long as we aim for perfect justice, it seems to me, rough justice is an outcome we can be pretty pleased about.

'What do you want me to do?' I asked, hoping sincerely that Dave's outing in the suit was not going to be compromised.

'Just don't lend him any money, Prof,' said Fergus. 'We'll be keeping an eye on him.'

My feelings after this conversation were mixed. On the one hand I was not unwilling that Rita should be defrauded, if only as a delayed vengeance on behalf of the colleague she had pestered — sexually harassed, indeed — on that long-past occasion. On the other hand, I thought a bit of police surveillance could only be a good thing in Poppy's interests, even if it meant frustrating Dave's designs on Rita. Or in Dave's interests, for that matter, given that I was beginning to suspect Poppy of Maxine-like tendencies. Reality was indeed a problematical thing. But my day of phone calls was not yet over. This time I did let it go to the answering machine, but picked up the phone as soon as I heard L's voice.

'Hello, darling,' I said.

'Hello, love; I just wanted to tell you not to make any arrangements for tomorrow. Poppy is going to be admitted to Santa Sophia, and Rita will be presenting a big cheque to the school for their appeal.'

'What appeal is that?' I asked.

'Don't be silly,' said L. 'Schools always have an appeal. And it's going to be happening at eleven o'clock.'

'I know,' I said.

'What do you mean, you know?' asked L. 'We didn't fix it up

more than half an hour ago.'

'Word gets around,' I said. 'But what on earth does it have to do with me? You're not asking me to join a demonstration are you?'

'Of course not,' said L. 'I'd be mortified if you were to dream of doing any such thing. But Gracie will be bringing Billy, and I thought it would be nice if you gave her a hand.'

'Of course it's always a pleasure to do anything for Gracie,' I said, 'but I'm afraid you've lost me. Why is Gracie going to be there — she isn't a Santa Sophia old girl? And why is she bringing Billy?'

'Santa Sophia is planning to establish a co-ed pre-school for littlies,' said L. 'I mentioned it to Gracie, and she was very interested, because of wanting to encourage Billy's feminine side, you know. And this is the first chance for her to have a bit of a look round.'

'If it is your wish,' I replied, 'nothing would please me more.'

But that was not quite the last phone call of the series. That came as I was out on the terrace a little later, enjoying the winter sunshine and appreciating the tracery of the frangipani against the afternoon sky. They were certainly not twigs, I thought, but branches didn't seem quite the right word either for the terminal elements of the tree. Could bracts be the word, or was that something else? Even in the afternoon light reality was hard to pin down. Not as hard to pin down, however, as the significance of the message which this time sounded from the machine.

'Hi,' it said, 'this is Bronwen from DoCS. We are trying to get in touch with the grandparents of a little girl called Billie. If you'd like to give me a call, my number is — ' at which point she gabbled something that submerged into a lot of static. Have you noticed the way people do that? They reach the one important part of the message, and then drop their voices and talk so fast that you can never work out what they're saying. My general conclusion is that if it's really important, they'll ring again, so I didn't feel any action was required. Contemplation of the import of the message, in any case, was abbreviated by the noisy arrival of Dave. I carried the suit out to the footpath, and explained Erna's plan.

'It's a beauty, mate, isn't it?' he said. 'I can easy fit it in the saddlebag.' He pushed the folded suit into the bag that was not full of chain. The flippers took a bit of pushing to get them in before the lid would shut, but Dave managed it after some effort.

'I should tell you, Dave, as mate to mate,' I said, 'I had a call from the cops. They seemed to think they ought to warn me about you.'

'No kidding?' said Dave. 'What did they reckon I was going to do to you?'

'They seemed keen for me not to lend you any money.'

'As if I would bludge off a mate!' said Dave. 'Well, see you tomorrow, I guess. Are you going to be there?'

'As it happens,' I replied, 'yes. I'll be keeping an eye on Billy.'

'Good kid, that,' said Dave. 'Well, I'll keep close till the action happens, and if Rita spots me she'll think I'm with you. See you then, mate.' And Dave departed.

That evening, I played the enigmatic phone message to L.

'Bronwen who?' she said. 'That's so annoying, the way people don't tell you their surnames these days. And the familiar way she said "Hi". If that woman imagines we have the time to trace round the whole of DoCS looking for a Bronwen when she can't even say her telephone number clearly, she's picked the wrong grandparents.'

'So you don't think we should worry Gracie about it?' I asked.

'Gracie has far too much of her own to think about,' said L. 'And if anyone's going to get into trouble over all that nonsense it will be you, not Gracie.'

'I seem to recall that you had some hand in it,' I said.

'No, I don't think so,' said L. 'I can't really remember — it's so long ago. I'm just looking forward to having some lovely meal you've made, and finding out whatever is going to happen in *Big Brother Live Nominations*.'

'Why?' I said. 'Is there someone you want to evict?'

'I just want to see what the impact of yesterday's eviction has been.'

'You admit now to following *Big Brother*?' I asked.

'Vice is a monster of so frightful mien,
As, to be hated, needs but to be seen;
Yet seen too oft, familiar with her face,
We first endure, then pity, then embrace.'

'I wouldn't say that I embrace,' said L, 'but it's interesting to keep an eye on what's happening.'

*

'This is going to be quite a big day for Santa Sophia,' said L the next morning. What with one thing and another, it was a while since I had started a new batch of sourdough going, so I was chewing on a commercial product. Though quite tasty, it didn't have the same kaleidoscope of breakfast-time flavours you get from the wild yeasts and ferments that float around your own kitchen.

'How so?' I said.

'Rita has promised a really staggering donation,' said L, 'and she'll be handing it over as soon as Poppy is admitted. Confidentially,' she continued, 'the school could do with a bit of a transfusion right now. The new headmistress has upset a lot of parents, and I hate to say it, but girls have been going "elsewhere".'

As you probably know, there is another girls' school quite close by, so the word 'elsewhere' had a special resonance to it.

'I suppose you know there's going to be an Angry Penguins demonstration,' I said. 'That's what the penguin suit was about.'

'Oh no!' said L. 'And you promised Erna, too.'

'Don't worry,' I replied. 'Honour has been satisfied; I will be able to give my full attention to Gracie and Billy. I did rather look forward to impersonating a penguin — and that I should do so at all, I would like to point out, was your idea — but I have hurled that torch from me, and it is to be carried forward by others.'

'I expect there will just be a few demonstrators around the gates,' said L, and if she was happy to think that, it was not my place to disabuse her; I turned the conversation to other things.

L left soon after, having issued my final instructions.

'I told Gracie to meet you at the gates at half past ten,' she said. 'You can mind Billy while she has a bit of a prowl around the school. Naturally she wants to get the feel of the place for herself when she is thinking of sending Billy there.'

'I will be in my position at the appointed hour,' I said. 'We meet at Philippi.'

*

In the event, I arrived at Santa Sophia with about quarter of an hour to spare. Quite a few nicely dressed mothers passed me as I made my way slowly along the street, and the odd father, too, successful enough to be able to excuse himself from the world of the learned or at least mercenary professions to attend a function at his daughter's school. There was a tall, off-white, cement-rendered wall with wrought iron gates, and to one side a well-grown loquat tree overhanging the entrance. I took up my position here, and waited for Gracie. Soon she appeared, Billy in a white lambswool jumper tugging at her hand. It didn't seem she gave much heed in dressing him to the possibility of dirt, but having been a sensible, well-ordered child herself, I supposed she would have no mental vision of her little boy being allowed to crawl round the floor of a pub.

'We're attending the function at 11 o'clock,' I said to the smartly dressed prefect at the gate. I could tell she was a prefect, because in addition to the jacket and tie in camouflage pattern worn by all the girls in accordance with the school's military theme, she had a peaked khaki cap, and flashes of rank on her shoulder straps. She gave us a programme. Gracie and I stood by the gate for a moment studying this, and some old girls – distinguishable by wearing the same tie as the prefect – passed in front of us. Though my attention was on Billy for the moment, I had the distinct impression that more than one of these might have had something draped over her arm that didn't look very much like a raincoat, but by the time I looked for them they were gone. In any case I was distracted by what had to be the approach of Dave. The bike came to a halt at the gates, and I heard Dave say to the prefect: 'I'm with Mrs van Tromp's party.'

'Ra-ra man, ra-ra man,' screamed Billy ecstatically.

Gracie shot me a suspicious glance, but the moment passed, for Dave glided past us, smoothly navigating his powerful mount between the pedestrians as he made for the new library.

This was to be the site of the festivities, it appeared. The older buildings of the school were in a style you could have described as Spanish Mission re-imagined by Leslie Wilkinson. They had a sort of stuccoed grace to them, in other words, and there were arcaded galleries on the side that faced the sun, and tiled walkways underfoot: altogether, I thought, had my life been otherwise, it would have been rather a nice place to go to school.

The new library was at first floor level over what had once been open space between two older buildings. Apparently council regulations decreed no more of the site could be used, or perhaps it was that the school had been naturally unwilling to encroach on its tennis courts or hockey field, and so this airspace had been coopted for the library. Some people might feel it not in keeping with the older part of the school, but I thought that if you granted an underlying Spanish theme, wasn't there a bit of wildness in the spirit of a nation that could accommodate Gaudi's Sagrada Familia and Gehry's Bilbao Museum? If the library stalked the playground on insect-like legs, didn't Dali's elephants do the same?

We reached the library just as Dave was finishing chaining the bike to one of the building's supports.

'G'day, mate,' he said. 'Can't be too careful with the bike in a place like this. G'day Billy.'

'Hello, Dave,' I replied. 'Gracie, this is Dave. Billy will probably remember that Dave called in that day when I was looking after him.'

'Ra-ra man,' said Billy again.

'Top kid, that,' said Dave, which, as any compliment to a parent will do, was enough to dissolve Gracie's suspicions almost completely.

'Thankyou, Dave,' said Gracie. 'Now perhaps you will be good enough to look after Billy for a little while, Dad, and I will have a bit of a poke around the school.'

'We'll take him with us,' I said. Dave was rummaging around in the saddlebag, trying to get the suit out without attracting too much attention. 'Just stay close by my side, Dave,' I said, as Gracie slipped away through the crowd, 'and with any luck no one will see anything.' We made our way upstairs and took up a position near the back of the room. I fancied for a moment I could hear a faint shouting that might have been 'What do we want? Penguins!', but the chanting, placard-waving crowds of Erna's imagination seemed to have left their run a little late. After all, it was the middle of Tuesday morning: most penguins, however angry, would have to have been at work. My attention wandering, I began to look around the room, now well-filled. On the other side, much nearer the front, were two figures in old girls' attire, doing their best to conceal what other eyes than mine would probably not have recognised as penguin suits. One of them had that distinctive sub-Meg Ryan haircut. In fact, they were none other than Elisabeth and Vicki, or Lili and Vovo as I was now inclined to call them in deference to their putative Gallic origins. It didn't surprise me that they would be mixed up in this affair – for the French, I reflected, are a devious race of people. I mean, what can you say about a nation that has the collective hide to refer to sour cream as *crème fraîche?* If the pair of them hid behind a spiral staircase you probably wouldn't see a thing.

And then, idly picturing the lithe figures of the two young women disposing themselves in the sinuous fashion such concealment would demand, I suddenly thought I saw the whole thing: the key to the Helen Garner business. The two sisters had launched me on this quest; now, thanks to them, I had the last piece of the puzzle. It was with the satisfaction of a Kekulé* that I turned my attention back to the proceedings.

The headmistress was taking her place at the front. She too wore a military style jacket, but hers, no doubt tailored to her own design, had gold epaulettes, braid around the cuffs, and rows of embroidered roundels on the left side where military medals would have been. Seen at a distance, they resembled the badges that Boy Scouts and Girl Guides used to win – or perhaps they still do. It's a long time since I've seen a Scout or Guide, and I'm not sure whether they still exist or not. Topping off the outfit was a khaki peaked cap with the school badge on the front. Caps apparently, though not usually worn, were part of the dress uniform for girls and mistresses alike.

The proceedings got under way. At girls' schools nothing of an official nature is ever allowed to happen unless preceded, and preferably also followed, by an item from the choir, string group, recorder consort or jazz ballet ensemble, and the programme of today's events made it clear that we were to be spared nothing. First we had the school song accompanied by a junior girl on the piano, and if the audience were a bit inclined to mumble through the verse, the animated shouts of *Feminari! Militare!* left nothing to be desired. Then there were announcements, read by the mistress MC'ing the proceedings, an older woman with rather untidy hair. Just at the close of these, a younger woman came forward and passed a folded piece of paper to the MC, who unfolded it, looked serious, and then bent over the microphone as if wishing to shield her words from unfriendly ears.

'I have just been handed a rather serious message,' she said, 'from an officer of the Department of Community Services who is at present conducting a search of the school premises. The Department is anxious to locate a child called Billie, who is believed to be at risk. If anyone knows the whereabouts of this child, please inform a prefect; she will pass the information on through the proper channels. The child may be severely disturbed, and the Department would like me to stress that no one should approach the child on their own initiative. I repeat, do not approach this child.'

Dave gave me a speculative glance.

'What do you reckon, mate?' he said. 'Might as well get the kid out of harm's way,' with which words he gathered Billy up and zipped him inside his jacket as before. Billy, no doubt looking forward to another ride on the bike, seemed happy enough.

Items came and went. Then Poppy appeared at the front, looking unwontedly schoolgirl-like, and the MC woman announced her.

'Headmistress,' she said, 'I present to you Poppy van Tromp for enrolment in this company of those who would contend to exalt their brains, proclaim their femininity, and vindicate the rights of women throughout the world.'

'Private van Tromp,' said the headmistress, 'I hereby admit you to this sisterhood,' and she placed a cap on Poppy's head and handed her a laptop got up to look like a haversack in a khaki carry-case.

'*Feminare!*' shouted the audience, or those of them at least who knew the protocol, '*Non cerebra in grallis!*'

Then Poppy retreated to a place in the front row while a group of girls sang a madrigal *a capella.* If the proceedings could be said to have a high point, it seemed we had now passed it. The MC took the microphone again.

'Headmistress, distinguished guests, parents and girls,' she said, 'I would ask you to join me in giving the traditional school welcome to Ms Rita van Tromp.'

The headmistress stood up, the audience applauded, and a girl down the front led a group of others who bent over and slapped one fist into the other open palm to the repeated warcry of '*Feminari, one, two, three!*' Rita came to the front; the headmistress made a long but trite speech of welcome.

Rita's response was to take the microphone, make a few remarks about her admiration for the headmistress and the ideals of the school more generally, and express her desire to show her appreciation of these ideals in the most practical way possible. She stepped back then with a theatrical gesture. Two prefects who had been standing in the wings now came forward, carrying between them one of those stage cheques about the size of a beachtowel that are beloved of local newspapers. So many cameras went off all around, it almost looked as if the audience had been equipped with sparklers. A group of lumpy post-pubescent girls in leotards began to file in – a jazz ballet presentation in honour of Rita's gift clearly imminent.

And then in the twinkling of an eye, as the apostle puts it, all was changed. From the top of the stairs where we had entered the library came a booming cry: 'Penguins before profits!' I would have recognised the voice as Erna's anywhere; turning towards it, like everyone in the room, I saw a tall and bulky penguin, who began to harangue the crowd through a loudhailer. Simultaneously, the MC woman began to speak into a mobile phone; L, I guessed, had passed on news of the demonstration, and some preparations were in place.

'Time to suit up, I reckon, mate,' said Dave in my ear, and put on his own penguin costume. He had to leave the neck unvelcro'd to avoid suffocating Billy, whose head now peeped out incongruously framed in white feathers beneath the penguin's beak. Whatever chimerical beast this figure looked like, it certainly didn't look like Dave; I was glad he was safe from recognition by Rita.

Dave was not the only one suited up. Two rather lithe penguins, who had appeared on the other side of the room nearer the front than we were, came forward at a quick shuffle and attempted to grab at the cheque and manhandle the prefects who were carrying it out of the way. The headmistress joined the tussle for one end of the cheque, the MC grabbed for the other. 'Penguins!' called the intruders, 'Santa Sophia' the others. Various of the audience, some of them clearly Angry Penguin infiltrators, committed themselves to the fight. I thought I recognised a few old libertarians from the funeral. Erna continued to rant. A siren was heard.

'It's the cops, mate – I'm out of here,' said Dave, and showing a remarkable turn of speed for a penguin, pushed towards the head of the stairs. There he unvelcro'd enough of the lower part of the suit to get his legs free and took the stairs at a run, flippers slapping the treads behind him as he descended. I followed – for Dave, after all, had performed no hostile or illegal act, and I didn't want him to get into trouble for nothing. On the other hand, he seemed to have forgotten that he still had Billy zipped up in his jacket and velcro'd into the top of the suit, and Gracie had specifically charged me with looking after the child. Then, from round the corner of one of the older buildings where she had been prospecting, just as Dave reached the bike Gracie herself appeared.

'If you take my baby you take me!' she shrieked, and with more agility than you might have expected of her lawyerly high heels she ran to the now roaring bike and jumped up behind Dave. In the drive a police car came into view. Dave gunned the bike and shot like an arrow past the police, down the drive, through the gates, and disappeared, Gracie with arms and legs wrapped around Dave and Billy like something out of *Twenty Thousand Leagues Under the Sea*.

Then all was still again — or not quite, for of course in his haste to get away Dave had forgotten to undo the chain, prudently locked around one of the architect-designed stilts of the library. As the bike had taken off, the unused length uncoiled from the saddlebag with the speed of a striking cobra. It stretched itself tauter than chain was ever designed to stretch. Resin and carbon fibre nicely calculated to defy Bass Strait were no match for the Harley at full throttle. The whole stilt delaminated and then disintegrated in a burst of black shards, and, as the library and all it contained settled into a corner-heavy slump, the chain, still attached to the bike, whipped around wildly in Dave's wake and disappeared with him to wherever Dave was going.

*

For reasons that I don't care to dwell on, not much speech passed between L and myself during the rest of the day. In the evening I deposited in front of her a plate of yesterday's tagliatelle dressed with a little oil, and shut myself in with the television. SBS was promising an Almodóvar festival: something that would have no attraction for L of any kind, and, if the theme of the day was to be Spanish, Almodóvar's modern baroque might be a good tonic after the Goya-like grotesqueries of the morning.

We met at breakfast.

'Have you got over your bad temper?' asked L.

'Bad temper?' I replied. 'What do you mean? I was naturally irritated that I couldn't find you, and that I had to walk the whole way home from Santa Sophia. You've no idea how far it is when you're walking.'

'You could have taken a bus or a train.'

'I suppose I could have, if I hadn't been so annoyed. Where did you get to?'

'I didn't "get to" anywhere, as you put it,' said L. 'But naturally I had things to do. Then, when I couldn't see you anywhere, I just assumed you'd stormed off in one of your passions, and I came home.'

Honours appearing to be even, it seemed appropriate to resume our accustomed relations.

'That was quite an affair yesterday,' I said, pouring myself a second cup of black coffee. L held out the paper.

'Look at this,' she said. 'You can't buy this sort of publicity.'

I looked at the article she indicated. It was headlined 'Terrorist attack at exclusive girls' school', and went on to give a circumstantial recital of the facts, noted that there had been no serious injury or loss of life, a result for which the old girl architect claimed all the credit, and got most of the people's names wrong. It ended by quoting the deputy headmistress, the MC of the previous day as I now saw from her photo, who said: 'These people hate us because they don't have access to the kind of exclusive education we offer at Santa Sophia.'

'If they were going to blame terrorists,' I said, 'Poppy might as well have worn the burqa as I suggested. It would have given a bit of local colour.'

'I'm sure enrolments will jump,' said L.

'But what about the headmistress; I thought she put people off?'

'Fortunately, that's no longer a factor,' said L. 'The headmistress is taking indefinite leave.'

'Fell down and dislocated an epaulette, I suppose,' I said derisively. 'I'm told that can be quite painful.'

'No need to be heartless,' said L. 'The poor woman has been under stress for a long time, and this was the final straw.'

'A few stilts short of a library, in other words,' I said. 'And is Gracie all right?'

'Gracie was full of thanks to Dave when she realised he'd saved

Billy from DoCS. She went in and saw the department in the afternoon and had that cheeky Bronwen grovelling for mercy. You know what Gracie's like when you get her all worked up.'

'In other words it's a win-win situation all round,' I said, 'and at the same time I have the satisfaction of having sorted out what to think of Helen Garner. I kept on looking at the words she uses as Professor J suggested, and trying to integrate Dave's ideas with what we were talking about before, but thanks to seeing the Lever sisters at the school yesterday, I think I've finally got somewhere. I've jotted a few things down on paper* that you may care to have a look at in due course.'

'Why don't you give me a summary?' said L. 'After all, I seem to have heard it suggested that if a thing can't be summed up in one sentence it can't be summed up.' And with that she stood up, carried her cup to the sink, and began to behave for all the world like a woman full of the most pressing affairs.

'You have spoken wiselier than you purposed,' I replied, 'because the thing about reality is precisely that it can't be summed up. And though I might feed you an offcut, I would suggest that you might regret a sandwich at 11, however tasty, if it spoilt your lunch at 12.'

'It's a rare day that a woman in my position has time for lunch,' said L; 'so bring out the sandwich, maestro, but go easy on the filling.'

'Well if we stick to the books for the moment,' I said, 'I think they are all about the search for understanding, but that our language itself only makes understanding accessible to a certain degree and in a certain order. The closer Garner gets to reality, the more intractable the material becomes. Now we put four of the books in order – and full marks to you for putting me on the right track – but on further reflection I have to say that your formulation, though elegant, wasn't as revealing as it could have been. The key thing was realizing that we needed eight categories at the very least for a proper understanding of those four books.'

'Eight categories for four books?' said L. 'What price reductionism now?'

'It served its purpose,' I said, 'but the time comes for any tool when its edge is dulled and it must be cast aside. So without making too much of it, you could say the books map out a winding path from the fictive to the real,* while the rabbits trace out an antiparallel trajectory.'

'You don't think this is just a lot of mumbo-jumbo?' asked L. 'Just go over "fictive" one more time for me, will you?'

'The more input we have into constructing something, the better we understand it. Something is most clear to us, be it material object or person, when we've embedded it in our own constructed view of the world. But once we've done that, what we're calling reality is just the stage set. And that, by definition, is fictive. We're like Jim Carrey in *The Truman Show*. He believes himself to be an autonomous individual in a world to which he reacts as if it was reality, but his situation is only truly transparent to the external audience watching him.'

'I've never much cared for Jim Carrey,' said L. 'He comes across as a distasteful kind of person.'

'It may just be that he's Canadian,' I said. 'As a race of people, Canadians can be a bit on the distasteful side – you only have to look at *South Park*. Substitute Hugh Grant if you like, though an unwashed British thespian can be distasteful enough in his own way. At any rate, Joe Cinque as played by Hugh Grant may think he is in the real world, but all the time Helen Garner is watching him and we are watching Helen Garner.'

'But Joe Cinque is, or was, in the real world,' said L. 'I'm not sure I'm happy about this fictive business.'

'Yet we only know Joe Cinque,' I said, 'as Helen Garner has imagined him. And the same could be said of ourselves. We can only know, or think we know, anything to the extent that we are characters in someone else's narrative – Joe Cinque or Truman Burbank.'

'And where do we get to in the end?' asked L.

'The source of all meaning,' I said. 'Which is to say life itself – but not individual life as we know it. The eternal unconscious where the first fire burns undiminished, not yet replaced by skill or jaded by repetition as it is in you and me. Real; intuitive; yin; in the shadows. Our narrator, beyond control or comprehension. Any inkling of it our conscious selves obtain has to come independent of our volition through its own emissary: anima, or animus, as it may be. Dante's Beatrice* – or, in Helen Garner's terminology, Maxine.'

'You're not telling me that those poor deluded drug addict girls in *Joe Cinque's Consolation* have something to tell us about ultimate reality?'

'No, not at all; qualities are inverted in the real, so they will be Maxines in name only. I think Jung would say they were inflated with the shadow: "possessed" in the medieval term. But Beatrice embodies the real Maxine. The anima really is the elusive dispenser of meaning – quite separate from the ego, and able to guide it towards understanding. The closest any character gets to being Maxine is Nicole Whatsy in *The First Stone* who dishes out meaning to Colin Shepherd.'

'But that's not how Helen Garner presents the story,' said L.

'No,' I said. 'Which is just the point. In the book we see the situation through the eyes of Helen Garner's persona, who sympathises with Shepherd. Meaning itself doesn't always have to be good, you know; but good or bad, there's always the chance that to us it may seem very unwelcome. Personally,' I added, 'I have always pictured Beatrice as a tall thin girl in a blue linen supper dress, but that's probably just a quirk of my own.'

It is always wise to tread warily where jealousy might be aroused, but I thought I was on safe ground here: L had no possibility of picking up the reference.

'I don't suppose your friend K would have owned a blue linen supper dress, by any chance?' she asked suspiciously.

'Not to my knowledge,' I replied. 'Nor was she a tall thin girl, as far as I can remember, though to be truthful I haven't thought about her for so long that it's hard to be sure.' You don't get to be married as long as I have been if you can't fake sincerity on demand.

'It's the autonomy of this anima/animus figure that worries me a little,' said L. 'That is, if all our conscious experience is mediated by language. Are you trying to sneak intelligent design or something in by the back door? You say there's an observer standing to our experience as we do as readers to Helen Garner's text, or as viewers do to the housemates, in a separate, controlling, reality we have no access to? It reminds me of that hymn that goes

> and behind the dim unknown
> standeth God within the shadow
> keeping watch above his own.'*

'Yes, scary, isn't it,' I said, 'but I didn't write the script. It's all there in the books. You'll understand when you read my extended treatment of the subject.'

L chose to ignore this invitation.

'I wonder what Helen Garner would make of Poppy and Dave?' she said.

'A rattling good yarn, I expect,' I said. 'I can see it as a film starring Pia Miranda and Craig McLachlan. Or if you think Pia Miranda's too old now, perhaps we should go with Emily Browning. It would put the Australian film industry right back on its feet. And whatever you think of those people as actors, I would venture to say their physical cleanliness would be unimpeachable. Until she does write it up though, I'm afraid I'm out of a job. But hey!'

'Don't use that stupid expression,' said L. 'It doesn't become you. But since you mention being out of a job, I had been meaning to tell you I was talking to Sarah Lever the other afternoon; we ran into each other outside Santa Sophia.'

'I'll bet you did,' I replied.

'What do you mean?' asked L. 'You said that in a very snide sort of way.'

'Just that she probably wasn't 100 per cent unconnected with the happenings at the school.'

'Well, whether she was or not, that's ancient history now,' said L. 'She's a charming woman, and it all worked out for the best. Anyway, she told me her younger daughter is floundering a bit at university, so I said you'd be glad to give her a few hints.'

'That would be Vovo.'

'What on earth are you talking about?'

'The daughter. Lili is the elder, and Vovo is the younger. Like the biscuit. Short for Victorine, I imagine.'

'Well you imagine a lot of nonsense,' said L. 'I believe the elder girl is called Sarah-Jane and the younger is Mary-Jane. A bit girly for my taste, perhaps, but not ludicrous, like those names you've dreamt up.'

I looked at her hard for a moment.

'Well, there you go,' I said.

It seemed the only possible response.

Notes

Chapter 1

p. 9   α – the initial situation: Vladimir Propp, *The Morphology of the Folktale*, p. 148. The narrator, dreamer, or 'hero' as Propp would call him, is found at the opening of the tale in a state of (perhaps only apparent) contentment and plenitude.

Boswell's life of Johnson seems to be a favourite text of the Dreamer. References to it will be passed over as too many to enumerate.

p. 11   *Sisters*, I thought: the Dreamer misquotes from *The Children's Bach*, p. 16. Considering he has not yet read the book, misquotation can probably be forgiven.

p. 13   is there a verbal reminiscence here of the passage which describes the departure of Voss and his party from this very spot? And if so, are we to take it as a hint at the illusory nature of the Dreamer's quest?

p. 16   careful tongs: the Dreamer's tendency towards transferred epithet remains strong, despite his earlier strictures.

p. 19   WILPF: the Women's International League for Peace and Freedom – what would once have been called a 'communist front organisation'.

The library received me with a rush of warm air: this sentence again seems to display foreknowledge of *The Children's Bach*.

p. 22   Either Dr Edith V's choice of motto came from proleptic knowledge of *The First Stone* (p. 155), or perhaps Helen Garner, or the woman in her eighties quoted in the passage in question, had the Santa Sophia motto in mind.

p. 24   *cradling the rabbit with my cardigan*: *Monkey Grip* p. 144.

p. 27   traveller's gingerbread: the gingerbread the Dreamer has in mind would be from Alison Uttley, *Recipes from an Old Farmhouse*, London, Faber, 1966.

p. 29   *They reminded her of the ankleboots…*: *The Children's Bach*, p. 72.

Chapter 2

p. 32   A – villainy: Propp, p. 149. The Dreamer is forced into an unwelcome situation.

p. 35   *at last he swallowed some which tied / itself in dreadful knots inside*: from Hilaire Belloc, *Cautionary Tales.*

p. 37   the careful darns in her jumper: *The Children's Bach*, p. 16.

Who sweeps a room, as for Thy laws, / Makes that, and the action, fine: George Herbert (1593-1633), 'Teach me, my God and King'.

p. 43   *The Great Fire*: by Shirley Hazzard (London, Virago, 2003). Perhaps the Dreamer's unduly harsh judgement is coloured by his circumstances at this point.

Barcroft Boake: Australian poet. "His last five months were the gloomiest. He returned home at the end of 1891 to find it a place of grief. His father was practically bankrupt, having lost the last of his money in Melbourne land speculations. Boake contributed his savings, some £50, to cover immediate household expenses. His father sums up the position: 'His grandma was invalided and confined to her bed and his eldest sister had found marriage a failure and was domiciled with me her husband being a helpless creature was dismissed from the Railway Dept., I myself was hopeless about everything and quite unfit to cope with the fiend melancholia that I plainly saw was opressing him'. He mentions a blow that Boake received: 'About this time he received a letter from the country, and in reference to it said to one of his sisters: "I hear that my best girl is going to be married".' A return to the outback might have saved Boake, but he seemed to have lost the capacity to make up his mind about anything. A few attempts to find work in the city proved futile and he sank into brooding inactivity. On 2 May 1892 he left the house. Eight days later his body was discovered in the scrub at Long Bay Middle Harbour, hanging by his stockwhip from a bough." *Australian Dictionary of Biography*, Vol. 3 1851-1890, (Melbourne, MUP, 1969), p. 187. These details seem to give the lie to Dave's belief that Boake was gay – but perhaps Dave was drawing on some other tradition; on the other hand, they present a poignant parallel with the past experience of the Dreamer.

p. 49   *There is little effort to respond…*: C. G. Jung, *Psychological Types*, pp. 176-177.

p. 50   *These ten years, no matter where he travelled…*: *Cosmo Cosmolino*, pp. 184-185.

p. 51   *Soon the old factory…*: *Honi Soit*, 2-6-2004.

p. 53   Dieter Brummer: one time star in the soap opera *Home and Away.* Most memorable line (from when his wife Angel, played by Melissa George, was working as a swimsuit model): "Almost decked a guy for pervin' at her this mornin'."

Diarmid Heydenreich: Dougie, Pizza Hut delivery boy, in a well-loved series of commercials.

p. 54   the word *movie*, used by no less an authority than *The Sydney Morning Herald*: the Dreamer's reference is probably to the issue of 28-9-1929.

Chapter 3

p. 55   D ^{9} – combat with a hostile donor: Propp, p. 151.

p. 62   *They brought her home white-faced and dumb…: Cosmo Cosmolino*, p. 121.

p. 67   Fodor and Katz: Jerry R. Fodor & Jerrold J. Katz, *The Structure of Language: readings in the philosophy of language*, Englewood Cliffs, Prentice-Hall, 1964. Good for a laugh.

p. 68   Grand Wailea Hotel: a circumstantial account of this establishment may be found in *The New Yorker* of 3-1-2005.

p. 69   Chomsky's dichotomy of competence and performance: the Dreamer is no doubt referring to the exposition of these ideas in the opening chapters of Noam Chomsky, *Aspects of the Theory of Syntax*, Cambridge (Mass.), MIT Press, 1965.

Chapter 4

p. 77   E ^{3} – favour to a dead person: Propp, p. 151.

p. 78   Perec (*Life: a User's Manual*) speaks of jigsaws cut in such a way that solving them becomes a contest of skills between the designer and the would-be solver. I know of none such.

p. 87   *some better, broader, freer, less rule-bound* gathering of the tribe…: *The First Stone*, p. 208.

p. 88   The Dreamer seems here to have a premonition of the underlying circumstances of *Joe Cinque's Consolation*.

p. 89   Le Lièvre: in the light of subsequent information, one feels this might itself be a rendering of the Irish O'Hare (see Chapter 6).

p. 91   *I think they felt that Shepherd...: The First Stone,* p. 43.

          Sexual harassment is an abuse of power. The First Stone, p.98.

p. 92   'we are not Ws on stilts': the Dreamer no doubt has in mind Lacan's opinion
          that 'There is no such thing as Woman: Woman with a capital *W* indicating
          the universal.'

Chapter 5

p. 98   G 2 – the hero rides, is carried: Propp, p. 152.

p. 107   *The Bulletin Reciter,* Sydney, Bulletin Newspapers, 1901.

p. 111   Hideaki Anno: creator of the animated series *Neon Genesis Evangelion.*

p. 112   *The fleets are converging...: The Aeneid of Virgil,* tr. C. Day Lewis, London,
          Four Square, 1962, p. 192.

p. 114   The words in the eight major divisions of Dave's sundial/clock are given in
          Appendix 2.

p. 116   Alan Kohler: financial journalist.

          "Those old Roman blokes...': Dave's statement is so compressed as to be
          positively misleading, for in the Northern Hemisphere, of course, the
          shadow on a sundial moves clockwise.

p. 118   This fragment produced by the Dreamer looks as if it comes from Ian
          Mudie.

Chapter 6

p. 120   I 2 – victory or superiority in a contest: Propp, p. 152. Using the magical
          weapon (reductionism) provided by the Donor (Professor J), the Dreamer
          defeats the police, here acting as surrogates for Rita.

Chapter 7

p. 141   KF 2 – the object of a search is pointed out, etc.: Propp, p. 153.

p. 143   Bronislaw: Bronislaw Malinowski. Started the First World War a German and finished it as a Pole, all without leaving the Trobriand Islands. 'The hero is transfigured,' indeed. In the process invented functionalism (or perhaps plagiarized the idea from his Australian mentors).

p. 150   *In the old brown house...*: *Monkey Grip*, p. 1.

           He wanted us to communicate...: *Monkey Grip*, p. 105.

p. 151   *You have to cup a breast in order to squeeze it*: *The First Stone*, p. 28.

p. 152   *I was walking through Martin Place and I said good morning to an old woman who was selling flowers*: *The Children's Bach*, p. 109.

           a hard-faced clerk inspected the ceiling...: *Monkey Grip*, p. 108.

p. 157   *great crocks and tureens of it...*: *Cosmo Cosmolino*, p. 185.

p. 158   *Lewis & Short: A Latin Dictionary, founded on Andrews' edition of Freund's Latin Dictionary, revised, enlarged and in great part rewritten by Charlton T. Lewis, Ph.D. and Charles Short, LL.D.*, Oxford, Clarendon, various printings since 1879.

p. 159   *The food...*: *Joe Cinque's Consolation*, p. 299.

p. 166   The Lady of Shalott: the Dreamer undoubtedly means the picture by J. W. Waterhouse, though whether the woman in the picture has red hair is doubtful. It might be necessary to inspect the original in the Tate.

p. 167   Charles Williams: the reference is to *The Greater Trumps*, London, Faber, 1954 – a tale of a gipsy lawyer, the tarot, and a fantastical orrery. Poppy's presentation appears to be based on a scene from the book.

Chapter 8

p. 168   U neg – false hero or villain pardoned: Propp, p. 154. This chapter could also be considered a second move in the tale, which takes the form of a difficult task (M). Perhaps this would make it easier to explain the premature transfiguration of the hero (T^4) in Chapter 6.

p. 171   Arthur Machen: early 20th century author of stories in the uncanny/horror mode. Among other things, responsible for inventing the Angels of Mons, and for writing the story that provided the idea for Daphne du Maurier's *The Birds*, which in turn...

p. 173   The Dreamer's superficial response here brings to mind Jung's strictures on the thinking type (*Psychological Types*, p. 444).

p. 180   Kekulé: Friedrich August Kekulé, 19th century German chemist – said to have intuited the structure of the benzene ring after having a vision of a snake biting its tail while riding on the top of a bus. Kekulé, that is, not the snake.

p. 186   I've jotted a few things down on paper...: see Appendix 1. The appendix goes rather further than the Dreamer's summary to L; perhaps his ideas are still inchoate at this stage. One notices that the appendix is not assigned to any particular time frame *vis-à-vis* the main story. Perhaps it should be thought of as taking place in some alternative reality.

p. 187   a winding path from the fictive to the real: it seems the Dreamer has moved on from Virgil and now already has Dante in mind: see *Inferno XXXIV,* 127ff.

p. 188   Dante's Beatrice: as Charles Williams would have it; see *The Figure of Beatrice,* London, Faber, 1943.

p. 189   L in her turn seems to be alluding, if unconsciously, to Lacan: that all discourse is the discourse of the Other.

Appendix 1

Sometimes when you are writing, the context seems to produce exactly the right word; other times there are two or three words that would do just as well. In the first case we are inclined to feel there is something about the meaning of the word that is uniquely suited to the context, in the second that the meanings of the alternatives are probably much the same. In other words, if we were trying to categorize meanings, we might just as well do it by categorizing contexts: words could be said to have something in common in terms of meaning to the extent that they tend to occur in the same contexts, or contexts could be said to have something in common in terms of meaning to the extent that they tend to contain the same words – or, which is much the same thing, to be different to the extent that they contain different words.

['I don't see where context comes into it,' said L. 'I thought you were trying to classify meanings.'

'Meanings are contexts,' I replied. 'Think of a word as a piece in a jigsaw – its meaning is the position that will fit that piece and no other: in other words, its meaning is its context.'

'I would have thought,' said L, 'that if I said the word *tree*, it's meaning was that thing with no leaves on outside the window, or anything else like it.'

'There's no difference,' I said. 'That's just like turning the bit of jigsaw over and looking at the other side. If you classify one side, you automatically classify the other – you can't separate them. If you'd like to say "value" instead of "meaning", that's all right with me, because as soon as classification comes up, that's what we're talking about.'

'But going about it your way,' said L, 'if you take one word out of a sentence, there are often lots of words you could put in the same place.'

'That's because a sentence gives you such a small amount of context. It would be like grabbing half a dozen pieces of a jigsaw – nine times out of ten none of them would interlock. But if you kept doing it over and over, eventually you would get a unique position for every piece.'

'It sounds like a slow way to do a jigsaw,' said L.

'But don't you see?' I said, 'That's exactly the position we're in with language. People only give us a little bit at a time.'

'And yet we understand it,' said L.

'That's because we each have a whole system of our own that lets us put ourselves in the speaker's shoes — but what I'm trying to do is to work out how that system fits together.'

'So you're trying to create something like those vocab lists we used to be given in French that were themed for the beach or the railway station or whatnot. It seems like a bit of a waste of time to me.'

'No,' I said. 'That's exactly what I'm not trying to do. Building upwards can never guarantee that you find the right answer. Remember that Ikea desk you bought where we ended up with two bits left over? What you have to do is start at the top and work down, following meaning as it ramifies in all directions like the frangipani. There will be boughs and branches, and twigs and twiglets. Bracts, even, if that's an appropriate word. And that way you will know you haven't missed anything.'

'But how do you know you're classifying things in the best way?' said L.

'Well there are techniques for doing this sort of thing which we needn't go into at the moment,' I said. 'A book called *Mental Maps* that came out about 30 years ago has quite an easy to follow explanation if you're really interested.'

'I never said I was as interested as that,' said L.

'Then why don't you just read on and see if it makes sense?']

The second of these strategies, i.e. the categorization of contexts, is the easier to implement, because the presence of a word is a fact. It's very easy to take a text, divide it into successive blocks, call the blocks 'contexts', which they are in the crudest sense, and count the occurrences of words in each block. If some blocks then turn out to contain words in the same kinds of relative numbers, those blocks can be considered similar contexts, and that information in turn can be used to define groups of similar words — words that are alike in meaning. No doubt the problem could be tackled the other way round, but it isn't obvious how you would go about it.

Taking the five Helen Garner texts and the 175 most common words, the most revealing way of dividing the contexts, ensuring that a context that contains any of the words in the first group is more likely to contain other words from that group than it is to contain words from the second group and vice versa, enables us to partition the words into two groups, like so:

ask, big, blue, body, boy, call, car, child, complainants, conversation, corner, dark, day, die, dream, drive, drop, drug, fall, family, father, feminist, find, finger, first, floor, friend, front, fuck, full, give, good, hair, hang, happen, hear, heart, hold, home, job, judge, keep, kitchen, last, laugh, lean, leave, left, let, letter, life, light, live, lose, love, mean, money, morning, mother, move, music, name, need, old, parents, party, person, phone, place, play, point, police, position, power, push, put, question, raise, read, ready, right, ring, run, say, seem, shed, shoulder, side, sing, small, smell, smile, son, speak, stare, start, stay, step, stone, stop, story, talk, tell, thing, trial, try, two, use, voice, wait, want, watch, way, witness, work, write, year

vs.

air, arm, asleep, bed, college, come, complaint, council, court, dance, door, evidence, eye, face, feel, foot, girl, go, hand, harassment, head, heroin, high, house, kill, know, lay, little, long, look, make, man, mouth, murder, night, open, pass, people, room, see, sexual, sit, sleep, stand, street, student, table, take, think, time, turn, wake, walk, wall, water, window, woman, young

This means that the most profound difference in meanings in these words is whatever unites the members of these groups with one another internally, and separates them from the members of the other group externally. Another way of putting it would be that the first group all contain the meaning-element A while the second group contain the meaning element a – that is to say, *non-A* – or that the choice between A and a is the most basic choice in meaning made by Helen Garner, by present-day Australian users of English, by Australian users of English in any period, or by users of English in general, just depending on how incautious you wanted to be.

Whether the finding has an interest beyond itself will rather depend on whether any of these generalizations is true, and whether the difference between the groups can be correlated with some objective feature of the meanings of the words that the groups contain. I will begin by dealing with the second of these questions.

The meanings revealed by this and by subsequent partitionings of Helen Garner's vocabulary I propose to explore by making use in the first instance of two concepts of M. A. K. Halliday's[1]

– that of *metafunction*[2] and that of *process*.[3] For Halliday the three metafunctions, *textual, interpersonal* and *ideational,* are features of the context of situation that work together to create and constrain the text; process, on the other hand, is a term loosely equivalent to *verb* which Halliday uses to classify the kinds of interaction between participants to be found in different kinds of clauses.

['If it's equivalent to a verb, why doesn't he call it a verb?' said L. 'I've never been able to see what was wrong with the grammar we learnt at school. I could understand what a verb was in 5th Class, but when Gracie was at school the teachers just filled their heads with a lot of double-talk.'

'I'm assuming you want your question answered and aren't just ranting for the sake of it,' I replied. 'As with many things there's both a respectable and a disreputable reason. The overt reason is that using the word *process* enables you to include in the category things that you mightn't want to call verbs.'

'Why would you want to do that?' said L. '*Verb* seems clear enough to me.'

'Suppose you have a sentence like "the east is red",' I said. 'What if you wanted to call *is red* a process? There's a case for doing so – in fact Halliday doesn't – but whether he does or not, *red* is certainly not a verb.'

'I can't see why you would want to say *is red* was a process,' said L.

'What's the difference between "the girl is red," "the girl goes red" and "the girl blushes" then? Isn't the same sort of thing going on in the part of the sentence that follows "the girl"? In Chinese there would be no reason to say *blushes* was a process and *is red* or *goes red* weren't.'

'But we're not Chinese,' said L.

'Is that a reason to deny ourselves something if it could be useful? But there's also the motive that dare not speak its name: if you used the word *verb* you might have to acknowledge that that position in the clause was defined by what it contained rather than vice versa, and once you did that the whole edifice would collapse. Like all Hegelians, functionalists like it when the system tells people what to do – they're crazy about hierarchy.'

'So why are you using these terms if you don't agree with them?'

'You can disagree with someone and still think they have something to offer. I'm not too proud to say that I'm standing on Halliday's shoulders, even if I'm looking in a different direction. I think that emerges a bit later in what I've written, if I could trouble you to read a little further.']

He divides processes into three basic kinds: *material, mental* and *relational,* with the transitional categories of *behavioural,* for those with both a material and a mental component, *verbal,* for those with a mental and a relational component, and *existential* for those with both a relational and a material component.

['When he has these three basic categories,' said L, 'and three others in between, do you mean it's like a colour wheel or something, with red for material processes and yellow for mental, let's say, and behavioural would be orange?'

'Odd that you should ask it in just those terms,' I said, 'because there's an illustration of the process types as a colour wheel on the cover of the second edition of *A Functional Grammar of English.* Though I won't swear that you've guessed the colours right. But I would sooner think of the processes as the vertices of a cube looked at corner on. That gives you two more points to play with – the origin of all the measurements and the place where they all overlap.'

'How do you mean?' said L.

'Look at this,' I said, sketching a diagram:

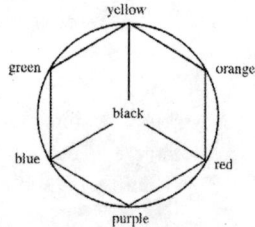

'You can have the same six points on a circle or at the corners of a cube, but using the cube gives you another dimension – from black, which has no colour, where they all originate, to white, out of sight round the back, where they all coincide.'

'I'm not sure it works that way with red, yellow and blue,' said L.

'Well just pencil in the colours it does work with,' I said. 'You know exactly what I mean.']

By my count, of 44 process words in group *A*, 24, or 55%, fall into the material, behavioural and mental categories, and 45% into the verbal, relational and existential, while of the 19 process words in group *a*, 19 – that is, 100% of them – fall into the material, behavioural and mental categories, and none into the verbal, relational and existential.

This observation at least shows it is possible to correlate *A* with the category relational and its side categories verbal and existential, and *a* with behavioural, and its side categories material and mental. Having done that, we may notice that it is not only process words in *A* that relate to the verbal and relational: *conversation, letter, money, name, position, question, story, voice* and *witness* may be added to the list — and in *a* similarly, *bed, door, eye, face, foot, girl, hand, head, heroin, house, man, mouth, people, room, street, table, wall, water, window, woman* all relate to the behavioural and material. One notices also that *father, mother* and *parents* — essentially relational words — are in *A* while *man, woman* and *people* are in *a*. One could go on, but I think the point is made: an objective criterion can be found which is reflected in the empirical categories *A* and *a*.

The next most revealing division of the words partitions them so:

['What do you mean "the next most revealing division"?' said L. 'Do you mean you can take your pick which way to divide the words?'

'Suppose the world of words was New Zealand,' I said, 'and imagine every word has an address somewhere there. Now the biggest division in the addresses would be between north and south wouldn't it — in fact there'd be a bit in the middle that had no addresses at all. So the biggest single piece of information you could give someone about your address would be how far north or south it was.'

'I suppose so,' said L.

'Then the next biggest piece of information would be how far east or west it was — but that information isn't an alternative to north and south, it's separate and independent. Every address has both.'

'I get the idea,' said L, 'and the next way would be up and down.'

'Exactly — that way you could distinguish the person in the first floor unit from the person on the ground floor. And so it goes on.'

'It couldn't go very much further,' said L.

'What about time share — "you can find me at this address but only on Wednesdays"?'

'I'd defy you to think of any more dimensions,' said L.

'What about the ironic — "I was only kidding"?'

'You'd be really happy to hear that,' said L, 'when you'd gone to all the trouble of writing it into your address book. But I get the idea.']

blue, boy, call, child, come, court, dark, day, die, drive, drug, eye, face, family, father, feminist, first, floor, foot, full, hair, hand, head, job, know, laugh, lean, let, life, look, make, man, mother, mouth, move, need, old, open, parents, people, power, say, see, seem, shed, shoulder, sing, sit, small, smile, son, stare, start, stop, story, take, think, time, trial, turn, two, voice, wait, walk, way, woman, write, year, young

vs.

air, arm, ask, asleep, bed, big, body, car, college, complainants, complaint, conversation, corner, council, dance, door, dream, drop, evidence, fall, feel, find, finger, friend, front, fuck, girl, give, go, good, hang, happen, harassment, hear, heart, heroin, high, hold, home, house, judge, keep, kill, kitchen, last, lay, leave, left, letter, light, little, live, long, lose, love, mean, money, morning, murder, music, name, night, party, pass, person, phone, place, play, point, police, position, push, put, question, raise, read, ready, right, ring, room, run, sexual, side, sleep, smell, speak, stand, stay, step, stone, street, student, table, talk, tell, thing, try, use, wake, wall, want, watch, water, window, witness, work

The first of these groups — let's call it *B* — contains 39% of the words as a whole, but 58% of the words for humans and 73% of the words for parts of the body; of other sorts of common nouns *b* contains 78%. It seems, then, that the categorical distinction here concerns the distinction of human from non-human.

The third most revealing division partitions the words so:

air, arm, ask, asleep, bed, boy, car, conversation, corner, dance, dark, door, drive, face, family, feel, finger, first, foot, friend, front, full, girl, good, hand, hang, happen, head, hear, high, hold, home, house, job, kitchen, know, lay, lean, leave, life, light, look, money, murder, old, open, parents, party, person, place, point, police, push, put, question, read, ready, right, ring, room, run, see, shed, shoulder, side, sing, sit, smell, son, stand, stare, start, stay, street, table, talk, try, turn, voice, watch, water, window, witness, work, year

vs.

big, blue, body, call, child, college, come, complainants, complaint, council, court, day, die, dream, drop, drug, evidence, eye, fall, father, feminist, find, floor, fuck, give, go, hair, harassment, heart, heroin, judge, keep, kill, last, laugh, left, let, letter, little, live, long, lose, love, make, man, mean, morning, mother, mouth, move, music, name, need, night, pass, people, phone, play, position, power, raise, say, seem, sexual, sleep, small, smile, speak, step, stone, stop, story, student, take, tell, thing, think, time, trial, two, use, wait, wake, walk, wall, want, way, woman, write, young

I am going to delay appending any labels beyond a simple *C* and *c* to the two halves of this division; instead, in the hope of further insight, I will at this stage combine the three ways of partitioning the words, to give eight groups:

ABC: boy, dark, drive, family, first, full, job, lean, life, old, parents, shed, shoulder, sing, son, stare, start, voice, year

ABc: blue, call, child, day, die, drug, father, feminist, floor, hair, laugh, let, mother, move, need, power, say, seem, small, smile, stop, story, trial, two, wait, way, write

AbC: ask, car, conversation, corner, finger, friend, front, good, hang, happen, hear, hold, home, kitchen, leave, light, money, party, person, place, point, police, push, put, question, read, ready, right, ring, run, side, smell, stay, talk, try, watch, witness, work

Abc: big, body, complainants, dream, drop, fall, find, fuck, give, heart, judge, keep, last, left, letter, live, lose, love, mean, morning, music, name, phone, play, position, raise, speak, step, stone, tell, thing, use, want

aBC: face, foot, hand, head, know, look, open, see, sit, turn

aBc: come, court, eye, make, man, mouth, people, take, think, time, walk, woman, young

abC: air, arm, asleep, bed, dance, door, feel, girl, high, house, lay, murder, room, stand, street, table, water, window

abc: college, complaint, council, evidence, go, harassment, heroin, kill, little, long, night, pass, sexual, sleep, student, wake, wall

['Wait a minute,' said L, 'before you go any further. Whatever the categories are, they're going to be pretty vague old categories aren't they?'
'There could be two reasons for that,' I said. 'The first is that superordinate categories of any kind are bound to be vague, if only because by their nature they're so inclusive. The second is that working with rare events, and even the most common words are quite rare, you can't help coming up with ragged edges. The information a person creates in the form of language is just so

sparse compared with their potential. What are these five books of Helen Garner's, 300 or 400 thousand words? And yet they take up what? Ten, fifteen centimetres on the library shelf. Think of how much that's in the library they don't contain.'

'Come to think of it,' said L, 'what do you mean by a word, anyway? Most of what I would call the most common words aren't even in your list at all.'

'Well I left out the empty words,' I said. 'All the *ifs* and *buts* and what not. And for the rest I'm talking lexical items rather than words as such.'

'Spare us the jargon, if you don't mind,' said L. 'What, pray, is a lexical item?'

'Good question,' I replied. 'If I may quote Halliday, he is on record as saying "the concept of the lexical item, therefore, is not wholly clearcut; like most linguistic categories, although clearly defined on the ideal, it presents many indeterminacies in application to actual instances" (M. A. K. Halliday and Ruqaiya Hasan, *Cohesion in English,* London, Longman, 1976, p. 292.).'

'That's a cheap trick,' said L, 'putting bibliographical references into a conversation.'

'Where else could I put it?' I replied. 'But when I say lexical item I mean for example that I lump *say* and *saying* and *says* and *said* in together. Things like that.']

I will begin with the fourth of these: *Abc*. This is the group that has the bulk of the words for relational processes, together with *name*, a word apt beyond any other to denote a floating signifier. I connect the meanings of this group with Halliday's relational process category, with his textual metafunction, and with Jung's category of the symbol – the thing we feel to be charged with significance even if we don't yet know what that significance may be.

The third group, it seems to me, is the category concerned with the *mise-en-scène* of Garner's narratives – Halliday's *field* – which is the projection of the ideational metafunction onto the text.[4] This group also contains the word *happen*, one of the few full words expressing existential processes in English, and the only existential process represented among these 175 words. Among process words I will therefore liken this third group to the existential category, the intersection of the relational and the material, and if this group is the projection of the ideational metafunction onto the text, this leads me to connect the seventh group with the ideational metafunction itself, and with the material category among processes.

Now, if the seventh group is *abC,* the category most different from it ought to be the second *(ABc),* and if the seventh group is related to material processes and the ideational metafunction, the second should be the intersection of the non-material categories of process — the relational and mental — namely the verbal, and the projection of the interpersonal metafunction onto the textual. In confirmation of this, we do notice in group *ABc* the verbal words *say, write* and *story,* and in the *aBc* group, which should correspond to mental processes, the word *think.* This in turn should mean a correspondence between the fifth group and behavioural processes, and we notice that six out of the ten items *aBC* contains are indeed words for behavioural processes or parts of the body. Let us sum up these correspondences:

Garner's categories	Metafunctions	Process categories
ABC	textual x interpersonal x ideational (mode)	—
ABc	textual x interpersonal (tenor)	relational x mental (verbal)
AbC	textual x ideational (field)	relational x material (existential)
Abc	textual	relational
aBC	interpersonal x ideational	mental x material (behavioural)
aBc	interpersonal	mental
abC	ideational	material
abc	—	—

['Would you just draw that out on your diagram for me again?' said L. 'I think I could follow it a bit more easily.'

'Nothing easier,' I said. 'It will be like this:'

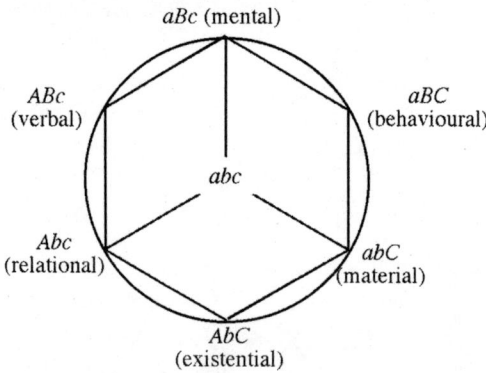

aBc (mental)

ABc (verbal) aBC (behavioural)

abc

Abc (relational) abC (material)

AbC (existential)

'So *ABC* is out of sight round the other side.'
'Just let me take it step by step,' I said, with only a slight effort to conceal a certain irritation at this tendency to rush on ahead.
'You can't blame me for getting overexcited,' said L, 'now that I've finally grasped what you're getting at. I'll be good now.']

In other words, a general relation can be discerned between *A* and the textual and relational, between *B* and the interpersonal and mental, and between *C* and the ideational and material. This is not to say that the categories objectively derived from Helen Garner's texts are the same as the categories constructed by Halliday's metafunctions, but to suggest they realize the same underlying distinctions.

['Wouldn't that have to be the case?' said L. 'You said that the configuration of the metafunctions you get in a particular situation constrains what you do − dictates it, in fact − so if you analyse what you do, you must get back the configuration that made you do it. One thing is just the other in a different medium.'
'You see deeply,' I replied, 'but Mr H is curiously sheepish about making that step. If you read what he says about collocation in *Cohesion in English*, you'll see that he's a bit puzzled by the associations it produces. He wants meaning to be somewhere else.'
'But meaning always is somewhere else, *n'est-ce pas?*' said L, rather flippantly, it seemed to me. 'You'd think he'd be grateful to have his ideas validated. I know I would be, if I were in his shoes.'

['You mean if I *was* in his shoes,' I said. 'The subjunctive is dead. But are they validated? That's the question I'm coming to.'
'Well don't take all day about it,' said L. 'I enjoy a bit of theoretical chit-chat as much as the next woman, but perhaps you academic people need to stop sometimes and ask yourselves how much that might be. You must realise that, however interesting it may be, it can only ever be interesting in a boring sort of way.']

So Garner's four groups *ABC* to *Abc* all have to do with the texts from which they derive — their personas, their concerns, their fields and their *textures*, as Halliday would say. Similarly, the *a* groups can be thought of as relating to analogous things which are not overt concerns of the text, namely the subjectivity, concerns, and environment of the author: *aBC, aBc,* and *abC* respectively. To what, then, does the point *abc* correspond? It is the origin of the metafunctions: that which is not textual, not interpersonal, not ideational. Logically, it should stand for those features of the context of situation that are not represented in the texts — except, of course, that the metafunctions exhaust all possible features both of the environment and of the text. It must follow that their point of origin is an empty category. Yet we observe that, as far as lexical items are concerned, this is not so. Far from being empty, it is not even the least populated category.

It might seem that, with the earlier Marx, we should allow a sphere of action for the individual outside the societal project of text-building, a sphere that, paradoxically, still creates text. In this case the metafunctions could be re-interpreted as ways in which the individual interacted with the human, physical and textual environment, with the reservation that the individual might act *sua sponte*. But it makes altogether more sense to move the point we consider the origin to coincide with the author — which is what I will now call *aBC* — the element of which the persona is the representative in the text.

['So if the author is the new black, what are you going to call the three dimensions now?' asked L.
'It doesn't really matter,' I replied, 'so I'm holding off for the moment. On the one hand it might seem a trifle insensitive to keep Halliday's names after junking his theory, but on the other it could be a gracious gesture to keep them, just to let people know where I was coming from. One thing you might

notice, though, is that if you had adopted the idea that the origin of the metafunctions was the sphere of action that remained to the individual, now that I've moved the goalposts you'd see that the individual was a constructed role like any other.'

'That wouldn't have pleased Mrs Thatcher,' said L.

'What do I care for Mrs Thatcher?' I said.]

As part of the justification for repositioning the origin in this way, I would draw attention to the numbers of items in Helen Garner's eight groups in relation to the diagram that follows them below:

ABC	19	22
ABc	27	26
AbC	38	37
Abc	33	31
aBC	10	11
aBc	13	13
abC	18	19
abc	17	16

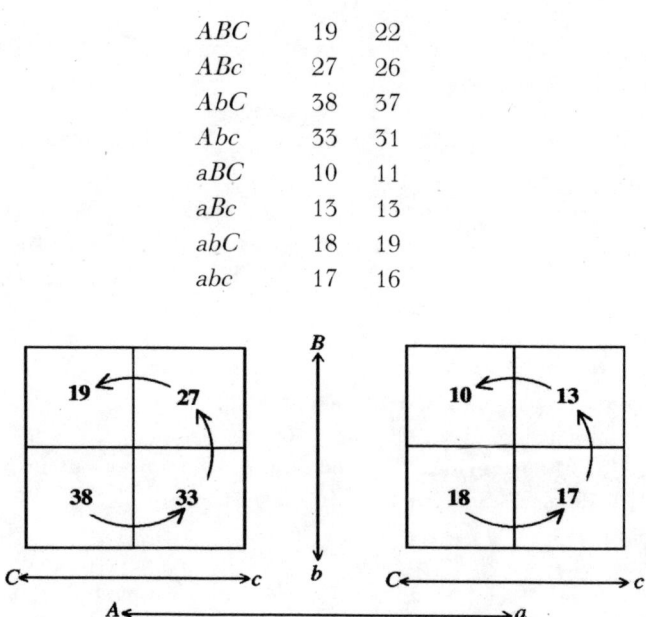

As the diagram indicates, the number of words in each group decreases by a regular proportion (the fourth root of 2) as we move step by step from the lower left of the left hand table to the upper left of the right hand table. The numbers in the right hand column above are what we would find if the proportion was exact.

The proportion means that when we have gone once round the circle the number of words is halved and so is the certainty with which we can know the contents of that area of meaning.

['Just run that past me again,' said L.

'Think of it like a galaxy,' I said. 'It spirals out from the centre; in the outer regions we can see millions and millions of stars, but in the middle, controlling the whole thing, there's a massive black hole. You can't see inside, but you know there has to be a lot of something there, because it balances everything that you can see. And that's the author. The further we get away from the author, the more the space is divided up into little separate meanings.'

'Don't tell me,' said L. 'This is where the books fit in, isn't it? *The Children's Bach* on the lower right of the left-hand grid, working round to *Joe Cinque* on the upper right of the right-hand one.'

'Exactly,' I said. 'And their meaning is harder to pin down the further you go. Like going down a spiral staircase into a cellar when there's only a light on at the top.'

'I still think it's disappointing,' said L, 'that it's not like New Zealand after all. I've always wanted to see more of New Zealand.'

'Well here's something that will cheer you up,' I said. 'What happens if you make a running total round the spiral, starting with 10?'

'You have 10, 23, 40, 58, 77, 102 – no, cancel that – 104, 137 and 175.'

'Now divide by two – or make that two and a bit.'

'This isn't one of those take away the number you first thought of things, is it?' asked L.

'No – just humour me for a moment,' I said.

'Well in round numbers, dividing by two it's 5, 12, 20, 29, 39, 52, 69 and 88. I'm afraid I can't divide by two and a bit without further information.'

'And so do the numbers say anything to you?'

'Are they supposed to?'

'Thresholds,' I said. 'Five, you start school; twelve: puberty, adolescence, big school; twenty: adulthood; 29: marriage – and so it goes on. Did you know that the mean age of marriage in Australia is twenty eight and a half? If you scaled the series to that, the last two numbers would be 67 for retirement and 86 for death. Or you could scale it to make retirement 65, and death would become 83, marriage 28 and so on. It's as if we live out the meanings. The first half of our lives – as far as marriage – we live for ourselves, and the second half as role models, symbolically. What do you think of that?'

'I think it's amazing,' said L 'what an unoccupied brain will come up with.']

So how general is this result? It is interesting to compare it with a study of the use of nouns in 200 Australian poems taken from *The Bulletin* over the years 1880-1897.

['This is that stuff of Dave's, then,' said L.

'Don't be dismissive,' I said. 'Dave's conclusions have objective correlates – his dial tracks the economic fortunes of late 19th century Australia more or less exactly, so you have to account for his results. The question of where Dave got them from – and I'd be the first to admit that he's quite capable of plagiarism – is neither here nor there.']

The two studies have 70 words in common. Those that for Garner belong in the *A* groups are scattered in the poems in ways that correspond significantly with Garner's *B/b* and *C/c* divisions, but when we look at the words that Garner puts in *a*, it is as if they have been mirror-reflected, with each such word on the average moving into the diagonally opposite quadrant. So we get a distribution like this:

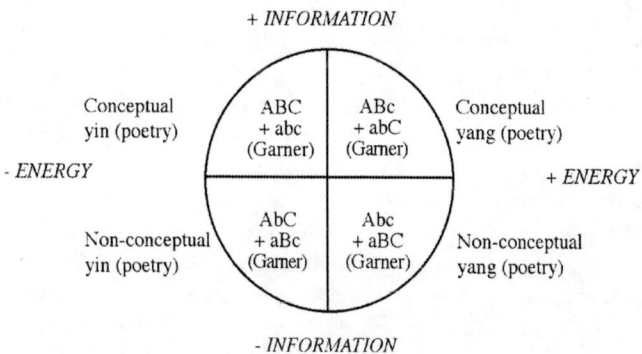

['Energy and information?' said L, 'Where did those words suddenly spring from?'

'Whenever we use terms,' I said, 'I think it's helpful to connect them if we can with things we know about already. And it seems to me that Ray and Alby, the statesmen and warriors, daytime people – they're the ones that have energy, while the Janets and Maxines are lying around moping and dreaming. And the other dimension will be information. Maxine and Ray have information within themselves, while Janet and Alby have to feel it or sense it. It's outside them. And I've always thought those two terms made a trio with meaning, which is what we're setting out to understand.']

From a statistical point of view, this coincidence between the two distributions is significant; how, then, to explain it? There are a number of possible lines one might explore. First, that Helen Garner is a woman, while the *Bulletin* poets were men: perhaps there are gender differences in the way meaning is conceptualized. Secondly, one set of texts embodies a temporal dimension and one does not. The corpus of poems is created in an eternal present: there is no sense in which a poem of 1895 is older than one of 1885, while the Helen Garner of 1995 clearly is older than the Helen Garner of 1985. Third, there is a real, if elusive, generic difference in Garner's work between fact and fiction; poetry shows no such division. A combination of the second and third of these explanations seems to me the most plausible, and with that in mind, I will revisit the question of what are Garner's dimensions and how they correspond with the dimensions that emerged from the poetry.

['Just hold your horses for a moment,' said L. 'What about this gender thing? You can't just assume it isn't important and hurry along as if you hadn't noticed it.'

'Well,' I said, 'you'll remember that Jung located creativity for both men and women in a counter-gendered archetype, the anima and animus respectively, so the idea of some degree of inherent gendering in the unconscious is commonplace to that extent. I'd like to think, though, that there's something more invariant at the centre of things. So if there is an inherent gendering there and everyone has it, we might have to promote the animus to a conscious category – equivalent to the ego. I always thought Jung was a bit shifty on the animus. Then if we were agreed on the possibility of an unconscious core that was gendered in some direction, we might say perhaps that it was the conscious that was counter-gendered for women, the unconscious for men.'

'That concerns me a bit,' said L. 'Wouldn't it mean that men and women are bound to misunderstand each other?'

'Talking to anyone,' I said, 'there's always some chance you're going to be at cross purposes.'

'Perhaps we should rely on non-verbal communication across gender lines,' said L.

'Many people find coarse gestures are quite effective,' I said.

'On that note,' said L, 'if you're including recommendations with your text, I think I've probably had enough. Any last words?'

'Be fair,' I said. 'I haven't even got to the conclusion yet.']

The diagram below shows the cube (or sphere) that appeared previously, rotated to place the point *aBC* nearest the viewer:

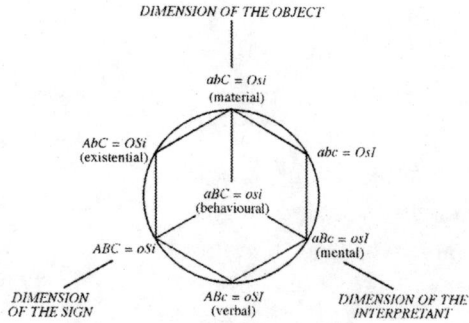

From this new perspective it is very plausible to identify the three dimensions radiating from the origin *aBC* as corresponding to different ways of knowing: sensory, systematic and intuitive respectively, or, to use Peirce's terminology, with things that we know *inductively*, with things that we know *deductively*, and with things that we know *abductively*.[5] Peirce's *object, sign* and *interpretant* are another triad of terms that may be useful in thinking about these distinctions.

> ['More new terms?' said L. 'What are these then?'
> 'Think of the footprint in the sand in *Robinson Crusoe*,' I said. 'The footprint is the sign; Man Friday is the object of the sign – what the sign is a sign of – and the interpretant is what Crusoe does about it.'
> 'That's rather like present, past and future, isn't it?' said L. 'The footprint is actually there, Friday has gone, and Robinson Crusoe still has to make up his mind.'
> 'Exactly,' I said. 'Which incidentally explains why planning, and trying to foretell the future in general, is such a waste of time. The future isn't just a linear projection of the past: it's off in another dimension entirely.']

Information, as it now appears, is a property of the categories (*OSi, Osi, oSI, osI*) in which the value for object is not equal to the value for interpretant.

> ['So that's a sort of "dog in the night-time" principle?' said L.
> 'You have it,' I said. 'The whole point about information is that you end up

with something different from what you started with. Anything you can predict already isn't information.']

Energy, on the other hand, is a property of those categories (*OSI, Osi, oSI, osi*) for which the value for sign equals the value for interpretant. The origin contains no information but it does have energy: an atemporal energy unlike the kinetic energy of the physicist that presents the object to our attention (*Osi*), unlike that energy we use to make the abductive leap from sign to interpretant (*oSI*), unlike the potential energy of Jung's *symbol* that hangs in the air like ball lightning, humming with immanent significance (*OSI*); it is an energy *sui generis*.

['So what is this energy?' said L.
'I'd say it's life, in the most general possible sense.'
'But the word *life* was in *ABC*, and *live* in *Abc* – as far away from the origin as you can get.'
'That's because life as we usually conceive of it is individual life: we assume it has a beginning and we know it has an end. But you and I and all the other individuals are no more than twiglets on the frangipani of life. Life in the big sense doesn't begin at conception or wherever the zealots would want to locate it – it began countless ages in the past, and will continue for countless ages in the future. Life has no meaning: life *is* meaning. The whole world as we know it could not exist without it, for life is the meaning of everything.'
'You're sure you've got it the right way round?' said L.
'Perfectly sure,' I said. 'Johnson and Berkeley were both on my side. When Johnson kicked the stone, what he was saying in effect was "Vivo, ergo est" – my life is the warrant of its existence. It's Descartes who gets it the wrong way round.'
'Just give me a moment to take that in,' said L.
'By all means,' I said. 'Take as long as you like – and while you're thinking, I'll just work in my last point']

There is one more point worth making. The four divisions of the *A* words, those in the domain of the sign, express the concerns of the text, and it's plausible to draw a grammatical analogy between them and the elements of clause or sentence structure. I have already suggested that group *ABC*, the projection of the author into the text, is like the subject, in which case *Abc*, the group most different from it, could be equivalent to the headword of the predicate: the verb, process, core, or whatever you want to call it. Now of the four groups with *A*, *ABC* has the lowest proportion of verbs (26%), while the *Abc* has the highest proportion of verbs (52%): it would seem that the word categories are distributed in a way appropriate to their typical grammatical roles. When we look at the *a* groups, though, we find that Helen Garner's author category has the highest proportion of verbs, and that this proportion diminishes in a regular way as we move away from the author. Group *aBC* has 60%, *aBc* 38%, *abc* 29%, *abC* 22%. At each step, effectively, the proportion of verbs decreases by the square root of 2. So while the persona is a noun, the author is a verb psychologically speaking, and – if we wish to make the identification with the anima – a woman.

> ['That's a rather striking contention,' said L.
> 'Like many of my contentions,' I replied, ' – or so I like to think – it's not as silly as it sounds. Nor as original, of course. I'll just tie together the strands by reminding you that Jespersen, in his *Philosophy of Grammar*, says, "the verb is a life-giving element." You'd be amazed at the gendered language people have used about verbs over the years, and at the arguments people have used to keep verbs out of the subject position. You'd think they were fundamentalists attacking women priests. Look at Fowler on the subject of what he calls the "fused participle" if you don't believe me.']

Conclusions:

1. We will have to conclude that de Saussure was wrong to say *'il n'y a que différence'*. Linguistic meaning – Saussurean *valeur* – has a structure with nameable dimensions and these dimensions are referable to an origin *aBC (osi)* – which is the ultimate *signifié*;

> ['I've never been able to see what it could possibly mean to say there was nothing but difference,' said L.
> 'Neither have I,' I replied, 'but you have to admit that French is a great language for epigrams. While people are still thinking you've said something

profound you've dodged the whole question of what the differences actually are.']

2. The proposition that all language is gendered deserves further investigation;

3. All users of the language share a meaning space which has three major dimensions. In order of their importance these can be thought of as the dimension of the sign, the dimension of the object, and the dimension of the interpretant, terms to be understood in terms of Peirce's semiotic theory. Examination of various texts suggests that as far as concerns their placement in these dimensions, some words may carry a more or less permanent weighting, whereas others move along and through dimensions as the particular author and text requires. The dimensions correlate with or are interconvertible with other descriptive or coordinate systems;

4.   The words that embody these dimensions, and from which the dimensions themselves were excogitated, are inseparable from affective content. This is because, unlike the – ultimately Malinowskian – as yet undifferentiated context of situation, life has an inherent content which will be served by promoting an environment receptive to its needs. Helen Garner's language suggested, beyond the textual, the usefulness of such terms as human/non-human and profound/superficial. In these terms, the origin/author was located as non-textual, human and profound. The semantic space is accordingly a space of affective value, aesthetic and moral, and the dimensionality of the value space will be a feature of the language if not a universal; the constancy of the placement of words in such a space creates an ideology, partly for the benefit of the individual, partly for the community that uses the language, but most importantly for the greatest utility of life itself.[6]

['I've still got some questions,' said L. 'For a start, what did you do with the *abc* group, the one that started out as the origin?'
'Did you notice,' I said, 'that Helen Garner makes that group a receptacle for words for things she finds unpleasant? And the same goes for the corresponding quadrant in the poetry. Look at *fight, fire, flood, scorn* and

216

shame just for openers. It's diametrically opposite the persona, so I think it has to be Jung's *shadow* – all the things the persona shrinks from and so pushes down into the unconscious. You'll notice how many pleasant words are in the groups adjacent to the author and the persona. They're a sort of comfort zone.'

'Isn't it rather a worry?' said L. 'The way these dimensions seem to have such a big, basic affective content? I know you wanted to do it from the top down, but I thought when you were talking about classifying meanings, at some stage you would say that a chair and a stool are both seats, and a seat is an item of furniture, and furniture is a sort of thing.'

'Look at it this way,' I said. 'You could say we are trying to answer the question, how do we know things, or what do we know things as? The affect is often the most important thing about something. If you say that *human* is one of the basic dimensions of meaning, being human is bound up with social pleasure and empathy and all that sort of thing. It's not just a biological label.'

'I suppose so,' said L.

'I wouldn't want you to think this is original,' I said. 'In *Roget's Thesaurus* words are basically classified according to which of the senses they appeal to. But he did it intuitively. We'd get down to the chairs and stools in the end, but maybe it'd be by way of relaxation and leisure and sitting about, and hanging with the homies.'

'Perhaps it would be if we were all so wedded to the language of the American ghetto as you seem to be.'

'Yo man, diss me naht,' I replied. 'But this is where Halliday loses his nerve; he can't regard collocational categories as lexical just because the distance between the broadest of brushstrokes, which is all you can ever get in a text, and the fine classification into chairs and stools and love seats and Welsh settles and whatever is so huge. It's taken me five novels and a lot of intuitive leaps of faith to get to this point, where if I squint and screw up my eyes I can just dimly make out a couple of the broad distinctions that are at work.'

'So any last words?' said L.

'Just this,' I said: 'I've pointed out how our lives are like a journey through a semantic space, and a text is much the same. In the three dimensions I've identified, each word has its own unique location, and the author takes us from one to the other and very frequently back again. So you could make a model of a text that way, like a game of snakes and ladders played in three dimensions. But you don't have to just go for the ride that the author takes you on: if you pick up the model and turn it round in your hands and look at it from different points of view you'll see that these dimensions are not just dimensions, they are directions. They come down from a common origin, and for every text that origin is the same.'

'Wait a minute,' said L. 'How do you know it's the same?'

'Because that's the direction in which the landmarks get further apart, or the slope gets steeper, or whatever metaphor you want to use. But although there are fewer features to know it by, you still recognise the occasional milestone or post or wayside shrine that tells you that it is the same road after all. And at last you are near the top: the sky is almost navy blue, and the snapping of prayer flags would be like rifle shots if the sound carried in that thin air. And there it will be: the source of all value – eternal, unknowable, unspeakable. The point without which there could be no meaning, for the meaning of everything derives from it.'

'Sounds like God.' said L.

'Perhaps "God" is just another word for perfectly fulfilled life as I have envisaged it. Certainly it includes many of the ideas the word "God" is conventionally used for. Don't forget, though, that this singular point is inscrutable from every direction, so anything we say about it is technically meaningless – "not even wrong" as the smart phrase goes. We proceed from it, not vice versa. So any attempt you might make to investigate meaning from the bottom up is at best futile, since it can't be proved, and at worst just rank Pelagianism. Dave's clock put *God* at about twenty past one in the morning, and look at the words it has around it. Things that can only be understood intuitively, which is to say by faith. Osgood and co. regarded alignment with this meaning space as an index of mental health – a theologian, I suppose might call it being attuned to the will of God.'

'Then you'd agree with the people that say understanding literature is a profoundly moral undertaking?'

'I'd say understanding anything is a profoundly moral undertaking. That's why teachers come in for so much stick. People get worried that their children might start to understand something – and where would that leave their authority?'

'You're probably right,' said L.]

Appendix 2

The words on Dave's 24 hour dial

10.30 p.m. – 1.30 a.m.

art, beauty, bloom, blossom, bud, care, colour, comrade, creature, cup, dark, desert, dew, dream, dress, evening, eye, fence, fern, figure, finger, flower, forehead, girl, God, gold, hair, hate, kiss, leaf, letter, life, lip, lover, madness, meadow, melody, mercy, mirth, morn, morning, music, nature, noon, picture, play, presence, rhyme, robe, sea, sheen, sigh, silk, sky, smile, song, sorrow, spring, stream, summer, sunlight, table, thirst, tide, train

1.30 a.m – 4.30 a.m.

angel, bird, body, bough, charm, cloud, crown, depth, ease, face, folly, frame, gain, glow, grace, grave, heart, height, honour, hour, hue, humanity, inch, iron, jest, laugh, look, maid, maiden, manhood, metal, moment, past, queen, ray, roar, room, rose, school, shade, smoke, snow, sob, speed, spirit, splendour, street, sunshine, thought, tongue, twilight, valley, voice, wail, wave, wine, wisdom, woman, worth, wreck

4.30 a.m. – 7.30 a.m.

answer, birth, brain, bread, brow, cheek, church, clay, cliff, daylight, deed, echo, faith, fame, foam, form, future, glare, goal, hand, head, hill, horror, king, knee, light, limb, line, mass, memory, midnight, mind, monarch, mother, mountain, mouth, neck, need, noise, ocean, pang, peace, pen, poet, praise, priest, rock, rule, scene, score, share, sister, son, speech, spot, state, steel, step, strength, strife, sun, tear, throne, tomb, tone, touch, trouble, vision, will, window, word

7.30 a.m. – 10.30 a.m.

beat, blood, blow, brand, brother, brute, cause, course, crime, crowd, dust, ear, fall, fear, flag, flame, flat, flesh, foe, foot, force, game, gladness, gloom, glory, god, home, host, house, hunger, law, loss, march, might, nation, power, pride, rain, right, season, shadow, shore, slave, soil, sound, sweat, thing, tooth, trace, truth, tyrant, virtue, wealth, weight, youth

10.30 a.m. – 1.30 p.m.

age, battle, beast, bed, breeze, bush, change, cheer, child, cry, curse, darkness, daughter, den, doubt, drum, end, father, field, freedom, friend, front, fruit, gully, justice, labour, land, language, lie, man, mile, money, name, part, people, pity, race, ruin, run, shaft, sight, stone, storm, toil, wage, war, water, woe, wrong

1.30 p.m. – 4.30 p.m.

air, anguish, back, band, bond, bone, burden, bushman, business, cattle, corner, creed, day, demon, duty, earth, fellow, fight, fire, flood, food, fool, ghost, homestead, hope, horse, joy, legend, load, lord, lot, master, mate, parson, pile, place, plain, range, rush, sadness, scorn, sense, shame, shanty, ship, side, sign, silence, station, story, subject, swag, tale, thunder, time, town, view, wall, wife, work

4.30 p.m. – 7.30 p.m.

ashes, banner, bar, beer, boss, breath, chain, chance, city, country, creek, dawn, death, delight, desire, despair, devil, doom, door, drink, folk, gate, hall, harvest, hat, heap, heat, heaven, hell, hero, hoof, hut, jaw, lady, laughter, length, lesson, lust, measure, month, night, paper, pleasure, pound, reason, rest, riches, ridge, ring, rise, river, road, roll, roof, scrub, shearer, shed, shoulder, skin, sort, soul, spell, store, struggle, sweetheart, track, vein, week, whisky, wonder, world, yard, year

7.30 p.m. – 10.30 p.m.

bank, bark, bell, bit, book, bosom, boy, breast, chorus, cow, dog, fancy, fate, floor, forest, garden, glance, glass, gleam, grass, leg, love, message, mist, moon, note, pain, passion, prayer, sake, sand, sin, sleep, space, spark, spray, star, strain, style, sunset, sword, tea, throat, tree, way, whip, whisper, wind, wing, winter, wood

Endnotes

[1] M. A. K. Halliday: holder of many academic appointments: ultimately foundation professor of Linguistics at the University of Sydney; a scholar prolific in thought-provoking ideas.

[2] See Christian Matthiessen, *Lexicogrammatical Cartography: English systems*, Tokyo, International Language Sciences Publishers, 1995, pp. 84ff., and Halliday in various places.

[3] M. A. K. Halliday, *An Introduction to Functional Grammar*, 3rd ed. revised Christian M. I. M. Matthiessen, London, Arnold, 2004, pp. 168ff.

[4] For field, tenor and mode and their relations to the metafunctions, see M. A. K. Halliday and Ruqaiya Hasan, *Language, context and text: Aspects of language in a social-semiotic perspective*, Melbourne, Deakin UP, 1985, p. 26.

[5] Or as *firsts, seconds* and *thirds*: see Charles Hartshorne & Paul Weiss (edd.), *Collected Papers of Charles Sanders Peirce*, Cambridge (Mass.), Harvard UP, 1931-58, particularly Vol. 2. It is tempting to take the further step of drawing a parallel between the members of the energy complex (*oSI, osi, Osi, OSI*) which form, as it were, the prime meridian of this sphere, and Lacan's S_1, $\$$, S_2 and *a* respectively. The four remaining points, *oSi, OSi, OsI* and *osI*, could then be related respectively to Agent, Truth, Other and Production. The equation of *OsI* with Other is helpful in understanding the typically unpleasant resonances of words in this category.

[6] For investigations that seem to lead to similar conclusions, see Charles E. Osgood, George J. Suci & Percy H. Tannenbaum, *The Measurement of Meaning*, Urbana, University of Illinois Press, 1957. It is interesting that those authors found that the possession by an individual of an uncharacteristic semantic space was an index of various kinds of sociopathy.